Wild Card

Wild Card

a novel by

JENNIE HANSEN

Covenant Communications, Inc.

Cover image by Spike Mafford © Photodisc/Getty Images, Inc.

Cover design copyrighted 2006 by Covenant Communications, Inc.

Published by Covenant Communications, Inc.
American Fork, Utah

Printed in Canada
First Printing: March 2006

12 11 10 09 08 07 06   10 9 8 7 6 5 4 3 2

ISBN 1-59811-075-6

I grew up on the stories my father, Jed Smith, told of frontier and cowboy exploits, especially of his grandfather who earned his living as a "hired gun" without ever shooting a man. I dedicate this book to all the cowboys who ever were and to all those who are now cowboys at heart.

CHAPTER 1

1872

"Shh!" Frank placed his hand over Beau's mouth. "Old Man Davis is coming." He glanced beyond the outhouse at the end of the path. Beau's shoulders shook with mirth. Together, the two boys watched a lamplight bob and weave its way through the trees. From their hiding place, they had a perfect view of both the path and the back of the small wood structure.

"Hurry!" Frank whispered encouragingly to the tiny flame licking at the weathered boards at the back of the shanty. Old Man Davis would wet his pants and make all kinds of threats when he saw the burning privy.

This was the third outhouse he and Beau had set fire to tonight. They hadn't stayed around to watch the first privy go up in flames, but had made a hasty retreat when they saw a man with a rifle run out of the rundown shack nearby where an odd assortment of mostly women and children had spent the winter. They were rumored to be Mormons on their way to a settlement in Mexico.

The second privy had been more fun. They'd gotten an eyeful when flames shot up the back of the outhouse behind the saloon and the mayor had burst through the door with his trousers almost tripping him. They'd beat a hasty retreat when a dozen men charged out of the back door of the saloon, armed with buckets and whatever else they could lay their hands on to extinguish the flames.

At last the schoolmaster emerged from the trees, waving his lantern and stumbling as he walked. Frank stifled a chortle. Davis, the high and mighty schoolmaster, was drunk! The man who was usually so prim and proper staggered toward the privy, tastefully concealed from his house by a grove of trees. He fumbled with the wooden peg that secured the door on the outside to keep it from flapping open should a gust of wind sweep through the small clearing. The thin little man stepped inside, and the waiting boys heard the latch that secured the door from the inside drop into place.

Frank peered through the dark at the back of the outhouse, wondering what was taking so long. There was a red glow, but it didn't appear to have taken hold. The dry wood of the other two privies had burst into flame almost instantly.

"It's not burning fast enough," he whispered. "Old Davis will finish his business and be on his way before this one takes off."

"Let's lock him in," Beau mumbled, and Frank grinned. Davis wasn't the only one who had drunk a little more than he could handle. Beau's ma would have him hauling water and scrubbing the wash tomorrow to teach him a lesson.

Beau was already on his feet, tiptoeing toward the privy door about as gracefully as an ox. Frank hurried after him. He wanted to scare the schoolmaster, but he didn't figure it would be a good idea to lock him inside the outhouse. Should the thin planks suddenly burst into flame, Davis might be injured. He found his own steps a bit unsteady, and Beau was reaching for the wooden peg when a whoosh of sound alerted Frank that something wasn't right. The kerosene lantern! Old Man Davis had carried a lit lantern into the privy! Frank lunged toward his friend, pushing him toward the ground. Together they rolled.

An explosion ripped through the soft, Southern night, sending a rain of fiery debris into the sky. It fell, pelting their backs, leaving scorched holes in their shirts and scattering flames into the woods. He could hear Beau's rough panting beneath him and knew his friend was winded, but all right.

A scream reached his ears, and he remembered Davis. He rolled off of Beau and straightened in time to see the schoolmaster tearing up the path, his flaming pants trailing from one ankle. Fire licked at the running man's shirttail, and Frank knew that in a matter of seconds, the flames would reach the queue of hair the fussy man kept tied at the back of his neck.

Gathering his legs beneath him, Frank lunged toward the fleeing figure, bringing him down with a resounding crash and rolling with him to extinguish the flames. He beat at the fire, ignoring the pain to his own hands until he was satisfied no lingering sparks remained. At last, he rocked back on his heels to survey the figure sprawled in the dust. He reached out a hand to turn the old man over, intending to help him to his feet, but a shout caught his attention, and from the corner of his eye he saw Beau disappearing into the bushes where the two of them had crouched earlier.

Frank rose to his feet. Someone was coming, and if he didn't run, they'd catch him. He looked at the unmoving figure lying at his feet and heard him groan. Angry voices carried on the night air, coming closer. They'd take care of Davis. He turned in the direction Beau had disappeared and began to run, annoyed that his friend had taken off without him.

He caught up to Beau at the woodshed behind Beau's house. The fight that ensued resulted in a black eye and a chipped tooth for Beau to have to explain to his mother the next morning.

"I yelled for you to run," Beau grumbled. He pulled a bottle from behind a pile of logs and rolled it across his throbbing eye for a moment before uncorking it and taking a deep pull. He held out the bottle to Frank, who accepted it and took a swallow before handing it back. Beau took another long drink.

"Think they'll know it was us?" Beau asked, wiping his mouth with the back of his hand.

"Probably," Frank answered. "Doesn't matter. Pa will blame me no matter what."

"Still plannin' to head for Galveston soon's you're eighteen?"

"Yeah. Two more months and I'm out of here." Frank reached for the bottle again, holding it absently without drinking. "No way am I going to be Uncle Dan's flunky."

"Thought you liked writin' essays and all that sissy stuff." Beau reclaimed the bottle.

"Uncle Dan's idea of an apprentice is someone to empty the slops, sweep floors, and clean the type. He does all the writing himself. He says all that stuff builds character and teaches responsibility."

"How come yer pa ain't sendin' ya to medical school in Boston? He always said he was gonna."

"I never wanted to be a doc like Pa." Frank slid to the ground, leaning his head back against the rough planks of the shed. "Anyway, Old Davis told Pa and Uncle Dan it'd be a waste of money to make me a doc. He said I haven't got what it takes and I should stay right here and work for Dan."

"Yer smart enough," Beau protested.

"Smarts isn't what he meant," Frank replied with a sneer. "Old Davis said it's fortitude and maturity I lack and likely always will."

"What'd your pa and Dan say 'bout that?" Beau slurred the words.

"Not much, so I suppose they agree. Uncle Dan just said he'd teach me responsibility when I started working for him."

"Ya think Old Davis is dead?" Beau changed the subject.

"Naw, he's not dead, but if he finds out it was us, he'll send the sheriff after us."

"Ma'll kill me iffen the sheriff comes lookin' fer me. Iffen she don't, Betsy will." Beau rose to his feet, casting an apprehensive glance toward the dark house. Beau was on the outs with his sister for telling their mother he frequently skipped school to go fishing. Frank hid a smile, knowing Beau would be in even greater trouble if Betsy learned Beau was doing more drinking than fishing on the days when he failed to show up at Old Man Davis's school house. He envied Beau in a way. He wished he had a ma and a little sister who cared whether or not he drank or went to school.

Frank turned back toward his friend, grabbed the bottle, and hid it behind a chunk of wood.

Beau seemed to agree that he'd had enough. Without a word, he took an unsteady step toward the house, then another.

Frank watched him for several minutes, then turned toward home, regretting that his own feet were somewhat unsteady. He figured Pa would be waiting up for him, and it might, at best, be a paternal lecture. As he approached the two-story frame house in which his mother had once taken so much pride, he could see there was a lot more going on than just Pa waiting up for him. Every room on the first floor level was lit up, and the front door hung open, spilling light onto the wide front veranda. A buggy and half a dozen saddle horses were hitched to the rail in front of the house, and several men could be seen lounging on the wide porch while others passed between the lights and windows inside.

Recognizing the buggy as Pa's and the big bay gelding as the sheriff's, he figured he was in bigger trouble than even he had expected. Leaving the alley, he slipped into his mother's overgrown garden to circle behind the house, choosing the darkest shadows to conceal his approach. If he could make it up the oak tree near his bedroom window, he might be able to pretend he'd been in bed all evening.

The sound of his own name caught his attention as he hunkered near the oak tree, so he crept closer to the parlor window to hear better. Raising his head slightly, he was able to see into the room that had once been his mother's pride. The room was filled to capacity with men, including several prominent figures.

"You don't know it was Frank." He recognized Uncle Dan's voice which went on with a definite sneer. "You were so busy trying to avoid being recognized, you didn't see a thing."

"The schoolmaster identified him." The mayor was properly clothed now. He scowled in Dan's direction.

"The schoolmaster didn't see who attacked him. He heard someone yell what might have been Frank's name," Uncle Dan argued. "Davis is so drunk, he can't be considered a reliable witness." Dan almost sounded as though he were siding with Frank.

"Everyone in town knows it was Frank Haladen and that Mason boy," someone else grumbled.

"And Doc Haladen admits the boy ain't in his bed like he ought to be," another voice added.

Pastor Longsworth added his solemn pronouncement, "We've been pretty patient with those boys for a long time, Doc. Beau losing his pa and your Frank his ma to the fever takes some adjustment, but they aren't boys anymore. They're almost grown and need to start taking their licks like men."

"Who but the Lord knows the workings of a boy's soul?" Pa said as though the whole discussion centered on a matter of philosophy instead of whether or not his own son was about to be locked up in the sheriff's jail.

"A night in jail might be the savin' of those two rascals," the sheriff's voice boomed. "Boys are apt to tip a few outhouses, maybe even set one or two on fire, but we can't have 'em beatin' folks up. Besides, if Alvin Tiltwater hadn't come along, the whole town could have burned from the fire that spread into the woods."

Frank noticed Pa wasn't saying anything in his defense. Pa didn't care about anything since Ma and Alice died, and certainly not about him. He wanted to jump up and tell the sheriff he hadn't beat up anybody; he'd saved Davis's life by putting out the fire spreading up the schoolteacher's clothing. He hadn't started a fire in the woods either. That old fool Davis had done that himself with his kerosene lantern.

"Look, you boys go on home." It was Uncle Dan speaking again. "Edmund is dead on his feet. He was up all night last night with Mrs. Frandson, birthing her twins. He saw patients all day, then Calvin Davis tonight. I'll stick around and talk to Frank when he comes in."

"That young hooligan needs more than a talking to," the mayor protested.

"A night or two in jail is what he needs," the sheriff put in. "I'm chargin' him with attempted murder and destruction of property."

"Don't be more of a fool than you can help," Uncle Dan shot back. "Even a boy has the right to be heard."

"Don't worry about Frank," Pa finally spoke up. "Davis said he won't have him back in the classroom. Come tomorrow, he'll be working at the newspaper office. Dan will keep him too busy to cause any more mischief." Pa's words didn't sit well with Frank.

"You can count on that." There was a grimness in Dan's voice that didn't bode well for any future working relationship with his nephew. Frank didn't know why it was any of Uncle Dan's business anyway.

His uncle was Ma's younger brother, but he always acted like he was the one in charge when he was only six years older than Frank.

Pa had pretty much raised Uncle Dan, and Ma was the only mother his uncle remembered. Ma had been nineteen and Dan just four when Grandpa Ellsworth died early in the war, leaving his newspaper to his children. Ma had worked at the paper most of her life and continued to manage it even after she married Pa a few years later. When Pa moved west, Dan had helped Ma pack up the printing press and came with them. Since Ma died of the fever two years ago, Dan had run the paper alone. He was always fussing about Pa working himself into a grave and Frank not helping enough. Frank was tired of it. Besides, it seemed to him that since half of the newspaper had belonged to Ma, it should be as much Frank's as Dan's anyway, but Dan never talked about Frank becoming a partner.

From what Frank could gather from the talk inside the parlor, he was through with school sooner than expected, so there wasn't any reason to wait around for the sheriff to put him in jail or for Uncle Dan to work him to death. It wasn't his fault drunken Old Davis had carried a lighted lantern into the outhouse. He wasn't going to be the one taking orders from Dan and sweeping out the newspaper office in the morning either. He could be in Galveston in three days. He'd heard there were plenty of opportunities there for a bright young man like himself.

Taking advantage of the raised voices, he climbed the tree and silently slipped through a window into his bedroom. It didn't take long to stuff a couple changes of clothing into a duffle bag and collect the small pouch of coins he'd been saving. He picked up the single shot rifle that Uncle Dan had passed on to him when they'd gone hunting last year. He started for the window, then turned back to pull from his bed the quilt Ma had made for him. For just a moment he paused with the quilt in his hands, thinking of his mother. It was almost as though she stood before him. He could clearly see disappointment in her eyes. He shook off the image, folded the quilt in thirds, then made short work of rolling it into a tight bundle, which he secured with a rawhide thong.

Back at the window, he could hear stomping and grumbling and knew Uncle Dan had convinced the men to leave, which meant he didn't have much time. Not daring to make any noise that might attract attention, he couldn't drop his bag and the quilt to the ground, but had to hang onto them and the rifle as he made an awkward struggle down the tree. At last, he felt the soft brush of grass. Once on the ground, he made his way to the springhouse.

One thing about Pa being the only doctor in town, they always had plenty of food. Two thirds of Pa's patients paid him in goods rather than cash, and the springhouse was always filled with a generous supply of meat and produce. He helped himself to a slab of bacon, a ham, and as many other supply items as he figured he'd need in a week. That would give him plenty of time to find work, probably on one of the ships where he wouldn't need to worry about room and board. In a few months, he'd be visiting the exotic places he'd only read about in the tattered geography book Old Man Davis passed from pupil to pupil.

Leaving the springhouse, he crept toward the stable. He didn't enter, but settled himself with his supplies in a clump of shrubs where he could watch the double doors. He expected Dan would soon lead Pa's buggy and mare to the small barn. He didn't have to wait long.

Dan soon showed up leading Pa's horse. He carried a lantern, which he hung on a nail just inside the doors, then began releasing the animal's harness. Piece by piece, he undid the array of straps and buckles, then hung the harness in its place, ready for Pa to grab from its familiar hooks the next time he was called out. Dan seemed to take forever brushing and currying the old nag, who stood patiently with her nose in a feedbag. When he finally finished, he led the horse outside and released her into a narrow, poled yard where she could move about freely. Two other horses made soft sounds of greeting to the mare as they moved toward her from the pasture that adjoined the corral. Dan didn't lower the pole gate separating the horses. Frank knew the mare was always kept in the corral at night in case she was needed in a hurry, but both his horse and Dan's roamed freely in the larger pasture edged by a new orchard he and Dan had planted and watered by hand three summers ago.

Dan leaned against the top pole of the corral and didn't move for several minutes. He stood as though lost in thought watching the horses, then slowly turned back to the stable where he hung up the brushes and reached for the lantern. Frank felt a twinge of conscience. Uncle Dan looked sad and loaded down with care. For just a moment, Frank considered calling to him and offering to help out at the paper, but Dan extinguished the light and closed the double doors before turning around, revealing a tight-lipped grimness. Frank watched him move with long strides toward the back porch.

Frank felt strange, knowing he'd probably never see his uncle again. Dan had been his boyhood hero, and later his disapproving jailer. For just a moment, he wished things could be the way they were before Ma and little Alice died. Dan hadn't been so serious then, and the two of them had been close friends, almost brothers. Now he took care of Pa like Pa was sick and bossed Frank around like he was Frank's pa.

Once he was certain Uncle Dan had returned to the house, Frank slipped inside the rundown barn. He didn't dare light the lantern, so he stumbled about in the dark, locating his saddle and bridle. Once back outside, he considered the two horses still stretching their necks over the corral fence as though gossiping with Pa's old mare. Ma's mare was the better horse. She was both larger and stronger than the gentle mare his parents had given him for his twelfth birthday. He eyed her for several minutes, then turned away. She was also harder to catch, and Pa needed her to spell off his buggy horse. Besides Dan had considered the horse his ever since the mare he'd previously ridden broke her leg and had to be put down. Frank wouldn't take anything for which Dan could fault him.

He approached his own mare and made short work of saddling Molly and stowing his gear. Dan had hinted that Frank might be getting a better horse when he turned eighteen, and for a moment, he regretted leaving without the better animal, but Molly would do. He wouldn't need a horse after he reached Galveston, and though the money he'd get for selling the old horse wouldn't be much, it would help tide him over until he started drawing wages.

He led the horse to the gate and didn't mount until he was a good distance from the house. He didn't want Uncle Dan coming after him or any of the townspeople being alerted to his departure. He approached Beau's house from the back and took the precaution of leaving Molly behind the ramshackle structure that served as the Mason's woodshed. He approached the house on foot, and when a handful of stones tossed against Beau's window failed to rouse his friend, Frank retreated to where he'd left Molly. Beau didn't own a horse, and Frank doubted his friend would leave his ma and little sisters to fend for themselves anyway. It was just that it didn't seem right to leave without telling his best friend good-bye.

A light came on in the room next to Beau's. That would be Betsy's room. He considered leaving a message for Beau with her, then decided against it. She'd likely throw something at him if he tapped on her window—either that or threaten to scream until he let her go with him. There was no telling with Betsy. He realized, with a start, that he'd miss Beau's towheaded little sister. She'd been following him and Beau around ever since she learned to walk. And just last Sunday, he'd seen her all dressed up for church and looking right pretty. He dismissed that train of thought. He had more important things to think about.

"Looks like we're on our own." Frank patted Molly's neck and swung into the saddle. He stroked the mare's neck again and looked back one last time toward Beau's window, then the window next to his. The light flickered out.

Frank didn't need Beau. Beau would just hold him back. Frank dug his heels into Molly's sides. He'd be in Galveston in no time. An exciting new life waited for him.

Once he left town behind, he urged Molly to her greatest speed for several miles, but when the horse tired, he let her pick her own pace, and they ambled slowly into the night. Stars shone above, the night was clear, and he had plenty of time to think. Being alone wasn't quite as easy as he'd expected. He considered turning back, but pride stiffened his resolve. He hadn't done anything so terribly wrong.

Probably every grown man in Willow Springs had tipped or burned an outhouse when he was young. He would be eighteen years old in a few days, but Pa and Dan treated him like a child. He'd show them.

* * *

It took longer to reach Galveston than he'd expected. He overslept twice, and he took the wrong trail and had to retrace his steps, which cost him a day. Preparing his own meals took longer than expected as well, and he quickly discovered he wasn't nearly as good a cook as Dan, who had done the cooking during their boyhood camping and hunting treks. When he finally looked out across the bay toward Galveston Island, he forgot the sore behind, sunburned skin, and half-cooked meals that he'd endured for almost a week. His fantasies of becoming a sailor and rapidly rising to become an officer filled his head. He'd contact several ship captains and see which one made the best offer.

Among the businesses near the causeway connecting the island city to the mainland, he finally located a livery stable. It was small, and the old man who greeted him looked him over, clucked a few times, then demanded payment in advance. Frank fished out the requisite coins, then stalked away, miffed, thinking the old man should have treated him with more respect.

Frank surrendered more of his supply of coins for a seat on the train. He'd never had the opportunity of riding a train before, and he found something both thrilling and frightening about crossing over water on the heavy train, but when he at last made his way down a city street to a wharf that stretched out over the water, his heart seemed to pound in his chest. The sun shimmered on white-edged waves rolling easily across the deep blue of the gulf. Even the air seemed to smell different. It was beautiful and exciting and he was about to realize his dream of visiting strange, exotic places. Someday he'd return to Willow Springs a rich and important man, an envied world-traveler.

After exploring the city for hours, the sun began to set and his stomach reminded him breakfast had been a long time ago. He turned his attention to looking for a place to purchase a meal. The businesses in this part of town appeared rough and crude, but at last he spotted a weathered wooden building that looked like a place where a man might find liquid refreshment and something to eat. Stepping inside the dim interior, he recognized the rank odor of unwashed bodies and alcohol. He straightened his shoulders and swaggered a bit. He belonged in a place like this, where brawny men ate hearty stews and drank a few mugs of ale while talking about the places they'd been. He didn't need more education or a dreary apprenticeship; he was a man now, and soon he'd be doing a man's work, earning a man's pay.

CHAPTER 2

Frank awoke with a pounding pain in his head and no idea where he was. The damp dirt floor appeared to be inside some kind of shed. Through squinting eyes, he made out a row of wooden barrels. A revolting stench filled his nostrils. Bits and pieces of memory flitted through his mind as he bent double with violent dry heaves.

At last, he sat upright. His first thought was of his horse. It had taken longer to reach the coast than he'd expected, and old Molly had been nearly played out when they arrived. He remembered the crafty old man who had demanded an exorbitant amount for stabling Molly—a whole dollar in advance.

His money! He slapped his pockets searching in vain for the leather pouch that held his few remaining coins. Panic led to another bout of nausea. As he bent double, all he could think about was that his money was gone! For a moment, he wondered if the old coot from the stable had followed him and stolen his money.

No, he leaned back against a shaky timber with a moan. It hadn't been the old man who had hit him over the head. He was certain of that. He'd spent a couple of hours wandering around town exploring the waterfront after he arrived on the island. He'd watched seamen loading ships and tried to guess their distant destinations and spent hours just staring at the huge expanse of water. He remembered that much. He remembered, too, that all that water made him a bit nervous.

A vague memory of swaggering into a bar near a long, wooden wharf flitted through his mind. With the long ride and camps concealed from the trail behind him, he'd felt as though he'd proven himself and was ready for the role of a man. He'd walked into the dingy place and scarcely sat down and ordered a drink from a well-padded waitress before a couple of seamen invited themselves to sit at his table. At first they'd seemed to be friendly fellows who answered his questions about getting work on a sea-going vessel. They'd fired his imagination with tales of foreign lands. The waitress brought his drink, and he remembered the way she winked at him like he was all grown, then bent forward to set his tankard on the table, offering a view that made his palms sweat.

After that, the whole evening became rather hazy. He thought he remembered the waitress snuggling up to him. She was helping him up some stairs. She'd been on one side of him and one of the sailors on the other. A dim recollection of sitting on the side of a bed, of reaching for his boots, flitted through his mind, then nothing more. Someone had hit him—hard. He felt the lump on the back of his head. His fingers came away sticky.

Anger consumed him as he pieced bits and pieces of the previous night together. He'd been set up and robbed! No doubt the waitress and those sailors were in cahoots. They'd spotted him for a greenhorn, gotten him drunk, and stolen every bit of his money. When he got hold of them he'd . . .

What? He wasn't a physical match for the two burly sailors. If he sought out the sheriff, he would likely be sent back home to face charges of attempted murder. Something brushed against his hand and he yelped. Then feeling foolish for being startled by a cat, he searched with his eyes through the dimness for the mouser. Even in the faint light, he could see glittering eyes watching him and almost screeched like a girl when he realized the cat-sized creature was, in fact, a huge rodent. A shiver of disgust had him scrambling to his feet. He had to get out of this place. He wasn't too certain how he'd gotten there or why he'd chosen to spend the night in such a disgusting place, but he must have had much too much to drink. Oddly enough, he didn't remember ordering more than one mug of ale.

As he approached the door, he could dimly make out that he was in a long, wooden warehouse. He could hear the slapping of water against wood and figured he had somehow made his way during the night to the wharf and been too befuddled to find his way back to the stable where he'd left his horse. Or maybe the train didn't run at night. He was fortunate he hadn't fallen in the gulf, he told himself with a touch of derision.

He reached for the latch securing the wide barnlike door and discovered that it wouldn't budge. Placing his shoulder against the thick panel, he pushed. Nothing happened. He pushed again with the same results. It took several attempts before he faced the fact that he was locked inside the warehouse.

Who would lock him up and why? His mind reeled. He'd heard of men being shanghaied, but that was in places like England or Boston, maybe even New Orleans, but not Texas. Besides, he'd planned all along to sign on with one of the ships in port. There was no need to shanghai him.

A sound caught his attention, and he pressed his ear against the door, hoping to hear something that would clear up some of the confusion in his mind. He wasn't disappointed. A woman's voice he recognized from the previous night said, "Here, set this inside the door."

"You think they're awake yet?" A male voice reached Frank's ears.

They? Could it be possible there was someone beside himself in this stinking place?

"Whassamatter? You afraid the kid will black your other eye?" A second male voice chimed in, and Frank recognized it from the night before too. It belonged to one of the sailors who had shared his table. He experienced a brief moment of satisfaction on learning he'd left one of the sailors with a black eye.

"For a kid, he's got a mean left," the first man retorted.

Frank grinned and stroked his swollen knuckles.

"It's too soon to worry about them being awake," the woman spoke in a matter-of-fact voice that hinted that this wasn't the first time she'd been involved in this type of action. "I gave the cowboy enough laudanum to keep him out until tomorrow. In a couple of hours, the boy will wake up, and it won't take long until he'll be hungry enough to eat this slop."

A masculine chuckle greeted her words. "Then he'll sleep like a babe."

"How long 'til Captain Dreymer picks this batch up?" the other man asked.

"Not until evening," the woman answered. "He means to put out when the tide changes after midnight."

Hearing the jangling of keys, Frank scrambled back to the spot where he'd awakened. It might be best to pretend to still be unconscious until he could figure out what to do. He wasn't stupid enough to think he could take on both of the sailors and the woman.

He threw himself on the ground and scarcely dared breathe as he listened to the door opening and the sound of rapid footsteps followed by the clatter of crockery. It took every ounce of willpower he could muster not to jump to his feet and confront the trio. Reason told him escape mattered more than revenge. He lay still, hoping the person delivering his breakfast wouldn't come any closer.

A few minutes later, he heard footsteps receding and the solid thud of the door closing again, followed by the scraping sound of a key being turned in the lock. He meant to lie still a few moments longer, but the skittering of small feet close by had him scrambling to stand once more. He hated rats! *The two-legged kind too.* He directed a scowl toward the door.

His eyes had grown accustomed to the dim light in the warehouse. That there was any light at all told him the sun was shining outside. From that, he figured he'd spent most of the night in the wharf-front shed. The only question now was how close the day was to becoming night again.

Once more, he moved toward the door. He found the tray his captors had left and discovered it held a tin cup and a bowl. A spoon was stuck in the bowl of what felt like thick porridge. The contents of the mug smelled like coffee. He was hungry—thirsty too—but from what he'd heard earlier, he figured one, maybe both of the items on his meager breakfast menu had been laced with laudanum. The notion of being drugged didn't set well with him.

He remembered the voices had referred to a cowboy. They'd only brought one breakfast, so maybe the cowboy was being held someplace else. But, he reasoned, if the cowboy had already been given the potent drug last night or early this morning, their captors might not have brought him anything to eat because they expected him to be unconscious a lot longer. If another person were being held in this prison, he should find him. Maybe together they could find a way out. He started a slow exploration of the warehouse. If he didn't find the cowboy, he might, at least find a way out.

He found the source of the stench in the confined space. It came from the barrels that filled most of the floor space. The smell reminded him of Ma's pickle crock, though it was kind of like rotten fish too, which drew him to the conclusion that the barrels held some kind of pickled fish. The barrels were stacked four high in places, and the stench made his empty stomach roil. He figured they held either incoming or outgoing cargo, and he began to wonder if he wanted to spend months, maybe years, around the stench that surrounded him.

A rat leaped from a tall stack of barrels, and Frank shuddered, remembering the old schoolmaster's descriptive words concerning rats on ships and how all ships harbored rats.

He thought of the two sailors who had tricked him into this mess. They weren't the mates he'd envisioned beside him as he explored the world. The life of a sailor was looking less inviting with each passing minute.

He made a circuit of the building and discovered bales of cotton as well as the stinky fish barrels. He was almost back to where he'd awakened, when he stumbled over a boot. In no time, he confirmed that the boot was attached to the leg of a body wedged into a narrow space between two rows of barrels. As Frank knelt for a better look, the man's high-heeled riding boots with sharp rowels were the first indication that the man was the cowboy his captors had mentioned earlier. He couldn't tell whether the cowboy was breathing or not, and he couldn't get close enough to place a hand on his chest, so Frank grasped the man's boots and pulled. It took several tugs before the body slid out of its hiding place. The grunts and groans coming out of the cowboy's mouth, he figured, were a pretty good indication that he was alive.

"You best wake up." Frank shook the man's shoulders, and when that brought no results, he slapped his face. He struggled to prop the inert form against a barrel in a sitting position. The cowboy groaned and slumped toward the floor. Frank caught him and persisted in forcing the man to sit.

"Look, mister," he whispered, "you met up with some bad folks last night. They gave you knockout drops, and if you're not planning on becoming a sailor, you better start looking sharp."

After a while, he gave up on the cowboy and returned to searching the warehouse. There were no back doors or attic leading to the roof. The shedlike structure was in good repair, and Frank failed to find any rotted boards that might provide an escape route. The few spaces that let in a little light were both too high and too narrow. He searched again, where he'd already searched, even climbing to the top of a stack of the stinking barrels, but it was no use.

His stomach growled, and he thought about the porridge and coffee his jailers had brought. It had been a long time since he'd eaten, and his stomach was rumbling. Maybe only one of the items held laudanum, and he'd be lucky and choose the other one. He made his way back to the tray. Several large rats surrounded the cup and bowl the woman had brought. He took a step toward them. They didn't retreat as he approached, and he decided he wasn't hungry enough to chase them away. He wasn't going to eat rat leavings, anyway. Besides, as bad as his head was hurting, he'd not be able to keep anything down.

He started to turn away, then he noticed one of the rodents attempting to crawl away. He couldn't help noticing that it was different from the others. It looked thinner for one thing. And it didn't scuttle, like it was sneaking at a run like rats usually do. It moved more like it was drunk or sick. Curious, he moved closer. When his movements didn't cause the other rats to run, he figured they were either dead or sleeping. He wasn't about to get close enough to see which. He turned his attention back to the one that was moving. Maybe it wasn't skinnier, just wet.

Once his little sister, Alice, dropped her cat into the horse trough. It had looked just like that; all skinny with its hair slicked back like a muskrat. *Only where would a rat find enough water to fall into in a locked warehouse? One of those stinking barrels?*

Or maybe the rat knew a way out Frank hadn't been able to discover. He took a step closer to the vermin. It moved away, and he followed. If the rat had been moving at a normal pace, he wouldn't have been able to keep up with it. As it was, he found himself scurrying around barrels and stumbling over obstacles as he followed it to the far side of the warehouse. Once, it stopped, seeming about to go to sleep. He clapped his hands together, and it began moving again.

Suddenly the rat disappeared. One moment, Frank was following it, and the next it was gone. He looked around, perplexed. *Where could that stinking overgrown mouse have gotten to?* He shoved at a barrel. Nothing. Heaving himself to the top of the barrel, he looked around but still couldn't see much. It was darker back so far from the door—or maybe it was getting to be night and that Captain something-or-other would be coming to collect him and the cowboy pretty soon.

He began to sweat. He'd lost all interest in becoming a sailor. And he didn't want to sign on with a captain who bought his crew like they were a bunch of slaves from Africa. Maybe old Abe Lincoln hadn't put an end to every kind of slave trade.

Angry, he jumped from the barrel. Expecting to hit the packed dirt floor, he was taken by surprise when he found himself sliding through thick mud. His hands flew forward to break his momentum, and he smacked up against one of the wooden kegs. He hugged the barrel for several minutes, then, catching his breath, he launched into a search for the source of the mud, hoping it wasn't just a leaky barrel.

The further he pushed into the dark corner of the shed, the squishier the mud became, until he found himself standing in ankle-deep water. He stood still, assessing the situation. This had to mean something.

If he had something to dig with, he might be able to tunnel through the mud and crawl right under the walls of the warehouse. Seeing as how the warehouse had a dirt floor, it couldn't be up on some wharf, where if he dug a hole in the floor he'd drop into the gulf. It might be that one corner of this place just got wet when the tide was high, or maybe it was built too close to a creek or something. *That rat found a way out.* He thrust out his chin and narrowed his eyes. Rodents could sneak through tolerable little spaces, but he wasn't going to be outdone by a rat! One way or the other, he was getting out before that shanghaiing captain arrived at the warehouse.

He started looking for something he could use as a digging tool. Remembering the food tray, he scrambled back toward it. This time he used his foot to boot the two big rats that slept near it aside. The bowl was crockery and wouldn't be much use. The spoon was a dinky little thing that wouldn't be much use either. He tossed them aside. The tray itself was so flimsy, it split when he tested it by snapping it against his knee. That left the tin mug. He grabbed it and started back toward the far corner of the warehouse.

On the way to the place where the rat had disappeared, he passed the cowboy and remembered the heavy metal spurs attached to the man's boots. *One of those spurs might prove right handy as a digging tool.*

He knelt beside the figure sprawled facedown in the dirt. If he could get those big Mexican spurs off . . . Grasping a boot with one hand and taking a firm grip on the shank of the spur with the other, he attempted to separate the two.

"What the . . . ?"

Frank sprawled backward as the cowboy's other boot hit his shoulder. A string of curse words accompanied the cowboy's struggle to sit up.

"Take it easy," Frank whispered. He could barely make out the man's face, which meant time was running out and he needed to enlist the cowboy's help if he was going to avoid sailing with the tide shortly after midnight. He scooted back to stay out of the cowboy's reach as the man flailed about, trying to get his senses together.

"Who are you?" the cowboy finally asked.

"Frank," was information enough, he decided. Before the man could begin to question him further, he went on, "We've been shanghaied. The folks at that saloon where I went to get a drink and some supper knocked me out and dumped me in here. I expect they did the same to you. Only it seems they laced your drinks with laudanum. They're planning to sell us to some ship captain around midnight."

The words that rolled out of the cowboy's mouth would have sent Ma to her grave if she hadn't already passed on. Frank memorized every one of them.

"Why was you tryin' to steal my boot?" the cowboy asked with a suspicious snarl.

"I wasn't stealing your boot," Frank defended himself and reached around until he found the cup he'd set down earlier. "There's no way out of here through the roof or windows, and the lumber's all too new to break out a board. I found a muddy corner, and I was going to borrow your spur to dig my way out."

"Maybe the two of us could bust the door down." The cowboy struggled to his feet and swayed uncertainly until Frank pointed him in the direction of the thick paneled door. It didn't take long for the cowboy to concede there was no way they could break the door or lift the bar that held it closed. With each thrust of his shoulder against the heavy planks, the cowboy's temper worsened.

Frank took his cup and headed for the corner where the rat had disappeared. He could hear faint sounds as the cowboy worked his way around the building. He'd told the guy—he still didn't know his name—there wasn't any other way out except by digging. He guessed the cowboy had to see that for himself.

The way Frank figured it, if he started digging in the soft mud as close as possible to the heavy timbers that held up the walls of the shed, he'd have the best chance of making a hole big enough to crawl through. He'd get wet and muddy, but he had a change of clothes in his saddlebags back at the stable where he'd left Molly. The important thing was to get as far away as he could get from this place before the woman and her henchmen came looking to sell him to the ship captain.

Frank had the beginnings of a good-sized pile of mud heaped up beside him by the time the cowboy worked his way around to where he knelt, scooping mud from the growing hole. Without saying a word, the man grunted and pushed until he had a spur free, then kneeling on the opposite side of the hole, he began digging. As they dug in silence, water seeped into their hole, but it didn't deter them.

"It's about time," Frank announced. He explained to the cowboy that he could feel with his mud-caked hands what he figured was the bottom of the log the builders of the warehouse had laid out for a foundation. The cowboy muttered something unintelligible, but dug faster. Frank started angling beneath the stout log.

"This ain't working," the cowboy complained. He stood up. "We gotta find a faster way." He stomped off.

Frank listened to the receding footsteps and his heart plunged. Even with the mud being soft and pliable, it was taking too long to dig a hole big enough to crawl through, and the mud he piled on the edges of the hole kept sliding back into his excavation. The whole pile needed to be moved farther back, out of the way. Wearily, he sat on the edge of the hole. Being a sailor might not be so bad . . . but he hadn't escaped being bossed around by Uncle Dan to become some ship captain's flunky! He kicked at the pile of mud. Maybe if he kicked hard enough, he could shove the whole blamed heap out of the way.

"Here! Use this." He looked up to see the cowboy had returned. He could barely make out in the dim light that the man was holding an armful of curved barrel staves in his hands. Frank took one and immediately noticed the rank odor permeating from the wood.

Using the staves as shovels, it didn't take long to push the piles of mud back from the collapsing edges of their hole. As the hole grew deeper, the cowboy used more of the barrel pieces as framework to keep the sides from collapsing or the piles of mud from sliding back into the hole. At last, Frank, being the smaller of the two, climbed into the hole and began shoving the mud behind him. The cowboy pushed it farther out of the way. When Frank's barrel stave snapped in half, he panicked for just a moment, then discovered the shorter piece worked more efficiently. He dug faster.

Frank was under the wall now, angling upward. *It shouldn't take much longer,* he told himself. The foundation log wasn't more than a foot and a half underground. The difficult part was moving all the mud that fell around him back out of the way, and the deeper he went, the sloppier the mud became.

"Hurry!" the cowboy's gruff whisper reached him. "Someone's comin'."

Frank gouged at the dirt, using his digging implement like a battering ram in his panic. Mud slithered across his face, and he wondered if he might die, buried in the thick, oozing muck. Still, he thrust the chunk of wood ahead of him and was startled when he felt his arm slide through a soft barrier, collapsing the sides of the tunnel around him. Mud and water rushed into the space behind him. He clawed his way out of the mud to find himself teetering on the edge of some kind of pond. The shallow water slapped against the side of the warehouse. He'd done it! He was out!

There was no time to check his bearings or celebrate. He began digging and scraping the mud that had fallen back into the hole out of the way. Water seeped in to fill the bottom. No matter, as long as the mud sides of the excavation held.

Hearing the tread of boots on planks, he looked toward the thick reeds surrounding the pond, then back at the hole. *I could be gone before anyone even knows I've escaped.* He couldn't do it. Instead of running for the concealing reeds, he sank back down into the hole. Blindly, he searched with his hands for the opening under the wall. When he located it with the tips of his fingers, he took a deep breath, and ducked his head beneath the water to wiggle his way back into the warehouse.

Blackness greeted him as he burst through the opening. When he scraped the muddy water away from his eyes, he still couldn't see anything. Using a finger to dig at the mud in his ears, he listened, afraid the footsteps he'd heard approaching might already be at the door. His captors might have already entered the warehouse and hauled away the cowboy.

"Cowboy?" he whispered.

"You ain't dead?" came the startled response from a short distance away.

"No, but we've got to hurry. Follow me."

"I cain't swim," the cowboy muttered, holding a barrel stave like a club. "That hole's all filled up with water."

"You don't have to swim," Frank explained. "Just hold your breath and follow me."

The cowboy may have protested further, but the grating sound of the key in the lock galvanized him into action, and he dropped his club before throwing himself flat on his stomach beside the murky hole.

"Follow me." Frank knelt in the hole they'd dug, then took a deep breath and thrust his head downward, using his hands to feel his way under the wall and into the space on the other side, which was nearly full of water again.

He felt a jerk at his pant leg and scrambled out of the hole to give the man following him room to stand. The cowboy sputtered and tore at his eyes and face to clear away the mud.

"Shh," Frank cautioned. "Let's get out of here." He started toward the reeds. Water splashed to his knees, but he was so wet already, he didn't pay it much mind. Behind him, he could hear the cowboy splashing after him. That worried him; if he could hear splashing, so could the shanghaiers.

A commotion erupted on the far side of the shed, and Frank figured the woman and the sailors had noticed they'd escaped. He started to move faster, but the cowboy reached out to touch his shoulder.

"Slow down, kid," the man spoke in a deep whisper. "We gotta hide, and we gotta be quiet. 'Sides, a few more steps that direction, and we're gonna be in the gulf."

Frank drew up and looked around. There was enough light to reveal the truth of the man's remarks, but he couldn't see any place to hide. There was nothing but water and a little bit of grass poking up here and there all around them.

"See that hummock of grass and reeds to the left?"

Frank looked in the direction the cowboy indicated, but he didn't see anything much different from the spot where they stood except the place where they stood was closer to open water. When the cowboy turned to the left, Frank followed. He hoped the man knew what he was doing. Seconds later, he found himself crouching in a shallow spot that was almost out of the water and where the reeds were thicker than they had at first appeared. Other than the occasional slap at the mosquitoes buzzing incessantly about their faces, they held still and didn't make a sound.

They watched as several men carrying lanterns circled the warehouse, and they knew the moment their escape hole was discovered. Frank felt a measure of satisfaction when he heard the woman's high-pitched screech of fury. He worried that someone might follow them into the slough, but no one seemed anxious to do so. It seemed to him that the half dozen or so men were in a hurry to leave. When a small wave washed over his backside as he crouched, peering through the reeds, it occurred to him that they might not be pursued if the captain and his sailors planned to sail with the tide, but he and the cowboy just might be washed out into the gulf if they stayed where they were much longer.

"They ain't comin', and I ain't stickin' around to drown." The cowboy started splashing toward dry land, some distance from where they'd been imprisoned.

Frank followed.

CHAPTER 3

They were well beyond the cluster of houses and businesses when they stopped running to collapse in a shallow depression filled with tall salt grass.

"How are we going to get off this island?" Frank gasped when he regained his ability to speak.

"We ain't far from the railroad."

"They took my money. We don't have any way to pay for tickets."

"I figure we got about four hours before the trains begin runnin' agin. We can make it across the bridge in that much time." The cowboy stood, reached toward his head, and swore again, raining down curses on the head of whoever stole his hat.

Not anxious to be caught on the railroad causeway by a train, Frank and the cowboy made the perilous trek across the rails as quickly as possible, reaching the stable where Molly dozed well before daylight. As Frank leaned across the stall gate to pat Molly's nose, he wondered where to go and what to do. He had no money to pay any more stabling fees or to purchase food for himself.

"Get saddled up and let's go," Jake urged. They'd exchanged names somewhere between Galveston and the mainland. Frank felt encouraged by Jake Pierce's assumption that they would continue to stick together.

"Molly's pretty old. I doubt she can carry both of us."

"Doesn't matter. There are other horses here. I'll borrow one." He picked up a saddle from the rail where Frank's saddle rested and proceeded toward a bay in a nearby stall.

"What if the livery man thinks you're stealing that horse?" Frank reached for his own saddle. He'd feel more comfortable if they waited until the old man who ran the place showed up and they could ask permission, but he suspected the stable owner would refuse to loan a horse without advance payment. Besides, he still felt a panicky need to get as far from Galveston as he could as fast as possible.

He buckled the cinch, grasped the reins in one hand, and swung aboard. Jake led the way, moving quietly for a quarter of a mile before giving the horse he rode its head. Frank's horse was hard pressed to keep up with the larger, stronger animal. Eventually they stopped in a grove of trees near a small town.

"Stay with the horses. I'll be back in a few minutes," Jake said as he swung down from his mount. Frank was so glad to stop, he didn't question the cowboy. As soon as Jake disappeared behind the closest building, Frank slid from his saddle and led the two animals to a spring where a trickle of water formed a washbasin-sized pool. He removed his canteen and filled it before allowing the horses to drink. They had just turned from the pool to begin grazing when Jake appeared carrying a flour sack with bulging sides. He fastened it to his saddle, then mounted.

Frank followed his lead, and the two again rode hard with only short breaks to rest the horses. Evening was approaching when Jake began picking his way deep into the scrub trees that lined one of the nearby hills. Eventually they came to a grassy area beside a stream.

"We can spend the night here," Jake suggested.

Frank nodded. His empty stomach was growling, and he was so tired, he wasn't certain he could eat if they had any grub to put in it. Molly quivered and shook as he removed her saddle and wiped down her sweaty sides. His own legs shook as he led the old horse to water and watched to be certain she didn't drink too much. All he wanted to do was roll out his quilt and sleep, but he took the time to string a line and attach both horses' leads to it so they could graze without the risk they might disappear before morning.

When he finished caring for the horses, he carried his saddle and quilt to a tiny fire Jake had built. He assumed Jake had helped

himself to one of the sulphurs Frank had stored in his saddlebag. To
his surprise, he found Jake stirring a pot of stew.

Frank never asked where the stew had come from or the coffee
and the green apple pie. He ate his share, then threw his quilt over
both of them as they lay back against their saddles. When morning
came, they rode west.

* * *

Jake proved to be a friend. He was a bit careless about what
belonged to him and what belonged to someone else, but Frank got
used to that. They'd been in a hurry and hadn't taken time to discuss
the matter when Jake traded Molly and the horse Jake had acquired
at the livery stable for a couple of fresh saddle horses a few days out
of Galveston. They traded their muddy clothes for some fancy duds
a washer woman had hung on a line just outside of some small town
a little farther west. And they acquired guns when they'd happened
on a couple of drunken cowboys sleeping off the previous night's
celebration in a cow town they passed. It proved a simple matter
after that to persuade the few travelers they met and the small town
shopkeepers to share their few coins. Sometimes Frank felt a twinge
of conscience for the things they did. His parents wouldn't approve
and neither would Uncle Dan, but they only took what they needed
to survive.

One evening, Jake produced a pack of cards to wile away the
time. Frank proved an apt pupil and soon discovered he could pick
up small amounts of cash by challenging the cowboys and ranchers
they met in isolated saloons and bunkhouses. Occasionally they
hired on to drive cattle, but Frank quickly discovered he hated the
dusty, dirty job and could earn more playing cards.

After Jake taught Frank how to play cards, it was seldom necessary to point their guns at anyone anymore to acquire funds. Frank
was willing to drift from town to town, winning small pots and
having a good time, until the Blackwell Gang held up a bank in a
town where he and Jake happened to be one afternoon, making off
with almost five thousand dollars.

That five thousand dollars stuck like a burr in Frank's mind. It was the same for Jake, and it wasn't long before Jake started talking about a man he'd met in a saloon, who claimed he'd ridden with Jethro Blackwell during the war and that he could put a couple of able bodied young men in touch with the outlaw if they were of a mind to ride with Blackwell's gang. The excitement and a chance to get rich appealed to Frank.

Riding with the Blackwell Gang was exciting at first, but dissatisfaction soon set in. Frank found himself to be nothing but a flunky. He was given the most disagreeable tasks and was left holding the reins of the gang's horses while the others held up banks and stage stations. He and Jake had been with the gang a couple of months when Frank finally got an opportunity to do more than hold the other outlaws' reins. This day their target was a prime herd of horses, and Frank was assigned to guard duty on a hill behind the ranch buildings.

With a rifle resting in the crook of his arm, he scanned the hillside while trying to force himself not to think about the things that had happened since the gang arrived at the ranch. He was glad he wasn't assigned to a task that kept him in close proximity to the other gang members. A flicker of motion in the tall grass on the hill caught his eye, and he snapped to full attention. A sudden movement prompted him to lift the gun to the ready position. Through the rifle sights, he saw a man leap to his feet and begin a charge down the hill. Not allowing himself time to talk himself out of it, Frank pressed a sweaty finger against the trigger. His aim was accurate, sending the figure collapsing back into the grass.

"Go after him!" he heard Jethro shout, and he dug his spurs into his horse's flanks.

Moments later, Frank reined in the animal, sending a spray of dust over the still figure lying halfway down the slope. Something in his gut twisted. He'd never shot a man before, and this wasn't even a man. Lying facedown in the dirt was a boy a few years younger than himself, his too-long hair still showing the towheaded paleness of childhood. Frank took a lot of teasing from the other men about being a kid, but the crumpled figure on the ground looked much younger than him, no more than fourteen or fifteen, just a boy.

Nausea threatened and stirred a hint of anger. He hadn't signed on with the Blackwell Gang to shoot children! Or women. He remembered the glee on Tom Blackwell's face as he'd fired repeatedly at the woman at the ranch, pinning shirts to the clothesline behind the house. Something about her had reminded him of his own ma, and he regretted everything that had happened since that wild night when he and Jake Pierce had escaped from Galveston.

At first it had been exciting to ride with the most notorious outlaw gang in Texas. There had been gunshots, and he'd listened to the men bragging about their deeds, but it hadn't been real until now. His ma had died when he was just this boy's age; now here was a boy who had died, knowing the pain of losing his ma. And it was Frank's bullet that had taken the boy's life. Frank felt his stomach churn. If he threw up, the men would laugh. He struggled for control.

"Put a bullet in his head! Make certain he's dead!" Jethro's voice drifted to his ears from below. Sweat trickled from beneath his hat, stinging his eyes until he could scarcely see. Frank raised his gun, never taking his eyes from the boy on the ground. His gun hand shook, and tears ran down his cheeks. He'd never done anything really bad before. Tom, Jethro's brother, and his taunts over the past weeks echoed in his ears. "Yer yeller. Nothin' but a lily-livered pipsqueak kid. Ain't good fer nothin' but holdin' horses while real men do the work!"

Frank fought to steady his aim. He'd prove Tom wrong.

"A man doesn't have to prove he's a man; that's the work of a boy." Pa's words echoed in his mind, and his gun hand shook. He'd left Pa and Uncle Dan because he'd had his fill of being told what to do. Anger now added to his turmoil. He'd had his fill of Tom's cruel taunts too. The boy was already dead. Another bullet wouldn't matter. He took aim, and at the last second, shifted his sights to fire harmlessly into the ground inches from the boy's head.

Jerking his horse's reins, he wheeled about. Moments later, his horse joined a large herd of horses, leaving the ranch at a wild gallop. As soon as he collected his share of the money Harrison Duncan had promised the gang for this job, he was striking out on his own. If Jake chose to come along, he'd welcome the company; if not, he'd head out on his own.

Shadows were growing long when the Blackwell brothers motioned for the fleeing outlaws to haze the herd of horses into a long arroyo filled with shrubs and trees that led to the river. He recognized the draw as the place where the gang had camped earlier in the week while Jethro and Tom rode off to meet the man who had arranged for the job they'd just completed. Frank veered away from thinking about the ranch they'd raided. If he thought about it, he'd be sick.

He did his part, turning the still-skittish herd toward the boxlike end of the arroyo, then rode slowly around the horses, checking for ways they might escape. Once he was satisfied that the only way out, other than the way they'd come in, was up a rocky, switchback trail that began behind a thick stand of trees and ended, presumably, in a stand of willows near the river, he dismounted and led his horse to where a handful of riders were gathered near their tack.

"The only way out at this end is pretty steep. It would take a good horse to climb it," he told them.

"They're settling down now, so we probably don't need to worry." A big, quiet man with long hair and a bushy beard turned his horse loose to make its way to the herd. The other riders followed his example. Shouldering their saddles, all but the big man walked toward the camp where the odor of beans and biscuits was beginning to fill the air. Frank watched the bearded man walk toward a spring in back of the camp before turning toward the one other rider who remained behind.

"Tom said you should remain with the remuda," Jake told him, looking apologetic. He stood holding the reins of his exhausted horse.

"I figured as much," Frank grumbled. He began removing his horse's saddle. "I hope we're staying here tonight. This nag is about to drop. She's no better than old Molly."

"Yeah, well, both of these nags looked better in the dark when I made the trade, but it won't be a problem after tonight. I heard Jethro say the horses we took today are the best horses he's ever seen, and he wants us all mounted on one of them in the mornin'."

A soft whistle escaped Frank's lips. "We're keeping them?"

"Not all of them. Jethro said there are enough geldings for a new mount for each of us. He plans to sell the colts and most of the mares. He figures they'll bring a good price. I heard him chewin' on Tom for not gettin' some big stallion the rancher was riding. He said it was worth a lot of money."

Nausea returned to Frank's stomach. He didn't want to think about the rancher Tom had ambushed. And he certainly didn't want to think about the woman and kid.

"You all right?" Jake put out a hand and touched his shoulder.

Frank shook off his friend's hand. "I'm fine, but I'm getting out of here. I'm not an outlaw, and I've had all of Tom's mouth I'm going to take. Are you with me?" He watched Jake through narrowed eyes. The two of them had been through a lot together, but he didn't entirely trust Jake. Honesty wasn't the cowboy's strong suit.

"If Jethro don't divvy up what Duncan gives him tonight, then I'm on my way. We been ridin' with this outfit nearly two months, and I ain't seen a cent of that bank loot we took. 'Sides, I don't hold with shootin' women. Tom claimed it was an accident and he didn't have any choice back in Killeen when he killed that woman bank teller, but killin' that little lady today was cold-blooded murder." Jake slapped his horse on the rump and sent it trotting toward the herd. "Since you're stuck here anyway, pick out a couple of good horses for us to throw our saddles on. I'm supposed to relieve you soon's I git through eatin' my supper. I'll bring you somethin' to eat, and when the camp is settled down, we'll light out of here the back way."

"What about our money?"

"Duncan's supposed to be here before sundown to pay Jethro, but I expect it will be just like all those bank hauls—Jethro will hang onto it, and all we'll get is promises. If Jethro don't divvy it up soon's he gets it, I figure he ain't going to ever do it, so's we might as well go before some sheriff hangs us," Jake answered before disappearing into the trees.

Frank continued rubbing down his horse, then tended to Jake's. When he finished, he looked up and let his gaze roam over the herd of horses. A big roan gelding caught his eye, and he wondered what it would be like to ride an animal like that. Scooping up a handful of the oats he'd stored in one of his saddlebags for his own mount, he extended his hand and began walking toward the big horse. The horse snorted a couple of times, shook his head, and warily watched Frank's approach. He'd almost reached the animal when he became aware the gelding wasn't the only horse eyeing the oats. Out of the corner of his eye, he saw a mare with long, slender legs edging toward him. She was a beauty with rich chestnut coloring and a wide splash of white forming a star between her eyes. White stockings lent her a deceptive air of delicacy, but Frank knew her deep chest and long legs were meant for both speed and endurance. As a boy, he had dreamed of owning a horse like her.

"Come on, lady." He redirected his attention to the mare. Just once, he'd like to ride that mare. She continued her slow approach. Frank stood still, hardly daring to breathe until he felt her velvet nose snuff against his hand. To his surprise, the gelding trotted toward him too, using his big head to nudge the mare away.

"There's enough for both of you," Frank whispered. He began to back toward his saddlebag that lay on the ground a few feet away. As he stooped to reach inside it, he caught a glimpse of a man leaving the fireside to disappear into the brush. He wondered if Jake was on his way back with a supper plate for him. When Jake didn't appear, Frank yielded to temptation, sliding his saddle onto the mare. She opened her mouth to accept the bit without any fuss, and Frank knew that she'd been trained by someone who knew horses. There was a smoothness to her, suggesting she'd been trained with rare expertise, perhaps for a woman. A dark shadow crossed his mind, and he attempted to brush it away by sweeping Jake's saddle onto the gelding. The gelding would suit his big cowboy friend.

Swinging onto the mare, he walked her in a tight circle, then galloped her a short distance with the gelding trailing behind. He knew he was setting himself up for disappointment. Jethro might allow Jake to keep the gelding, but there was no hope the outlaw brothers would agree to Frank claiming the mare.

A couple of quick gunshots caught his attention. He turned his head in time to see Jethro slump to the ground near the outlaws' cook fire. Chaos erupted with guns blazing from the rim of the arroyo. Men and horses ran every which way. The outlaws returned fire, but silhouetted against the fire, they were easy prey. Frank's heart slammed inside his chest. Someone had followed them, perhaps a sheriff's posse. If he were caught, he would hang. Drawing back into the trees, he attempted to stay out of sight. He considered making a run for it, but he didn't know this area. He remembered the man he'd seen disappear into the brush a few minutes earlier. If he were Jake . . . Frank gathered up the gelding's reins and moved toward the spot where the man had likely gone to relieve himself.

The man leaped from the brush, grabbing for Jake's saddle. "Duncan double-crossed us," he hissed. "He means to cover his tracks by murdering us all." Too scared to dwell on the bad luck that catapulted Tom Blackwell instead of Jake onto the gelding, Frank turned the mare toward the trail he'd scouted earlier. It was his only hope. They passed the milling herd in a blur.

The sure-footed mare responded to Frank's lightest touch as they bounded up the steep trail with the gelding close on her heels. Frank crossed his fingers, hoping Duncan's gunmen weren't waiting at the top to pick off anyone attempting to flee over the almost nonexistent trail. They burst into the open, and Frank encouraged the mare to run. She skimmed over the ground faster even than he'd imagined she could run. Any other time, he would have reveled in the sensation of flying.

Frank clung to his horse's reins, and each time she seemed to slow, he dug in his heels, urging her to continue running. Under the circumstances, he couldn't accurately judge the distance they covered, but he guessed they were miles from the arroyo before no amount of encouragement could force the mare to continue her lightning pace. She was spent. He looked to his fellow fugitive but didn't dare suggest they stop. Instead, he allowed the mare to slow. Finally, the other man headed for a small grove of trees. The big gelding's sides were heaving, and his mouth was flecked with foam. He was glad Tom realized they'd kill their horses if they continued to push them as they'd been doing.

"No sign of anyone following," Tom grunted as he turned to check their back trail.

Frank wondered why, if only one other outlaw were to escape that massacre back there, it had to be Tom when he, more than any of the others—except maybe that double-crossing rancher, Duncan—deserved to die. The only one of the outlaws he'd miss would be Jake Pierce. He'd miss him a lot.

"First thing we got to do is get some cash." Tom spoke his thoughts aloud.

"You're not doing nothing about that double-crosser who killed your brother and Jake and the others?" Frank didn't even notice how the fine grammar Old Man Davis had drilled into him, and Pa and Uncle Dan had insisted he use, had deteriorated since he'd left home.

"I'll get him," Tom promised. "But right now we gotta look out for our own hides. I'll be back one day, and that snake will die. You can count on that."

"What about burying the others?" Frank asked. He didn't want to think about Jake lying in the sun or of wild animals getting to him.

"Don't worry about that!" Tom spat for emphasis. "Duncan will tidy everything up all nice and neat. He won't want anyone to see what happened. He's probably already buried that horse breeder and his family where no one will ever find them."

* * *

Frank and Tom huddled near their horses without unsaddling them as deep shadows turned to night. They didn't speak, but Frank supposed they'd both been awake more hours of the night than they'd slept.

He thought longingly of the quilt he'd carried with him when he left home. He wished he had it now. The quilt had been nearly worn out for some time now, and he'd bought a couple of blankets in Waco weeks ago, but he'd hung onto the quilt because it was all he had left of his mother. It was gone now as were the blankets, left behind when Duncan ambushed the gang.

That was one more reason to despise both Jethro Blackwell and Harrison Duncan. Fortunately, his saddlebags and rifle were attached to his saddle, and he had the gun he wore strapped to his hip. He didn't doubt Tom would claim Jake's saddlebags now. Tom also wore a gun low on his hip, and there was a pistol strapped to his ankle.

Frank understood now why the crooked rancher had generously allowed the outlaws to claim the dead rancher's horses, which were the finest horseflesh the men had ever seen. Duncan had planned all along to claim the horses after the outlaws were dead. Frank felt a moment's satisfaction, knowing he had beat Duncan to two of the best horses in the herd.

He shifted to his back, staring at the starry sky. He was exhausted, but sleep wouldn't come. No matter how hard he tried, Frank couldn't get the picture out of his mind of the young boy he'd left lying on the side of the steep hill back at the ranch they'd raided.

The sun was just beginning to show when Tom spoke. "There's a bank in Hewitt. If we hit it fast, before Duncan has a chance to come after us, we'll have enough funds to reach Mexico. Then we can lay low there for a few years. Duncan will figure out we got away and come after us. He ain't the type to leave any witnesses alive. It won't be safe for either of us in Texas for some time."

Frank didn't know what to do. He didn't want any part of holding up a bank. He'd made up his mind during the long night to leave his outlaw life as far behind as he could put it. But if he rode away now, Tom would shoot him in the back. Tom wasn't the kind of man who left witnesses behind either—and he'd had it in for Frank from the day Frank joined the Blackwell Gang. Reluctantly, he stepped into his saddle, knowing that by saying nothing, he was agreeing to Tom's plan.

Hewitt wasn't much of a town, just a narrow, dusty Main Street with a handful of trails for side streets. Most of the buildings were of recent construction and looked as though the first good wind would flatten them. One short block, boasting boardwalks, housed a general store, a saloon, a clothier, and a bank on one side and a sheriff's office, a two-story hotel, and a barber shop on the other. A few other ragtag businesses and houses fronted directly onto the street. Tom stopped his horse in front of the bank.

"Here!" He thrust his reins toward Frank. Frank accepted them, relieved for the first time that he wouldn't be going inside. He watched Tom until he disappeared inside the bank, then let his gaze wander up and down the street. Not many people were out, and none appeared to be paying him any attention. For a moment he toyed with the idea of simply riding off, but he didn't doubt Tom would come after him. Besides, where would he go and how would he live?

A rush of activity erupted in front of him as Tom burst from the bank followed by two men in black suits. Frank drew his pistol just as Tom fired. The first man staggered to his knees, then fell face-down. The second man darted back inside the bank.

"Let's go!" Tom shouted at Frank as he swung into the saddle and spurred the big gelding hard, sending him plunging down the street.

Frank touched his booted toe to the mare's side and felt powerful muscles spring into action. The mare caught up to the gelding and nosed ahead in seconds. Wind streamed past Frank's eyes, but a movement just where the boardwalk ended caught his attention as he flew past. A boy with two horses ducked into an alley. The image froze in his mind, but gunshots behind them had him urging the mare to greater speed.

Once they cleared the small town, Frank thrilled at the speed the mare put out. He had to rein her in to allow Tom to catch up.

"I knew that rancher's horses were good!" Tom flashed him a smile, showing yellowed teeth. "Put a smaller man on that mare, and she'd take every purse anyone was dumb enough to put up. Too bad we don't have time to use her to make a little money."

Frank's heart sank. He suspected he wouldn't have the mare long. Tom would be looking to sell her.

"I never had a horse as good as this one," Tom crowed. "You did well choosin' these two. This'n is big enough to carry a big man like me, and he almost kept up with that long-legged mare. I think we can slow down a bit now, give the horses a chance to catch their second wind. There ain't a horse alive that can catch this pair—'cept maybe that big stallion the rancher was ridin'. He was likely both these animals' sire. Wish we coulda caught him."

A flash of memory brought a picture of one of the horses in the alley back in Hewitt to Frank's mind, but as quickly as it appeared, he dismissed it. There would be a posse after them, and because Tom had shot the banker, they would both hang if they were caught. He let Tom set the pace, but he frequently turned to glance over his shoulder. He couldn't get the picture of that boy and the two big horses he held in that alley out of his mind. Besides, a nagging suspicion in the back of his mind told him he and Tom Blackwell were being followed more closely than Tom thought.

He noticed with a touch of bitterness that Tom never mentioned the man he'd shot at the bank or the bag he'd tied to his saddle.

Tom knew this country well and left the road several miles out of town to lead the way to a river that hadn't dried up in the summer heat. They followed the river for several miles, wading the horses through the shallows not far from the bank. About dusk, he pointed to a dark spot on the river and urged his horse into the deeper water. Frank's horse followed with little urging.

When they reached the island, they made their way away from the shore to find shelter in a grove of trees that covered one end of the narrow wedge of land. Once the horses were rubbed down and tethered where they could graze without being seen from the riverbank when daylight returned, he and Tom split the last of the hard tack and jerky that Frank had stored days ago in his saddlebags. Frank and Tom hadn't discussed it, but they both knew having a fire would be too dangerous to chance. They would have to settle for a cold camp. The scorching daytime heat had given way to a chilly night, and they huddled together to eat their cold supper without complaining.

After eating their meager meal, Tom set the bag he'd carried from the bank on the ground between them and opened it. He reached inside to draw out a thick wad of bills, which he handed to Frank. Thrusting his hand back inside the bag, he pulled out a couple of gold pieces which he also tossed to him. Frank stared at the paper bills and weighed the gold pieces in his hand. The gesture startled him. He'd seen none of the money the gang had stolen since he and Jake had joined the group. Jethro had been generous with providing mounts and supplies, but little real money had been handed out, though Frank had heard plenty of promises concerning the good times they would all have when they reached Mexico.

"All right, that's your share of the loot," Tom said. "You're gettin' it now cause it's never a good idea to keep all the money in one place. If Jethro had divvied up, instead of doling out little bits of change whenever we went to town, we wouldn't a had to hold up that bank right under Old Duncan's nose. We would have had a few coins jingling in our jeans already." He sounded bitter. "You done better than I expected back there, and I figure I owe you for helpin' me escape Duncan's trap, but once we reach San Antonio, we're splittin' up."

That suited Frank fine. He took the bills and coins without comment. It wasn't half, but he didn't care to argue with Tom. Any complaints were more likely to bring a bullet than an even division of the loot. He wasn't sorry Tom wanted to go his own way once they got clear of Duncan and the posse. It was what he wanted too.

"Course taking that money weren't really stealin'." Tom's bitterness was turning to anger. "Duncan owns that bank in Hewitt, and he took more'n that from Jethro and the boys when he killed them. Jethro had over twenty thousand dollars in a couple pockets inside his vest. I bet Duncan kept it all and took back the thousand bucks he give us to get rid of that ranch family. And he got the horses he promised us—'cept these two."

Frank stuffed part of the bills in a pocket in his jeans and placed the rest inside his saddlebags, then he lay back against the bags, using them for a pillow. He closed his eyes and pretended to sleep, though he was really trying not to react to Tom's casual assertion that murdering the rancher and his family, not the acquisition of horses, was the real reason Duncan had hired them.

Out of slitted eyes, Frank watched Tom tie the bank bag to his saddle horn then lean his head against the hard leather. Minutes later, Tom reached for the saddle blanket to cover himself, but finding it wet with horse sweat or river water, he tossed it aside. In minutes, he was lying in the grass snoring.

Frank didn't find sleep so easily. It wasn't the first time he'd wondered if he would have been better off if he hadn't escaped that warehouse in Galveston. His mind shut down and he refused to think about Pa and Uncle Dan. To remember Ma and little Alice was unbearable. When Ma's sad eyes persisted in catching him unaware, he screwed his own eyes more tightly shut. It did no good. He knew she was disappointed in him. He tried to tell her he was sorry. He wanted to promise her he'd change; he'd be good again. But how could being sorry change the things he'd done? He'd become a thief and a murderer. There was no going back for him.

Thinking of Ma made him wonder if he could pray his way out of the mess he was in. Ma believed in praying, but he wasn't sure God even existed, and if He did, Frank didn't figure He'd listen to the prayer of someone who had done the things he'd done. Ma's eyes continued to plead with him, and finally he mumbled a few hasty words asking for deliverance from the mess he was in.

At last Ma's face faded from his mind and he drifted to sleep, but he didn't sleep long. A dream, maybe it was a memory, had him sitting bolt upright. It was a boy's face he saw now. He didn't know whether to tremble with fear or shout with joy. Something he'd seen earlier had registered in his mind as he relaxed in sleep. Seconds after leaving the bank, he'd turned to see if they were being followed. He'd seen a figure staring back at him from between two buildings. It had been a boy hiding in an alley with two horses! He looked a lot like the boy he'd shot at the ranch, and he'd caught a glimpse of the Crossed C brand on the flank of a horse that looked a great deal like the big stallion the ambushed rancher had been riding. Maybe the boy hadn't died! Hope filled his heart and tears burned his eyes. He vowed he'd get out of the outlaw business. When Tom Blackwell rode south for Mexico, Frank was heading north.

CHAPTER 4

1878

A cold wind, laced with hard-driving rain, blew across the open grassland as Frank made his way into one more bleak West Texas town. He had a little money, enough for table stakes, but unless Lady Luck smiled on him, he might have to look for another line of work, something that didn't involve cattle, cards, or bank robbery.

Discouragement hit him. He'd earned a living with cards for more than three years now and barely made enough to keep a roof over his head and food in his stomach.

He rode past a small square building with a sign that proclaimed it the Wallace Creek Bank. He wasn't ever going back to robbing banks. That life ended when Tom Blackwell sneaked off with Frank's rifle and most of their ammunition from the island in the Brazos River where they'd hidden from Harrison Duncan and his posse. He'd spent two days too scared to leave the island, then with the $200 in stolen bank money Blackwell left him and a horse wearing the Crossed C brand, he'd spent a nightmare night floating down the river. He passed Hewitt in the dark, and finally, with the dawn, he'd pointed his horse toward shore. It had taken another four days of running and hiding, surviving on a few chews of jerky and water from the muddy springs he'd stumbled onto to reach civilization—if you could call a town that consisted of ten adobe structures civilization. Life hadn't been easy since that day. Much as he'd hated to part with the mare, he'd accepted an offer of fifty dollars and a steady but not so flashy stock horse. Until now, he'd made himself believe a better life, filled with money and adventure awaited him. Now he looked down a bleak corridor of time filled with cheap whiskey and little pieces of cardboard.

He knew he could make more money gambling if he used the little tricks he'd found that fancy gamblers employed, but something about cheating at cards didn't set well with him. He wasn't sure the practice wasn't a whole lot different from robbing banks. He wasn't religious, but he'd never forgotten that night on the Brazos when he'd felt his ma urging him to pray. It had left him with a permanent phobia for stealing. He tried to forget the boy he'd shot, but the memory had become a permanent ache.

Rain dripped from his hat and ran in rivulets down the slicker that was doing a poor job of keeping him dry. He could have stayed in Abilene, but he'd had an attack of conscience and had decided he no longer wanted to take the hard-earned pay of the drovers who ended their trail drives in that dusty, dirty town.

He'd spent short intervals of several days in a lot of towns since then, usually leaving about the time potential players grew reluctant to play against him or a local sheriff dropped a few broad hints that he was no longer welcome.

Nothing stirred in this town. Not even a mongrel dog dashed into the street to welcome or warn him away. He'd figure the town for a ghost town, except for one faint light at the end of the street he could just make out through the haze of rain. The light was coming from a squat adobe building, most likely the local cantina. There didn't seem to be a hotel in town, the saloon was closed, and the cantina looked too small to let rooms. He sighed. At least he could get a drink to warm him, and he could ask about a place to stable his horse.

When he got closer, he saw the crude sign above the door that read Wallace Creek Gazette and Printing. A newspaper! For a moment, he felt he'd come full circle, and he half expected Uncle Dan to come to the door. Blinking his eyes to clear them of the rainwater that blew in his face, he could see that this was nothing like the prosperous business Dan ran. He couldn't imagine what kind of man had hauled a printing press to this nowhere place. As he moved closer, he figured he didn't stand much chance of finding a dry bed for the night, but since the newspaper office was the only place in town that appeared to be open, he dismounted and looped his horse's reins to the pole that ran in front of a couple of planks that served as a walkway leading to the door.

He stomped his boots to shake off the mud they'd collected and stepped up to the door. Uncertain whether he should knock or just walk in, he finally settled for a short rap on the door before lifting the latch. He noticed first the familiar scent of ink permeating the air, bringing with it memories of a life he'd struggled for nearly six years to forget. In retrospect, those years back home didn't seem so bad. The room was smaller than Uncle Dan's office, but it held the same sprawl of paper and print trays. The press occupied most of the room. A wave of homesickness swept over him as he looked at the press and breathed the scent of ink.

A curtain separated the front office from a back room. He stepped toward it, and the unmistakable sound of the hammer being drawn back on a shotgun froze him in mid-step. A pair of gun barrels poked through a hole in the curtain, and he noticed two more slits in the heavy fabric, which no doubt provided a man with a shotgun an ample view of the room where Frank stood. He recognized the snub barrels of a Greener, the infamous sawed-off .20-gauge shotgun favored by bartenders the length of Texas. Slowly he moved his hands well away from his body, lifting them, palms out, in a suggestion of surrender.

"Who are you? What do you want?"

It was the voice, rather than the questions that startled him. It was deep and husky, but there was no doubt it belonged to a woman. Unconsciously, he began to lower his hands.

"Keep them up!" The woman sounded more cautious than frightened, though something in her voice told him only a fool would push his luck. Since he wasn't a fool, he lifted his arms a little higher.

"Ma'am." He would have removed his hat, if he'd deemed that much movement practical. "I don't mean you any harm. I just rode into town, and everything seems to be closed up for the night. I saw your light and was hoping someone might point me to a livery stable where I can put my horse up for the night out of the rain—and perhaps a hotel where I can get a few hours sleep."

"Unbuckle your belt."

Her order was a good sign. She wouldn't shoot an unarmed man; at least he hoped she wouldn't. Taking care not to move too quickly, he reached for the buckle that held his six-shooter low against his right thigh. He knew that in a fair fight, he could draw as fast as most men, but *most* had never struck him as great enough odds where his hide was concerned. Besides, this woman, whoever she was, had the drop on him. And there were too many variables. The fact that it was a woman holding him at gunpoint didn't mean she couldn't shoot, and the gun she held wasn't any tiny derringer such as a number of ladies of his acquaintance hid in their stockings and he kept hidden in his sleeve. He'd discovered more than one woman in this vast land could wield a double barrel shotgun as well as any man could, and there was no way a Greener would miss anything it was pointed toward. There was also the possibility the woman wasn't alone.

Once his belt was free, he held it out with one hand and slowly lowered it to the floor.

"Kick it this way." Her voice hadn't warmed any, and he did as she instructed. "Now march right back out that door," she instructed. "I'll throw your gun after you, once you've cleared the hitching rail."

"Ma'am, I'd be happy to, but could you just tell me where I can find some shelter for my horse. It's raining hard out there, and we've come a long way. We're both tired and hungry, as well as cold." He tried to inject as much humbleness into his voice as possible, but inside he was seething. He hadn't made a threatening move or said one disrespectful word. He considered pulling his sleeve gun. He could shoot the old harridan before she knew he'd even moved. He paused, one hand on the door, the other poised to drop the sleeve gun into his hand.

"There's a barn out back."

The reluctant offer surprised him. He left the derringer where it was. "Thank you, ma'am." He resisted an urge to turn around. Instead he opened the door and stepped back out into the rain. Pulling his hat low over his face, he took a step toward his dejected looking horse. Before he reached the animal, a thud, followed by the slamming of the door, told him the woman had kept her word. With two fingers, he picked up his gun belt and strapped it around his waist. Still moving with care, he reached for his horse's reins, unwrapped them, and leading the horse, trudged around to the back of the building. Through the rain, he picked out a darker square and led the animal toward it.

As barns go, this one left a lot to be desired. It was really more shed than barn and only boasted two stalls. Once he'd bedded his horse down in one empty stall, he rolled out his bedroll in the other and adjusted it a few times to avoid as much dripping water as possible. There was no straw to soften his bed, but he fell asleep almost at once to the drumming sound of rain on the roof. Somewhere in his dreams the sound of rain changed to the thump and clang of Uncle Dan's printing press.

* * *

A sliver of light found its way through the thatched roof to awaken him much too soon. He didn't hear the rain any longer and assumed the storm had blown itself out. He stretched and looked about the crude shelter. He guessed it had been some months, maybe a couple of years, since it had last sheltered a horse. The small amount of tack hanging from hooks on one wall looked old and neglected. His horse shifted impatiently and he rose to his feet, rolled his blankets into a tight bundle and set them beside his saddle and valise. He stroked his horse's nose while he gathered his thoughts. He hadn't seen a pump last night, but there had to be one close. Once he'd washed his face and watered his horse, he'd have to decide whether to move on or try his luck in town.

Outside, puddles dotted the ground and sunshine promised to return the sleepy town to its former dusty state before the day ended. He breathed in, reveling in the fragrant air, as he studied the fresh-washed look of the prairie that spread beyond the little town. Covered with spring bluebells, it reminded him of the rolling ocean waves he'd once dreamed of, bringing a strange nostalgia for what might have been.

He found the pump and rusty trough midway between the newspaper office and the barn. After pumping enough water to fill the trough, he returned to the barn for his horse. While the animal was noisily drinking, he glanced toward the small adobe structure and was surprised to see a woman carrying a bundle of newspapers slip out its door then, staggering beneath her load, start toward the other businesses on the street.

She had long auburn curls that reached midway down her back, hastily tied back with a strip of leather. Her shirtwaist must have started out white, but it was now smudged and wrinkled, as was her long black skirt. She wasn't much larger than a child, but her stride was strong and sure. Was this the woman who had threatened him with a gun the night before? Somehow he'd pictured that woman as middle-aged, large, and masculine in appearance. This woman was nothing like that. To begin with, she was at most five feet two and probably weighed less than a hundred pounds. Her apron was tied tightly, revealing a shape that would turn most men's heads and belied any suggestion she might be a child. He wasn't close enough to be certain, but he suspected she was in her early twenties. Had he been misled by the woman's husky voice, or could this young woman be the other one's daughter?

A tingle of excitement coursed through his veins, and he found himself drawn to the woman in a way that no other woman had ever interested him. Tethering the horse's lead rope to the pump, he started toward her, keeping a wary eye on the print office door. When he caught up to the young woman, she ignored him, though she couldn't have failed to hear his boots on the boardwalk that lined the street.

"Good day, ma'am." This time he did lift his hat. With her arms weighted down by two large bundles of newspapers, he figured he was safe from the pistol that he could now see sagged the pocket of the printer's apron she wore over her skirt and shirtwaist.

She nodded her head in a quick, jerky movement in acknowledgment of his greeting but kept walking. He matched his steps to hers.

"I'd be happy to carry those papers for you," he said, reaching for the bundles, "in exchange for a little information about where a man might find a bite of breakfast."

"I don't need your help." The woman resisted his attempt to take the papers, but her one sentence refusal gave away her identity as the woman who had held him at gunpoint a few hours earlier. Her husky voice sounded neither intimidating nor middle-aged now. With an endless ocean of bluebells behind her and the glory of a Texas morning after a cleansing rain serving as her backdrop, that husky voice sounded like music.

He angled to get a peek at the face partially hidden beneath a well-worn felt hat. One look at her scowling face caused him to stumble. She was not only young, but beautiful. Her curls framed a heart-shaped face that would forever haunt his dreams. Thick, dark lashes framed the greenest eyes he'd ever seen. Her down-turned lips were full and pouting. He found breathing difficult. Struggling to recover his wits, he grasped the papers more firmly, tugging until she released them.

"You may not need my help, but I need yours," he responded to her earlier refusal of help as he settled the papers firmly in each hand. "Lead the way."

She glared at him through narrowed eyes, clearly suspicious of his motives. He noticed the way her long lashes formed little half moons against her upper cheeks. Her mouth revealed her anger and irritation, but even so, he was glad his hands were otherwise occupied or he wouldn't have been able to resist reaching out to skim a finger across the cutest pout he'd ever seen. Her skin was the color of a porcelain doll his little sister had gotten for her birthday when she turned six. That fine skin told him she hadn't spent a lot of time in the hot Texas sun.

When he simply stood there staring at her, she finally turned away with an irritated motion that came awfully close to stomping her feet and began moving briskly up the boardwalk. Her dainty boots tapped a sharp staccato beat with each step she took.

"Leave four here." She pointed to the front step of the mercantile. He did as she commanded. A dozen papers were left at the first saloon, one at the blacksmith shop, one at the sheriff's office, another couple at the stage stop, two at the bank, and so on until the business district was covered. Still without speaking beyond peremptory instructions, she turned back toward the newspaper office. He followed, saying nothing either, since it might be that silence on his part would prove to be the best tactic.

She didn't invite him inside when she reached the small adobe building, but she didn't seem particularly surprised when she found him still waiting after she emerged a few minutes later with two more bundles of newspapers. He held out his arms, and with a show of reluctance, she let him take them.

She led the way to the few homes scattered through the town, establishing a pattern as she paused at each house, took a paper from one of the stacks he held, folded it, and tossed it toward a front porch. It seemed to him that they'd fallen into a rhythm as familiar as though they'd been working together for years. Hoping she felt just a small part of what he did, he introduced himself and paused, waiting for her to tell him her name.

"Amelia Carlisle," she muttered, making it clear that introducing herself went against her better judgment.

It was a start, he congratulated himself.

"My uncle owns a newspaper in East Texas," he struggled for a topic that might engage her interest. His attempt to start a conversation paid off as she turned to look him full in the face for the first time. It might have been easier if her eyes had been the brown he'd expected earlier, but they were the sage green of the hill country, and they held his as nothing had ever done before.

"Did you work for him?" she asked.

"A little. I was pretty young, so I mostly swept up around the office and ran errands." He wished he could dazzle her with his experience as a newspaperman, but he sensed she would see through any lies he might tell her. That same instinct told him she wouldn't be impressed by his experience as an outlaw nor the years he'd bummed across Texas playing cards to eke out a living. It wasn't that he'd never spent any time around a pretty woman—he'd known plenty of saloon girls, but they were nothing like Amelia Carlisle.

Conversation was halting at first, but as they walked and delivered papers, they drifted into a casual exchange of information. He learned that her father had bought the newspaper office sight unseen, then died before he could move west to claim it. Her mother had remarried a few months later, and her stepfather hadn't welcomed a grown daughter, so with few resources and no family to turn to, she'd sold her few belongings and purchased a book about newspapers, and a combination of train and coach tickets that brought her to Wallace Creek. The long journey had provided ample time to study her book and increase her thirst for journalistic triumphs that had been ignited by her father's dreams and her own strong sense of justice.

She'd been in the small town for five months. Something about those five months of running a newspaper single-handed troubled her, but he didn't ask any questions. He did make up his mind to find out what had caused the appearance of two narrow lines above her pretty little nose and a wary hint of fear in her eyes.

Frank chose to be selective in revealing his own past. Since neither gambling nor riding with the Blackwell Gang were attributes that would gain him the attention he sought from Miss Carlisle and he'd already mentioned Uncle Dan, he told her about his father, who was a small town doctor.

"Pa had plans for me to go to school and become a doctor too, but Uncle Dan wanted me to work with him in the news office. I didn't know what I wanted to do," he told her. "I had big dreams about seeing the world and experiencing life, so I headed West to gain that experience."

"And did you discover the excitement you thought you would?" she asked.

"I discovered trailing a herd of cattle north to the railheads isn't as romantic as the penny novels make it sound, sleeping in the rain is cold and uncomfortable, and money and honor are scarce commodities on the Texas frontier." He finished with a self-deprecating laugh.

She joined his laughter, and he found himself enjoying strolling beside her discussing any and every topic that came to hand. At one house, she stopped to rap on the door. A large woman wearing an encompassing gingham apron responded after just a few moments' wait. She handed a towel-wrapped bundle to Amelia that smelled like fresh-baked bread, making Frank's stomach growl and his mouth water. He hadn't had anything to eat since the previous morning. He never had got the hang of campfire cooking and spent as few nights as possible on the trail.

By the time they returned to Amelia's office, which he now knew was also her home, he was praying she intended to share her loaf of bread with him. Though if she didn't, he would understand. He'd been able to deduce from her conversation that she was barely making a living from her newspaper. He'd also figured there were those in town who objected to her presence there, and he was curious to know who and why. She hesitated only a few seconds before inviting him inside to share her breakfast.

Frank looked around the small back room where Amelia led him. It boasted little more than a cot, a Franklin stove, a table and two chairs, a box nailed to the wall for use as a cupboard, and a row of hooks where a few articles of clothing hung. Beneath them, pushed up against the wall, was a black trunk. Amelia lifted a coffeepot from the top of the pot-bellied stove and poured them each a cup of the hot liquid. Then she unwrapped the bread and sliced it. From her cupboard, she produced a small crock of butter and a pot of jam.

He'd had more elaborate meals, but he'd never enjoyed one more. Whether it was the simple fare or the woman sitting across the table that touched a soft spot in his soul he didn't care to examine too closely, something told him to savor the moment, and he stretched out the meal as long as he dared.

"There doesn't seem to be a hotel in town," Frank said, setting his cup down at last. "Do you know anyone who rents rooms?" He surprised himself with the question, but the moment the words were out of his mouth, he knew the question had been inevitable. He wanted to stay in Wallace Creek more than he'd wanted any particular thing in a long time. He hadn't thought beyond finding shelter for the night when he'd arrived last night, but now he suspected that riding on was something he simply could not do.

Amelia toyed with her cup for a few minutes before speaking. "Mrs. Bronson, the woman who trades a loaf of bread each week for her paper, sometimes takes boarders. Her husband was killed a few years back on a cattle drive. She has two almost-grown boys, but they don't earn a man's wage yet, so she has to do all she can to support them. The older one sometimes helps me on press day."

"I'll go see her this morning."

"For a little extra, she'll provide meals and laundry."

"I can afford that for a while, if she doesn't want too much for the extra service." He rose to his feet. "Thank you very much, Amelia, for both the use of your stable last night and for breakfast this morning. I'll go right over and have a talk with Mrs. Bronson."

He got as far as the door before turning back. "Would you mind if I leave my horse in your barn a little longer?"

"That would be fine. I don't have an animal, so there's no reason you can't make use of the barn and the small pasture behind it as long as you're in town."

"If you'll let me, I can pay for his board by helping with your paper. I had a little experience with a press like yours when I helped my uncle." His uncle hadn't actually let him do much beyond inking, but he was aware that pulling the bar and tightening the mechanism required strength.

Frank scrutinized her face, waiting for some kind of response. He noted the dark shadows under her eyes and the weary slump to her shoulders and recognized the signs that she'd been up all night printing her papers. She was exhausted. He saw her eyes drift toward the cot on the other side of the room, then back to him. She nodded her head almost imperceptibly, but that small acquiescence to his suggestion filled him with elation. He excused himself and let himself out the door. The sound his boots made on the boardwalk was the happiest rhythm he'd felt like making in a long time. He smiled, and in his mind he pictured Amelia asleep on her little cot before the sound of his footsteps died away.

Frank was amazed as he made his way back to Mrs. Bronson's house by how much he'd picked up about the small town and its inhabitants from Amelia and by how much better the town looked in the morning sun than it had in last night's rain.

He turned a corner and recognized the house where Amelia had gotten the loaf of bread. Two young boys sat on the front stoop. Amelia said they were almost grown, but they looked about ten and twelve to him.

"Howdy, fellas," he greeted them. "Could you let your ma know I'd like to speak to her?"

The younger one rose eagerly to his feet, while the older one stared at Frank in a less than friendly fashion.

"Are you Miss Carlisle's beau?" the older boy gathered his courage to ask.

Frank hid a smile. "Miss Carlisle was kind enough to let me use her stable for my horse. She doesn't know me well enough to consider me a friend just yet." He didn't add that he intended to stick around long enough to see if he might become something more than a friend to the lady.

The door slammed behind the other boy. It opened again moments later, and the large woman he'd seen earlier stood framed in the doorway. She probably wasn't more than thirty years old, but she looked older as frontier women tended to do. Hard work, worry, and too much blazing sun aged women faster than it did the men. He thought for a moment of Amelia's delicate skin and felt regret that her chosen profession and the unforgiving West Texas sun would soon turn it to the leathery consistency of this woman's.

"Ain't you the young man that came around with Miss Carlisle this morning?" The woman eyed him with obvious curiosity.

"Yes, ma'am." He elected to get right to the point. "She said you sometimes let rooms, and that for a little extra you might provide meals and laundry."

"That I do," she responded. "No offense, but I insist on payment in advance."

"No problem." He couldn't blame the woman for being cautious. After riding for miles in the rain last night, then sleeping in a leaky shed, he didn't suppose he looked very presentable.

"Do you want to see the room?" She issued the invitation in an offhand manner as though she didn't care one way or the other whether he took the room, but something in her eyes revealed an almost desperate hope.

Frank stepped onto the porch and followed the woman inside. Sight unseen, he knew he was going to take the room.

He was relieved to see that the house was clean and neat. A large table with a half dozen chairs took up most of the front room. He caught a glimpse of a big, old Aga stove at one end of the room and judging from the loaf of bread he'd helped Amelia eat for breakfast, he knew the woman could cook. The prospect of home-cooked meals held a great deal of appeal.

She led him through a narrow doorway to a short hall. A door opened on either side, and a narrow flight of steps led upward to what he presumed was a sleeping loft where her two boys doubtless slept. Mrs. Bronson opened one of the doors, revealing an iron bedstead, a washstand, one straight-backed chair, and an armoire. A large oval rag rug filled the space between the bed and the door. On the wall were two framed watercolors depicting an English garden flanking a larger sampler with a carefully stitched Bible verse. He glanced quickly at it, reading the first and last lines.

No man can serve two masters . . . Ye cannot serve God and mammon. St. Matthew 6:24.

He found the words troubling, but he didn't have time to think on it now. Mrs. Bronson was talking, explaining that the room got the morning light, but was cool and comfortable in the afternoon.

He turned his attention to the rest of the room. It was simple, but neat and clean. For some reason he couldn't precisely fathom, it felt like he was coming home. Perhaps it was the contrast to the many nights he'd slept outside or in cheap hotels and boarding houses. He hadn't been inside a real home for six years. And perhaps it was a reminder that he'd grown up in a world of neatness and order where the scent of baking bread wafted in the air, neatly stitched samplers adorned the walls, and Sunday called for a stroll beside his mother to a white clapboard church with a steeple pointing toward heaven. For the first time in years, thoughts of his mother failed to bring him pain.

CHAPTER 5

After handing Mrs. Bronson a five dollar gold piece, Frank walked the few blocks to the barbershop he'd spotted earlier while helping Amelia deliver newspapers. A shave and a haircut, and if he were lucky a hot bath, might make him a bit more appealing to a certain young lady. Sprucing up would certainly do wonders for his own sense of worth.

A short, balding man looked up from the beard he was trimming when Frank walked through the door. He nodded briefly but didn't speak. Frank could see he and the man in the barber's chair were deep in conversation, so he settled himself in a chair near the door to wait.

"Be with you in a minute," the barber called after a few minutes, then went back to snipping at his customer's beard and expounding on the pros and cons of barbed wire.

"You new around here, mister?" the man in the chair asked, directing his question to Frank. Frank eyed the man's black trousers and the fancy vest with a silver thread forming a series of scrolls across the front. If not for the vest, he would have placed the man as the town banker, but the vest said saloon.

"Just arrived," Frank conceded as he settled back against the wooden chair the barber kept for waiting customers. He didn't want to appear unfriendly, but he knew it wouldn't be a good idea to show too much interest in a man who could determine whether or not he'd be welcome in his place of business.

Noticing a newspaper on the floor, Frank picked it up. It was one of the papers he'd helped deliver earlier. Considering the opportunity to read the newspaper a lucky break, he eagerly scanned the head-lines, then began to read. He liked Miss Carlisle's style. Her articles appeared to be well researched and the presentation simple and straightforward.

He read with interest about the debate over whether or not barbed wire should be allowed in the county, which he concluded was the impetus behind the conversation he'd just overheard. He read, too, that the mayor had received word from his son-in-law in Macon, Georgia, that he was now a grandfather, the Handley's goat had been apprehended by the sheriff for stealing sheets from Mrs. Walker's clothesline, and Reverend Donaldson's Sunday sermon would be on the subject of "rising above temptation."

He groaned when he reached the editorial. Amelia was a prohi-bitionist. She clearly didn't approve of strong drink or saloons. If she had her way, the "cesspits" and all "liquid misery" would be abol-ished. Her editorial certainly should have been enough to discourage his interest in the young lady, but strangely it didn't. He still wanted to know more about the feisty, young woman with such strong opinions and the courage to express them.

A deep chuckle had him lifting his eyes to the man who was just climbing down from the barber's chair. "Silly woman! She's got no business running a newspaper. Folks around here won't put up with such nonsense for long." Obviously the man with the fancy vest had read Amelia's editorial and found it both irritating and amusing.

The man's reaction stirred an opposing response in Frank. He wanted to speak up in her defense. It took considerable effort to restrain himself, but years of poker playing had taught him not to show his hand prematurely.

"Name's Bart Williams." The man held out his hand and Frank took it. "I see you've discovered our local newspaper." Turning to the mirror, the freshly barbered dandy checked his sideburns for symmetry. He patted an invisible hair into place. "The little lady gets quite agitated over issues which are none of her concern. That's what happens when one of those do-gooder ladies gets above herself and tries to do a man's job." There was a condescending element to the man's remarks that grated on Frank's nerves.

"Lots of folks disapprove of strong spirits," Frank pointed out, surprised at even tepid support for prohibition coming from his mouth. "Come to think of it, most every preacher I've come across has had at least one sermon in his repertoire concerning the evils of 'demon drink.'"

"Preachers are one thing, but these suffragists are something else." The man's jovial expression changed to a scowl.

Frank started. Was Amelia a suffragist? He'd heard the term a few times and equated it with wild-eyed women carrying banners and marching down Eastern streets demanding the right to vote. That description didn't fit Amelia, did it? And if it did, did it matter? Ma always believed women should have as much say as men about government.

"Crazy woman thinks all the saloons should be shut down, Sally's place too, and that women should vote like men! She's always snooping in things that are none of her concern." Bart Williams slammed his hat on his head and strode out of the shop.

"He and that brother of his over at the bank think they own this town." There was enough resentment in the barber's tone to suggest that not all of the town folks thought as much of the two men as they did of themselves.

Frank watched the dandy cross the street and enter one of the few buildings on Main Street that wasn't made of adobe brick and which was two stories high, proving his earlier guess right. The building was the largest saloon in town. He turned back to the barber. "Any chance I could get a bath as well as a shave and haircut?"

"The bath is two bits extra."

Frank flipped the barber a couple of coins, and a short time later, he sat in hot water up to his chin. He leaned back, letting the steamy water ease the aches of what he hoped was his last ride for some time. His mind turned to Amelia, and the saloonkeeper's words flitted through his mind. *A suffragist?* He thought about it and decided the word didn't evoke the horror in his mind it did for other men. Ma had claimed more than once that the day would come when women would be senators and governors. She'd threatened more than once to run against that pompous fool Mortimer Steadman for mayor of Willow Springs.

Her threat had always amused Pa, but Uncle Dan had egged her on. At the time, the whole argument had embarrassed Frank, but as he thought about it now, he figured Ma would have made a better mayor than old Steadman. And Frank certainly had no objections if pretty, little Amelia Carlisle wanted to vote, but shutting down the saloons was another matter. The saloons were where he made his living.

An hour later, feeling like a new man with his cheeks smooth, his hair trimmed, and sporting the black, ready-made suit he always wore when he sat down with a deck of cards, he made his way back to the newspaper office. He didn't see any sign of Amelia and decided she was probably still sleeping, so he turned his horse into the pasture and gathered up his saddlebags and the few belongings he'd left in the barn with his saddle. He turned back toward the street, carrying the meager possessions he could call his own.

Once settled at Mrs. Bronson's, he'd check out the saloons. For some reason, he cast a guilty glance over his shoulder toward the newspaper office. But the fact was, he'd need a few good wins in order to stay in Wallace Creek more than a couple of weeks—and he had definite plans to stay.

* * *

In the coming weeks, Frank dropped by the news office every day on some pretext or another, and he made certain he was free Wednesday nights when Amelia printed her paper, then showed up at her door Thursday mornings to help her with delivery. At first, she seemed suspicious of his motive for hanging around, but gradually she relaxed and seemed to enjoy his company as much as he enjoyed hers. There was something exhilarating about being around Amelia. Frank found himself laughing more than he had since before his ma died.

They argued too. Amelia was strong-willed and firmly committed to women's rights, which she loudly proclaimed through her paper. She also had strong opinions about almost every issue that affected Texas and the whole United States of America.

"I'm not against women getting the vote," Frank told her during one of their many discussions on the topic. "I just think a more subtle approach would be more effective. Why can't you write a series of articles pointing out the accomplishments of progressive women without tying in Women's Emancipation? If men hear or read about successful, intelligent women, they'll start to see women as equals and be more willing to trust them with the vote."

"Too many men like the Williams brothers will never see women as intelligent equals without being hit over the head and forced by law to recognize us," Amelia scoffed at his suggestion. She reached for a tray of type to set her editorial for the week's edition.

"The Williams brothers and some of the other men you've antagonized could be dangerous," Frank warned. "Narrow-minded individuals tend to feel they're being attacked when a difference of opinion is stated with a great deal of bluntness."

Amelia lifted her face to look directly in his eyes. "I know you think I'm hopelessly naive, but I'm not. Journalism is all about finding the truth and stating it with boldness. Newspapers that only reflect popular opinions, that shy away from pointing out wrongs and sidestep important issues, are only good for wrapping yesterday's garbage. I intend to be a real journalist, and that means printing the truth as I see it."

"I'm only saying to be careful."

"I won't placate the Williams brothers just to make my life easier." She scowled and ducked her head back to the tray of type. "There comes a time when a person has to decide what he or she believes, then stand up for it."

Her words brought a wince to Frank's conscience. How long had it been since he'd stood up for anything he strongly believed in? For that matter, how long had it been since he'd held any strong views? He stifled a sigh, then asked, "What do you want me to do?" He'd come to help since this was Wednesday and he was well aware of how hard Amelia worked on Wednesdays to finish up the last minute details of her paper before she began printing. He supposed that if he had strong feelings about anything, Amelia was quickly becoming that something.

"You could start writing the story on this fall's election. Several candidates for governor have already announced, then there are our local races for mayor and sheriff."

"Me? You want me to write the story?" Frank stared at Amelia, expecting her to burst out laughing and proclaim it all a joke.

"You can write. I've seen you correct my spelling more than once." Amelia stood her ground. "I've got to finish the article on the church supper and set the type. That leaves you to piece together an election story from those telegrams I received and the candidate bills that came on the coach."

Frank felt an odd thrill as he pulled a sheet of foolscap closer and reached for a pen. It had been a long time since he'd held a pen in his hand. To his surprise, the words came quickly to his mind. He paused only when he saw the name Harrison Duncan as one of the candidates for the state senate. He read the description on the poster and knew it for a bunch of lies. It made Duncan sound like some kind of wise guardian of the land and the people of Texas. Frank considered including the truth in the piece Amelia had asked him to write. He'd like to tell the world that Duncan was a thief and a liar. A murderer too. He didn't doubt Amelia would do just that if she knew what he knew about the rancher-turned-politician. But he couldn't do it. Amelia might wonder how he'd gained the information. He couldn't risk letting her find out about his past.

He settled for leaving out the glowing account of Duncan's so-called farsighted endeavors and simply wrote: *Harrison Duncan, a relative newcomer to Texas, claims one of the largest ranches in the hill country portion of the state near Hewitt. The fortuitous sale or abandonment of the ranches surrounding his initial small parcel of land led to the rapid expansion of his Double Bar D brand.* Frank considered for several moments before he added, *Duncan's estranged wife and son remain in New York with her family.* He added the last, knowing Texans remained suspicious of anyone with Yankee connections. There was no mention of Duncan's family in the bills, but the information he'd learned from Tom Blackwell would be easy to confirm by telegraphing a New York newspaper. It was also as far as he dared go toward exposing the man whom he had good reason to hate and fear.

He finished the story with a glow of pride. For just a moment, he considered adding his byline and sending a copy to Uncle Dan. *Better not,* he decided. He didn't want his name associated with Duncan's in any way. He carried the article to Amelia, who, much to his disappointment, didn't take time to read it immediately. She was busy forming lines of type. He watched her for a moment and remembered his mother's flying fingers selecting letters and stringing them together without seeming to even glance at the trays before her. He'd learned to spell using his mother's trays of type.

Hearing the front door open, he wandered to the front of the shop in time to see his landlady's son step into the room.

"Howdy, Clarence," he greeted the boy. Clarence merely grunted and moved to where Amelia kept the supplies she needed for the press. He selected an oilcan and a rag and went to work preparing the machine for tonight's run. Frank watched the boy in exasperation. He'd tried everything he could think of to befriend the lad without any luck. His younger brother, Timothy, was more than eager to be Frank's friend, but not Clarence.

Grabbing his hat, Frank left the office. If he hung around the news office, Clarence would glare, spill oil or ink, and make more noise than necessary as he inked the plates, distracting Amelia and setting Frank's teeth on edge.

Frank whistled as he walked down the narrow Main Street of the town he'd begun to think of as home. He tipped his hat to a couple of ladies exiting the mercantile, then turned to enter the boot shop. The smell of leather and boot polish hung in the air, and he breathed it in deeply, enjoying the rich scent.

"Howdy, Frank." A small, balding man rose to his feet, wiping his hands on a leather apron. "I've got it right here." He scurried behind a counter to produce a piece of paper. Frank examined it and nodded approvingly.

"It looks good and is bound to bring more customers to your shop." Frank pocketed the ad and the silver dollar the shoemaker handed him. They chatted a few more minutes, then Frank said good-bye and left the shop to wander on down the street.

He passed Sally's and smothered a grin when she called to him with her usual offer of a quarter-page advertisement. He laughed

and shook his head to show there were no hard feelings. The sound
of her laughter followed him down the street. They both knew that
Amelia would never run the "sporting" madam's ad.

He collected a few more ads for the newspaper, then made his
way back to Amelia's office, feeling slightly smug. Both the
number of ads and payment for them had doubled since he'd
begun helping Amelia sell advertising for her paper. He wasn't
certain whether he was a better salesman or if the merchants were
more comfortable dealing with a man concerning financial
matters. Basking in a glow of accomplishment for both the article
he'd written and the increased revenue he'd brought the paper, he
wondered if Dan had been right all along and he did have a future
in newspaper work.

He passed the sheriff's office. The lawman appeared to be
sleeping, tipped back in his chair in front of his office. Something
about Joel Rivers bothered Frank. He was almost as new to Wallace
Creek as Frank and, according to Amelia, hadn't been elected sheriff,
but had suddenly shown up one day with a badge on his chest and a
letter of appointment from the governor. He was a loner who didn't
seem to elicit strong feelings pro or con from the community. Still
he managed to convey an air of disapproval toward Frank. It may
have been Frank's imagination, fueled by his well-grounded wariness
of lawmen, but he couldn't help sensing Rivers felt some personal
antagonism toward him.

Clarence scowled and put down the broom when Frank reen-
tered the shop, but Amelia handed the boy a dime and sent him on
his way. He lingered at the door for several minutes watching
Amelia, then casting Frank a dark look, he shuffled out, making his
way slowly down the boardwalk.

"I don't know what has gotten into that boy lately." Amelia
shook her head, watching the boy trail down the street with
slumped shoulders.

"I do." Frank grinned when she turned to face him with one
eyebrow raised in query. "He's jealous and thinks I've moved in on
his territory."

Her cheeks turned red, and Frank's grin widened.

"I can't really blame him. In his shoes, I'd be jealous too." His eyes met hers, and a thousand words seemed to fly back and forth. Amelia was the first to look away.

"Well," she rubbed her hands down the front of her apron. "We better get to work."

Frank merely chuckled and followed her to the stack of papers waiting to be fed into the press.

Hours later, Amelia brushed her damp hair back with one hand while she used the other one to brace her back. "That's the last one," she groaned. Before she could reach for it to fold and add to the stack, Frank picked it up and completed the task.

Amelia lifted a rag from the pile she kept handy, but Frank took it from her hand.

"Sit down," he told her. "I'll clean the ink off the press. It will only take a few minutes."

"But . . ."

He gently pushed her toward her chair. She sank onto it and watched him for a few minutes.

"Won't you be missed at Bart's tonight?" The thrust of her chin told him the way he spent most evenings was a sore spot with her. He'd known from the start that it was something he'd eventually have to explain to her. In a town as small as Wallace Creek and with her curiosity about everything, there was no way he could expect her not to know he spent almost every evening at Bart Williams's saloon. He gave the press a few more buffs, then deliberately returned the rag to the bucket.

Approaching the desk behind which she sat with as much confidence as he could muster, he pinched the crease of his trousers and settled himself on a corner of her desk. She turned her head away.

"Amelia, look at me," he started in a quiet voice. When she raised her eyes to meet his, he went on. "I know how you feel about saloons, and I share many of those feelings. But the only way I know to earn a living is with a deck of cards, and saloons are where I play. Not everything about a saloon is bad."

"I've heard all the arguments for saloons—that they provide places for lonely men to meet over friendly games of cards, that with men vastly outnumbering women in the West, men need the feminine company prostitutes provide, that alcohol is necessary for men to relax and have a good time after working hard. I don't believe those arguments. Men like Bart Williams don't build saloons to provide recreation for men—all he cares about is getting rich. He doesn't provide a charitable service for lonely cowboys. He takes advantage of their youth and loneliness to strip them of their hard-earned pay! And the men who have families are wasting money that would be better spent on food and better living conditions for their families. I don't like knowing you frequent his place, helping him entice men to gamble and drink." Her fingers fumbled with a piece of lead, and she looked away to hide her sudden nervousness.

That gave Frank encouragement. Amelia always spoke her mind, and if she was concerned about hurting his feelings, she must care for him at least a little.

"I tried to earn a living chasing cows," Frank told her. "But I'm no good at it. I'm not a farmer either. Out here, there aren't many ways to earn a living. I'm good at cards—I don't cheat, and I never leave a man without the means to feed himself. I've thought about moving farther west to try my hand at mining, but it holds little appeal. I'd leave off gambling in a minute if I could support myself some other way."

"Sometimes you have to take a stand, even if you don't know where you'll land," Amelia said in a low voice, and he thought of the leap into the dark she'd taken when she risked everything to travel to a strange town to begin a career as a journalist. He thought of his own rush to leave home, but it wasn't the same. He'd been running away more than pursuing a dream.

"Are you trying to find something else?" she added after a moment.

"Yes, I've got an idea, and if it works out, you'll be the first to know." He smiled coaxingly, hoping she wouldn't ask too many questions or send him out of her life. He didn't particularly trust Bart Williams, and he was becoming more aware each day of the contrast between the joy he felt being with Amelia and the darkness and profanity that surrounded him as he sat at Bart's poker table.

Too much of the gambler's life brought him into proximity with men like Tom Blackwell. But he really did have an idea. It would involve exploring a little farther afield than Wallace Creek, but with luck, he'd know before the summer ended.

"Will you trust me for awhile?" he asked and held out his hand to her. If he could just keep up this double life a little longer, everything would work out fine. He could ease out of one way of life and into a new, more satisfying one if he played his cards right.

Finally, she nodded and took his hand. He wasn't certain whether she'd decided to trust him or if she was too tired to argue any more.

"You're tired, Amelia. I don't want to keep you up talking, but there is one more thing I'd like to say." He lifted her hand to his lips. "Would you please accompany me to the box social Friday night at Conrad Williams's house? He's nothing like his brother, and his wife is a kind and gracious lady. If you want to think about it, we can talk more after you get some rest." He kissed her fingers, then straightened. "I'll be here early in the morning to help you deliver papers," he promised before stepping from the office.

A short time later he was whistling his way up the path to Mrs. Bronson's front door. He let himself in quietly, since the household had settled in for the night several hours earlier. He didn't light a lantern until he reached his room, where the first thing he saw as the light flared brightly was the hand-stitched sampler on the wall. Its words made him wince, and long after he blew out the lantern and laid his head on his pillow, he found himself wondering whether he was one of those attempting to serve two masters.

* * *

The night of the box social, Frank arrived at the newspaper office dressed in his best suit and was delighted to see Amelia in cream-colored muslin with a green satin sash encircling her tiny waist. She appeared lighthearted as they walked the short distance to Conrad's two-story house located just beyond town. More than one pair of eyes looked askance to see the newspaper editor and the gambler arrive together, but Conrad and his wife were gracious hosts, making them feel comfortable and welcome.

When the time came to join the others on the wide veranda to share their box lunches and the pastor and his wife invited them to join them at their table, Frank experienced a sense of well being he hadn't known since he was a boy. He hadn't realized until that moment how much he'd missed being part of a community.

He watched Amelia nibble on a piece of chicken and was struck again by her beauty. For the first time since he'd fled Galveston, he dared to dream. Wallace Creek would be his home from now on. It was an up and coming new town with a steady flow of new businesses. He'd make a place for himself in the rapidly growing town, and his fortune would grow with it. He even dared to hope Amelia would be part of the future he was beginning to envision.

"If the ladies will come with me," Mrs. Williams spoke, holding the door that led to the inside of the house, "I'd like to show you the lovely painting Conrad had shipped here for my birthday. Mr. Eastman Johnson is quite in demand in Boston this season."

Frank hid a smile, seeing the quick flash of annoyance in Amelia's eyes. He didn't doubt she would much prefer to join in the gentlemen's conversation to sighing over a painting, famous artist or not. To be quite honest, he would have preferred to keep her by his side all evening.

He paid scant attention to Conrad's announcement that he and his brother had bought up two parcels of land on the north side of Wallace Creek or to their plans for building stockyards in anticipation of the day when a railroad spur would be extended to the growing community they expected would someday serve as the hub of the West Texas cattle industry. Conrad was a bit of a blowhard, and though he'd always been friendly to Frank, Frank suspected his civilized veneer didn't go much further than skin deep.

When the ladies rejoined the men on the veranda, talk turned to lighter matters, and Mrs. Williams entertained her guests with two light opera pieces while the pastor's wife accompanied her on a small spinet from just inside the wide veranda doors.

It was with a sense of relaxed comfort that Frank took Amelia's arm to walk her home down the town's Main Street when the evening, which was brightly lit by stars and a full moon, ended. It was only a little past ten o'clock, and tinkling piano music and saloon lights spilled onto the street. He carefully steered her away from the businesses he knew she found objectionable.

"Frank." He knew at once from the tone of her voice that she wasn't sharing his romantic thoughts. Instead, she was writing a story in her head, one that was bound to antagonize the Williamses. He wished he could make her understand that antagonizing the brothers was akin to poking a bear with a stick. "While Carolyn was showing the ladies that silly painting in the library, I saw something sticking out of a drawer of Conrad's desk that interested me."

Frank groaned inwardly, but his silence only encouraged Amelia to go on. "There was an envelope with the return address of the Santa Fe Railroad Company protruding from the drawer. I was standing next to the desk and, being bored, I shifted a few books and papers about. Beneath a ledger, I saw the letter that had arrived in that envelope. It seems Conrad is negotiating with the railroad to sell a right-of-way across eight ranches."

"He mentioned he and Bart had purchased a couple of tracts of land outside of town in anticipation of the railroad's arrival," Frank said.

"But Frank, I know those ranches. None of the owners wished to sell, but the bank foreclosed on two of them quite recently, and a third belonged to a man who died last spring when his horse shied at a rattlesnake and threw him. Conrad bought the land for a pittance. The fourth was a farm that was abandoned last fall when a renegade band of Indians supposedly stole stock and burned the family out. The other ranches have similar stories. I find it odd that they all somehow fell into Bart and Conrad's hands."

"This is a small town, and neither Bart nor Conrad Williams are wealthy by most standards. Where did they get the money to buy up so much land?" Frank mused in spite of his determination to stay out of the Williams brothers' affairs. Talk of acquiring ranches from unwilling sellers brought back painful memories that he'd worked hard to leave behind.

"I'm not certain what it means," Amelia said. "But it appears from something said in the letter that the Williams brothers have a wealthy backer. I'd like to investigate that further."

"Be careful you don't antagonize Conrad," Frank warned. "He's quieter than Bart and appears more gentlemanly, but I think it would be a mistake to underestimate him."

"Are you saying that if I pursue this story, he might find a way to shut down my press?"

"I'm just saying he's not a man to trifle with."

CHAPTER 6

By midsummer, the paper's circulation had doubled, partly because Frank had convinced Mrs. Bronson to allow her boys to make a circuit on horseback to ranches within a day's ride of Wallace Creek to drop off papers, and partly because the stage that came through town twice a week began ordering a supply of papers to leave at the various stage stops along its route. With wider circulation came more advertising, and Amelia's paper began to make a profit.

Even Clarence was happier and made tentative peace with Frank, since it was Frank's horse that the boy rode to deliver papers, and the paper route was earning him enough coins to make him feel like the man of his family. Amelia became the darling of both the Methodists and the Baptists, and Frank was often beside her as she gathered notes on their various socials for the society page she instituted. He even occasionally attended Sunday services with her as she alternated between the two denominations, depending on which traveling preacher was in town.

The only one who wasn't happy was Bart Williams. The saloon owner was becoming increasingly vocal in his complaints about Amelia Carlisle snooping into affairs that were none of her concern and her editorials that denounced his line of work. A group of ladies went so far one night as to picket his saloon after reading in the *Gazette* of ladies in the East who were picketing local taverns. Williams threatened them with the shotgun that the bartender kept behind the bar, then embarrassed himself further by having to back down when the ladies refused to move. He lost a little business as well, due to the ladies' husbands choosing for the sake of their happy homes to stay home that night.

A few nights later as Frank dealt cards, he heard Williams's raised voice mention Amelia's name, and he paused to listen. "Someone ought to teach that little girl a lesson. She has no business interfering with men's right to run things. She's nothin' but a troublemaker without enough brains to see the big picture," he said, denouncing Amelia to a pair of ranchers at the bar, both known to have uncertain tempers. Bart said something that Frank didn't quite hear, but from the raucous laughter that followed, he surmised the remark had been suggestive or worse. He rose to his feet and stepped to the bar.

"Bart," he said, "you may not like what Miss Carlisle has to say about saloons and the troubles made worse by drinking, but I can't see that she's hurt your business any. If you can't leave her name out of this place, I'm leaving. I expect most of the regulars who stop by for a game of cards once or twice a week will follow me across the street to the Red Rooster."

"Seems for a gamblin' man you're gettin' kind of sweet on that trouble-makin' . . . female," Bart observed. His eyes narrowed, and a nasty sneer accompanied his words.

"My feelings for the lady don't enter into this discussion. What will it be? Do I sit back down, or do I take my game across the street?" Frank held his breath and forced a calmness to his demeanor. He couldn't believe he'd actually challenged Bart. A small glow began to build in his chest, and he grew more confident. He'd taken whatever path was easiest for so many years, it was a novel experience to actually stand up for someone other than himself. For Amelia, he discovered, he could take a stand.

After a few muttered curses, Bart agreed Amelia Carlisle was off limits as a topic in the Golden Garter, and Frank made his way back to his usual table. He felt an urge to exhale deeply, but instead assumed the relaxed stance he'd learned kept his opponents off guard at the gaming table. He knew Bart was too astute as a businessman to drive away his star attraction. Word had spread among cowboys and ranchers alike that they wouldn't be cheated at cards at the Golden Garter. Business flourished. The men who tried their luck at Frank's table never left with full pockets, but they weren't drained to desperation either, and they even occasionally made modest gains which they turned around and spent on drinks and women. It was an arrangement that served the Golden Garter well.

Bart's overall profits had risen nicely during the months Frank played at his table. His establishment had taken on an almost reputable shine. Frank hadn't done badly either, and his growing account at the Wallace Creek bank was carrying him closer to the goal he'd set to win Amelia.

Frank glanced at the glass at his elbow. It was still nearly full. He'd learned to sip a single drink slowly enough to make it last all evening. Whether it was Amelia's disappointment should she smell alcohol on his breath that curbed his taste for whiskey or the demands of the carefully controlled game he played, which required his full attention, he didn't know, but he found himself wanting a drink less each night. There was an added bonus to the reduction in his drinking as well: his game had improved so much, he was winning far more than he ever had before.

For some reason, he found himself thinking about Pa. Pa would have agreed with Amelia that alcohol was behind more human woe than all of the Indian tribes put together, and he would be disappointed if he knew his son spent so much time in a saloon drinking and gambling. *Only a little longer,* he told himself. Then he could fling the cards in the nearest fire and never touch another drink.

* * *

One Monday morning in mid-August, he boarded the coach for Midland to put his plan in motion. A week later he traveled west. On returning to Wallace Creek, he sought out Amelia. She was sitting at her desk, writing furiously with a squeaky pen.

On seeing him, she set aside her pen to welcome him with a joyous smile, unmindful that she was holding up the story that would be the lead article in the following morning's paper. When she remembered, she pushed the article she'd been laboring over toward Frank.

"This is really exciting," she told him. "I've been collecting information on the various outlaw gangs that have operated in Texas since the war. There are quite a few former soldiers turned gunmen who are robbing banks and holding up stages. It will be a great article. Two articles, I should say. I printed the first one last week while you were away. It featured the infamous Blackwell Gang that mysteriously disappeared six years ago. This one is about a new gang that seems to be led by one of the Blackwell brothers, who reappeared a few months ago."

Amelia's words raised a warning flag in the back of Frank's mind, but only slightly dimmed the optimism he felt. It was the first time in years Frank had really felt good about himself.

"Here, I've been busy too." Hoping to distract her from further discussion of outlaws, he brushed aside the concern her newsgathering had stirred by handing her the stack of papers he carried in his hand. "It may be a little difficult to read. Bouncing around in a coach didn't do much for my penmanship, but it didn't seem right to waste time staring out a window, when I could provide you with stories about some of Wallace Creek's neighboring towns and leading citizens."

She smiled the way most women would have done had they been handed flowers wrapped in fancy paper. She began thumbing through the sheets, pausing to read a line here and another there.

"This is good. I wonder if we could do a follow up." She pointed to a scrawled paragraph about four Mormon families who were attacked by rowdies while they were en route to Utah from one of the Mexican settlements where they'd taken refuge following the assassination of their leader, Joseph Smith, prior to the war. The hapless families had lost their stock and two of their wagons had been overturned. Just as he'd expected, her attention shifted from outlaws to Mormons and he smiled as she vowed to find out more about the group and their treatment. An unexpected twinge of conscience reminded him that he had once been guilty of harassing adherents of the much-maligned religious group by setting their privy on fire.

"Here's something else I thought you might be able to use." He placed a stack of advertising orders on her desk. "And they're all paid for." He placed a small leather bag beside the ads.

She reached for the bag, carefully loosening the drawstring to look inside. Seeing the amount of money inside it, her eyes glistened with unshed tears, and she rose to stand in front of him. One hand touched his forearm. "That's more money than I made in all the months before you came, more than enough to pay off my loan at the bank. But it wouldn't be right to keep it all. I want you to keep half of it." She began dividing the money.

"I won't refuse a commission," he told her, placing his hand over hers to stop her dividing the money, "but I won't accept half. I think ten percent is standard. Besides, your expenses are bound to go up with adding another page to the Gazette."

"Another page?"

"You'll have to add another page in order to have room for all these articles and advertisements."

She stepped closer, and his arms folded around her. She leaned her head against his chest. They stood locked together until a rattle of the doorknob alerted them that Clarence had arrived to sweep out the shop and ink the press. Pulling guiltily apart, Amelia resumed reading the pages he'd given her, and he set to work proofreading a stack of papers Amelia had left on the desk he'd come to think of as his own.

Later, after the boy had gone, Amelia and Frank worked with an easy rhythm as though they could read each other's mind, setting the lines of type and laying out the pages. Still, it was after midnight when Frank pulled the lever for the last time and Amelia folded the sheets together and added them to the stacks that filled every available space in the small office.

Amelia sank to her chair. "I don't know why I'm so fatigued. We finished a full two hours ahead of when I finished last week while you were away." She smiled tiredly at him.

Before Frank could join her in his customary spot, perched on one corner of her desk, the sound of shattering glass brought their heads up. Reacting instinctively, Frank shoved the curtain to Amelia's private quarters aside and dashed inside the room. A puddle of flames burned brightly atop the stove where a whiskey bottle lay shattered. The stench of kerosene filled the small space.

Snatching a towel that hung over the back of a chair, he wiped up the rivulets of kerosene that ran toward the edges of the stove and beat out the tongues of flame that followed the streams of fuel. He worked with speed and care to prevent any of the streams from dripping to the floor, knowing they would be followed by flames which would spread rapidly across the wood floor. Only when the flames at last disappeared did he turn to Amelia, who had followed him into the room to help him beat at the flames. She stood amid shards of glass from the back window, breathing heavily.

"Stay back," he told her, "until I get this swept up."

"I can clean it up." She reached for the broom that Clarence had left leaning in a corner. Frank took it from her hands and completed the task. She watched him for a moment then started for the door, carrying her shotgun.

"You can't go out there!" Frank shouted, grabbing her by the shoulders and forcibly seating her in one of the two wooden chairs beside the table. "If someone wants to kill you or scare you off, he could still be outside with a rifle waiting for you to open that door."

"I don't understand." She stared at the pile of debris he was sweeping into a bucket.

"You don't understand why the fire didn't burn the whole place down, or why someone threw burning kerosene at your home and business?" He spoke through clenched lips, so angry he wanted nothing more than to find who had done the cowardly deed and thoroughly thrash him. If he found out who had tried to kill Amelia, he was angry enough to borrow her Greener himself.

His mind grappled with possible suspects while trying to appear outwardly calm and discuss the matter rationally with Amelia.

"Both, I guess." She sounded as angry as he felt.

"Well, first of all, the fire didn't do more damage because the person who threw the bottle threw it too hard, striking the stove on the opposite side of the room, which, being August, wasn't in use. Had it been thrown with less force, it might have landed on your bed or rolled against the curtains, and with the ink, oil, and paper around here, the fire would have been out of control in less than a minute. To answer the second question, I don't have any idea who did this, but I intend to find out." He wasn't being entirely truthful. There was one person who openly held a grudge against Amelia. Frank had every intention of confronting Bart Williams with a few questions.

* * *

He hated leaving Amelia alone even after the fire was out and the mess cleaned up, but he felt an urgency to see Bart as soon as possible. The night air was cool, and it served to calm his temper as he made his way down the street. When he pushed the batwing doors aside and stepped inside the Golden Garter, he noticed at once that Bart wasn't in his usual place behind the bar. Scanning the room, he spotted two men, one old and one young, huddled together in a far corner. The older man was downing whiskey, one drink after another in rapid succession, while the younger man seemed to be berating him. He hadn't seen either of them before. They'd likely arrived in town while he was away working on his plan to expand Amelia's newspaper. He hadn't seen the cowboy who slouched low, seemingly asleep, at a shadowed table a short distance behind the two anytime before either. His tied-down gun suggested he might be one of the fast guns who drifted through West Texas like dark shadows. Drifters were common in Wallace Creek, but he'd make it his business to learn more about these newcomers.

He recognized Joel Rivers, the local sheriff. He was a big man, who seemed to spend an inordinate amount of time in the Golden Garter, though he never played cards and he could nurse a single shot of whiskey all evening. Frank suspected he did odd jobs for the Williams brothers in addition to his lawman duties, and he suspected they had a hand in his sudden appointment to sheriff.

He sat alone, though an empty glass across the table suggested he hadn't been alone long. Frank made his way to the table Rivers occupied.

"Mind if I join you?" Frank made his voice as casual as possible.

Rivers looked up and asked with a sneer, "Your lady friend throw you out?" Frank stiffened in spite of his determination to appear unruffled. Bart and all of the townspeople were well aware Frank spent Wednesday nights assisting Amelia with the newspaper that hit the street every Thursday morning. A snatch of gossip concerning Rivers he'd heard earlier came to mind. Rivers was suspected of paying more than casual attention to Amelia before Frank's arrival. That, he decided, would account for the animosity Rivers seemed to direct toward him.

"Finished early," Frank responded in an even voice. "Mind if I sit down?"

Rivers made a grandiose gesture toward the empty chair across from him. "I've no reason to stop you, and it's not likely Bart will be back tonight. Just don't think I'm stupid enough to try to beat you at cards," he finished with a warning.

"I'm not looking for a game—just a little conversation."

Rivers eyed him suspiciously as Frank made himself comfortable at the table.

"How long have you lived in Wallace Creek?"

"What's it to you?"

"Nothing. Just making conversation. I thought it might be good to get to know each other a little better."

"You got something on your mind. Ever since you arrived in Wallace Creek, you've had your eye on the main chance, but you aren't fooling me." Rivers leaned forward. "I've noticed the way you shuffle those bits of pasteboard so you don't clean out the locals and they keep coming back. You want something."

"Sure, I want something." Frank smiled congenially. "I plan to make Wallace Creek my home."

"I never heard of a gambler making any place his home," Rivers scoffed.

"Maybe I don't plan to be a gambler forever."

"Once gambling gets in your blood, it's like liquor. A man doesn't change."

Frank suspected Rivers was referring to something more than gambling. "He does if he has a reason," he countered, keeping his voice smooth.

"Are you saying that bit of skirt running the newspaper is reason enough to change?"

Rivers appeared amused. Frank merely smiled a tight-lipped smile. Rivers turned his face away as though inviting others to share the joke, yet Frank suspected he was really scanning the room for something else entirely. He was almost as good at camouflaging his intent as the cowboy he had observed earlier, who appeared to be sleeping, though Frank suspected he missed nothing happening in the room.

"Let me tell you something." Rivers leaned across the table. "You aren't as smart as you think you are. That newspaper woman has been sticking her nose in dangerous matters. Bart knows about the inquiries she's been sending to various state offices, and I don't think you're going to like the trouble she's likely to stir up."

"Is that a threat," Frank struggled to remain calm, "or an admission that Wallace Creek's sheriff was hired to see only what the Williams brothers want him to see?" He wasn't certain Rivers's statement was an admission of his complicity in the attempted torching of Amelia's office or a swaggering attempt to put Frank down. Frank had learned to read other men's faces, but Rivers left him puzzled. He was hiding something; Frank was sure of that. But he often made comments that implied he expected Frank to read a deeper meaning in his words.

"You're thicker between the ears than that newspaper woman." There was disgust in Rivers's voice, and Frank had an uneasy suspicion the man was warning him of some danger—or warning Amelia through him. He wasn't sure why the man would do that if he was Bart and Conrad's man and they were responsible for trying to run Amelia out of town. But then Rivers was a strange man, and Frank couldn't begin to guess what was behind his cryptic remarks.

He'd thought to report the attempt to burn Amelia out to the sheriff and ask for his help in finding the responsible party, but now he could see that would be a waste of breath.

"Where's Bart?" He was tired of fencing with Rivers, and it seemed the only way to get answers was to confront Bart directly.

"Oh, he's around." Rivers didn't meet his eyes. Instead he let his gaze once more roam across the saloon.

Frank resisted the urge to seek physical satisfaction from the smug lawman. He made it a practice to avoid confrontations with the law, crooked or not. He rose to his feet. "I think I'll take a look around."

"You do that," Rivers responded, but his attention seemed focused on something behind Frank. A sensation at the back of his neck suggested someone was watching him.

Turning slowly to keep the illusion of unhurried casualness intact, Frank scanned the room once more. Nothing had changed unless it was the two strangers he'd noticed earlier. There was something a mite too deliberate about their avoidance of his glance. He'd probably interrupted a discussion of his skill at cards. He turned to leave.

Rivers stood too. "I'll walk out with you."

"Suit yourself," Frank shrugged and turned toward the door.

Rivers followed a step behind. Once he reached the boardwalk, Frank turned toward Amelia's office. He'd sleep better if he checked on her once more.

"Been doing a little listening to Indian legends lately," Rivers's voice was almost conversational. "Seems the Indians around here believe that when a warrior escapes death on the battlefield, all the other warriors who died that day keep an eye on him from their new home in the sky. If the surviving warrior escaped because his medicine was powerful, they help him in subtle ways to defeat his enemies, but if he escaped because he was a coward who ran away, they aid his enemies."

"I can't say that I've ever paid much attention to Indian legends." Frank tipped his hat and moved away.

"You should," he thought he heard the sheriff say before he turned away from the lights of the Golden Garter and began moving slowly down the dark street.

CHAPTER 7

Frank leaned back in his chair, giving his cards a brief glance, then returned his eyes to the big rancher sitting across from him. Carson was struggling to hang onto his temper and was likely close to depleting his cash supply. Frank had learned during the previous weeks that Carson accepted small losses graciously, but he suspected a major loss would bring an eruption better avoided. He discarded an ace and continued closely watching the other players.

Johnson, who ran the mercantile, played badly even when he held a good hand and never seemed unduly upset when he lost. A fussy little man without a family, he only came to the saloon to play cards for the companionship he found in a few hours at the table. He never played more than a few hands and would soon drop out. He didn't concern Frank.

Two local cowboys had started out the evening joking and amiable, but they were both devoting more attention to the girls keeping their glasses filled than to the game. He wasn't surprised when they both folded and followed the girls upstairs.

The drifter who had joined their game more than an hour ago appeared more interested in keeping his glass full than in winning, though earlier he'd won enough pots to make Frank nervous. He couldn't be sure how old the man was. His hair was gray and slicked back with some kind of grease. His skin had the flushed softness of a habitual drinker. His clothes were shabby but looked as though they might have once belonged to a wealthy gentleman. Sober, he'd played well, suspiciously well, but as his consumption of whiskey increased, his ability began to slip. A belligerent note had crept into the drifter's voice during the last hand.

Frank suspected that he could win this hand easily, but it might not be wise to do so. He discarded another card.

Taking care to throw in his cards before the stakes grew high, he lost a couple of times to the rancher and once to the drifter, who was now mumbling almost incoherently. If Frank were moving on in the morning, he'd take advantage of the drifter's inebriated state and coax the locals into ever higher stakes, but he was staying, and prudence warned it wouldn't do to pocket any really large winnings. Besides, Bart kept an eye out for professional gamers who might give his business a bad name, and he and Frank had developed an understanding. As long as Frank made certain the house got its cut and he kept his winnings from inciting talk, he was welcome to play at the Golden Garter.

"That's all for me." He tossed his cards on the table and started to rise. As he did so, he caught part of a phrase mumbled by the drunken drifter. One word stood out—Blackwell. It had been three weeks since Amelia wrote that story about outlaws, and Frank had begun to relax, thinking he'd worried over nothing. There had been no further attempts made against Amelia or her business in that time either.

"Come on, friend." Frank helped the drifter to his feet and steadied him. "Where are you staying?" He did his best to sound concerned. Truth was, he was concerned, but not about whether or not the drunk made it to his bed. He needed to know what the man knew about Tom Blackwell. He'd heard a few rumors that the outlaw was back in Texas and that he and the new bunch of desperados who rode with him were holding up banks again. He'd also heard that this time the bank robber wasn't leaving any witnesses alive.

After asking directions from the bartender, he took the drifter's arm and led him outside. The man staggered and cursed while clinging to Frank with a deathlike grip. As they made their way down the street toward the edge of town, Frank attempted to draw the man into conversation, hoping he could get him to talk about Blackwell. If the outlaw was anywhere in the vicinity, Frank wanted to know. He had no desire to renew his brief acquaintance with Tom Blackwell. In fact, he would just as soon be as far away as possible should Blackwell show up in this part of the state.

His major concern was Amelia. She stopped in regularly to check with the sheriff for news that she might include in her newspaper. Frank usually accompanied her. She'd insisted on telling Rivers about the attempt to burn her newspaper, and Frank was convinced it was news to the sheriff. Rivers was furious that Frank hadn't told him about the attempt the night the incident occurred, yet Frank sensed a softening in the man's attitude toward him.

On a recent visit to the sheriff's office, Rivers had shown Amelia and Frank a new wanted poster that had just come in showing an outlaw who had shot a man in Odessa and another during a holdup in Midland. There was an almost speculative look on Rivers's face as he handed the wanted poster to him. The poster named the gunman as Tom Blackwell and said the outlaw who had disappeared for almost four years was now back with a new, more deadly gang than the one who had ridden with his brother years earlier. The sheriff also produced a dusty wanted poster from a thick stack on his desk with Blackwell's picture on it and a description of his last known companion at the time the poster was produced. Frank had recognized the description as that of himself. Someone had recalled the rider who had held Tom Blackwell's horse during the Hewitt holdup.

Fortunately there was no picture or name given for Blackwell's mysterious companion, and as far as Frank knew, no one other than Blackwell and possibly Harrison Duncan could identify him. Even Duncan didn't know his name, though he was most likely the source of the description on the wanted poster. A nagging memory told him one other person could perhaps identify him. His mind flashed back to the frightened face of a boy cowering in an alley.

The posters had intrigued Amelia, and against Frank's advice, she'd dug into Blackwell's past to write the feature story about the outlaw and his exploits. Frank had resisted correcting her errors or refuting any of the yarns she accepted at face value from the sheriffs and bank officers who answered the flood of inquiries she sent out for further information. Remembering Tom's arrogance, Frank feared what might happen if the outlaw happened on one of Amelia's newspapers. If he was back in Texas, he just might pay a visit to the reporter who told the world that Blackwell's actions proclaimed him a coward.

Frank also feared his own part in the outlaw's exploits might come to light should Blackwell show up and recognize him. No way did he want his past association with the Blackwell Gang to ruin his budding romance with Amelia. There was also the possibility of going to jail or hanging for his part in that long ago bank robbery.

Then there was the boy back at the horse ranch. Had he killed him? He'd never learned whether or not the kid had survived. If he were dead, and if Frank were identified as the man who had shot him, he'd hang. He clung to that brief glimpse he'd caught of a boy and two horses in an alley. In order to live with himself and dream of a future in Wallace Creek, he had to believe the boy he'd seen was the same boy he'd supposedly killed and that he wasn't a murderer after all.

Summer was almost over, and there was a crispness to the night air that served to sober the drifter somewhat. Or perhaps he wasn't as drunk as Frank had thought him to be. The old man's steps became brisker, and he appeared to be in a hurry as they moved toward a crumbling shack on the edge of town, and in spite of Frank's attempts to elicit what the man knew about Blackwell from him, the drifter evaded his questions with chatter about the great partnership the two of them could form if Frank would throw in with him.

A lamp flickered in one window of the shack, and a shadow flitted briefly on a drawn curtain, alerting Frank that the man didn't live alone. If the man had a wife, he pitied the woman, being married to a drunken gambler. If the man didn't have a wife, then who waited up for his return? He remembered his first glimpse of the old man. He hadn't seen the man who had sat with him earlier, but that didn't mean he'd left town.

Caution, borne of his years alone on the harsh frontier, suggested he might be walking into a trap. Since the attack on the newspaper office, Frank had become particularly vigilant. Bart had insisted he'd had nothing to do with that attack, and Frank believed him, though he reserved a hint of skepticism. Now it crossed his mind that Amelia might not have been the intended victim of that flaming bottle of kerosene. Was it possible someone had discovered his own past and was seeking to silence him?

"I'd best be getting home myself," Frank said, releasing the other man's hold on his arm. "You'll be fine now, so I'll be on my way. My landlady doesn't like me coming in late, disturbing her boys' sleep." He backed up a couple of steps while keeping his eyes alert to any movement in or around the shack.

"Thank 'ee, lad. Would 'ee care to step inside me humble abode for a wee tip o' the bottle?" The drifter did a poor imitation of an Irish brogue while clutching at Frank's arms in an attempt to detain him, further raising Frank's hackles. In the saloon, the gambler's drawl had hinted at more than a passing acquaintance with the Deep South.

"Not tonight. I've got to be up early tomorrow," he made a hasty excuse and took another step back to where the shadow of a spindly tree spread itself across the ground. He welcomed the darkness it offered as a shield.

"Me daughter's a lovely lass, and she'd be pleased to meet 'ee," the old man called after him.

Frank shuddered and left. He felt naked and exposed until he was safely back on the boardwalk that ran the length of the town. He paused outside the Red Rooster, contemplating another game. He usually didn't play at saloons other than the Golden Garter, but he might make an exception this once. After further consideration, he didn't want to test his luck. He couldn't shake the feeling he'd had a close call tonight. Besides, he really did need to be up early in the morning. He had plans to take Amelia for a drive. He'd already arranged with Conrad Williams for the loan of his buggy and team. Ever since the supper and dance at Conrad's house, Frank's relationship with Amelia had grown more personal, and he harbored high hopes of sharing his future with her.

He turned toward the opposite end of town. He'd just make a quick check of Amelia's place before turning in. Since the night someone had attempted to burn the office, he'd managed one or more surreptitious strolls past the news office each night, but there had been no repeat of the attack or any kind of further threat made against her or her newspaper. A couple of times, he'd caught a glimpse of Joel Rivers watching, too, from across the street.

* * *

Frank slapped the reins across the team's backs and laughed when Amelia frowned at the faster pace. He'd been surprised to discover that spitfire Amelia Carlisle was afraid of horses. She'd admitted to him on one of their long strolls through town, delivering papers, that the big beasts made her uncomfortable. He'd learned she really was afraid of the animals when she refused to accompany him anywhere on horseback. Only a sedate drive behind Conrad's plodding team had proved an acceptable mode of transportation beyond strolling the dusty streets of Wallace Creek on foot.

The sun bore down from a relentless blue September sky, and a dust devil whirled across the road. A lark called from a nearby thicket. Frank whistled a tune from long ago, not remembering a time when he'd been happier.

Once they reached a place Frank had begun to think of as "their place" along the sluggish creek that had given the town its name, he pulled the team to a stop and hurried around the buggy to lift Amelia out. After settling her feet on the ground, he reached back for the basket Mrs. Bronson had packed for them. He'd given her an extra four bits to ensure that she not only packed a delicious lunch for the occasion, but to gain her cooperation in keeping her boys occupied and unable to follow on the pony he'd helped Clarence purchase with his increased wages, as they'd done on previous occasions when he had set out with Amelia for a picnic. Today he wanted to be alone with her.

Amelia spread the quilt in a shady spot beside the shallow stream that still trickled between its banks in spite of the lateness of the season. In minutes, their boots were off and their feet dangling in the cool water. They sat like children with the basket between them, enjoying the water lapping at their feet as they dug into fried chicken, flaky rolls, and baked beans. They took turns drinking from a jar of tart lemonade.

Amelia was the first to lean back with a sigh. Fearing she might fall asleep before he could give the speech he'd prepared, Frank took one last bite of a fat raisin cookie Mrs. Bronson had provided for dessert, then set it down. Amelia gave herself one day off after she completed each edition of her paper, but following a rigorous week of collecting news, writing articles, and operating the press, she generally slept most of her day off.

"Frank, I think it's time I started paying you a wage." Her sleepy voice drifted to his ears. "You write as much of the paper as I do now, and with your help, it no longer takes all night to print the papers."

Frank groaned inwardly. They'd had this argument before, and he didn't want to fight with her now. "Boarding my horse is pay enough."

"But the barn and pasture were just sitting there not being used." She sat up to launch into her usual argument. "And if you let me pay you, we could expand the paper to cover Heston too," she named a neighboring town that had recently sprung up just fourteen miles away. "If we became partners, you wouldn't have to play cards at the saloon anymore."

He froze. He didn't want to talk about cards. She'd made her aversion to what he did for a living abundantly clear. That was why he'd waited to ask her to marry him until he could afford to buy half her business. He was only surprised that she was the one to bring up the possibility of a partnership.

"Amy," he shortened her name as he'd done in his mind so many times in the past few weeks. With one hand, he reached across the basket to take her hand. "I've been thinking along the lines of a partnership too. But I don't want you to give me half control of your paper." He reached into his pocket to produce a stack of paper bank notes. Turning her hand over, he placed the money in her hand. "I do want to be your partner, but I want to *buy* a half ownership in the *Gazette.* And I don't want to be just your business partner, but your husband as well. Will you marry me?"

Her eyes widened, then her glance dropped to the basket between them. He cursed himself for a clumsy fool.

"Amy," he paused and placed his hands over her two much smaller ones, bringing them close together. "That wasn't the speech I've been practicing all week. First, I meant to tell you I've grown to love you since that night you held a Greener on me and sent me to sleep in the barn."

The corner of her mouth twitched, giving him hope.

"You're beautiful and smart and more than I deserve for a wife. I suspect I should get out of Wallace Creek and leave the field open for a better man than me, but I can't move on without telling you how much I've come to care for you. If you tell me you care nothing for me, I won't keep bothering you, I'll move on to another town, but I'll leave here less than half a man. And if you agree to marry me, I promise you that the day you become my wife will be the day I'll not only become the luckiest man in the world, but it will be the end of my gambling days."

"Oh, Frank." Tears shone in her eyes as she scrambled across the basket to land in his lap. "I love you. I just never thought . . . well, I'm not ladylike or . . . I know I'm terribly outspoken and men don't like—"

He stopped her words with his mouth.

* * *

On the ride back to town, they laughed a lot with Amelia sitting as close to him as she could get. In her excitement, she forgot about the horses and failed to chide Frank when he allowed them to break into a trot. Frank felt like the biggest man in Texas when Amelia blushed at his suggestion that he build a bedroom onto the one-room living quarters at the back of the newspaper office. "Later," he told her, "I'll build you a house."

Frank offered to drop Amelia off at the newspaper office, but she insisted on accompanying him to the banker's home to return the team and wagon. After unharnessing the horses and giving them a well-deserved brushing while Amelia watched, he turned them into a pole corral. Placing the basket and quilt over one arm, he offered the other to Amelia. Arm-in-arm they strolled down the street to the bank to let Conrad know they'd returned his property.

"Your money is going right back into the bank," Amelia promised and clutched her reticule tighter.

"It's your money now," he laughed.

"Soon it will be *our* money and *our* newspaper." She looked up at him, and he noticed the slight flush on her cheeks and the light in her eyes. She'd never been more beautiful.

They were almost to the bank when Frank caught sight of the drifter he'd played cards with the night before. Something about the way the man glanced hastily up and down the street before disappearing into an alley raised an alarm in Frank's mind. The man was up to something.

"Amelia, there's something I have to do. Would you mind letting Conrad know I've returned his team?" He stepped back, loosening her hold on his arm.

"Of course, but—"

"I'll meet you back at the *Gazette* office in less than an hour." He smiled, gave her arm a final squeeze, then hurried toward the alley where the phony Irishman had disappeared.

At the end of the alley, he saw the man approach a line of horses and begin gathering their reins into his fists. Frank went cold. That had once been his job.

Doubling back, he kept to the shadows until he reached the street. He glanced both ways, then made his way to the bank. A peek inside confirmed his suspicions. Two men with scarves hiding their faces held pistols directed toward the tellers and a small group of customers who were huddled together to one side, Amelia among them. Amelia appeared more curious than scared. A large, familiar figure backed into the room from the direction of Conrad's office. He held a gun to the banker's head, drawing him with him into the bank's public area.

Tom Blackwell! Somehow Frank had known Blackwell was involved. He considered rushing the room to rescue Amelia, but if he did, there would be gunfire, and she might get hurt. Besides, the only gun he carried these days was his sleeve derringer. It would be no match against the outlaw's Colt six-shooter. Taking care not to be seen, he backed up, then raced across the street.

"Tom Blackwell is holding up the bank," he shouted as he thrust his way into Rivers's office. The startled sheriff looked up as Frank cast a glance through his smudged window toward the bank, then dashed back outside.

The old man was bringing the horses to the front of the bank from which came the muted sound of gunshots. A figure, hugging the shadows, followed behind. Impervious to the curious people beginning to crowd onto the street, Frank tugged his hat lower to keep the sun from interfering if he had to shoot. He shook his arm, and the small pistol slid into his hand as he strode toward the bank doors through which two men emerged, sprinting toward their waiting horses. Blackwell followed more slowly with his arm around a hostage—Amelia.

Frank had to reach her. She was the only good thing in his life, and he couldn't lose her. He walked toward the outlaw.

"Let her go, Tom." The outlaw looked startled, then laughed as he shoved Amelia toward him. Surprised at Tom's quick compliance to his request and the force of Amelia's body smashing into his chest, they tumbled toward the street. Before they landed in the dusty street, a shot sounded, and he watched in horror as a burst of crimson spread across Amelia's blue dress. He had no recollection of the impact when they hit the ground. His whole attention was focused on Amelia. He cradled her in one arm and tried to stanch the flow of blood with the other.

He lifted his eyes once to see Blackwell leaping for his horse, twisting as he did so to send a shot toward Frank. Frank palmed his derringer once more and aimed it back at Blackwell. He fired, catching Blackwell in the shoulder, spinning him around to face Rivers. One blast from the sheriff's pump action shotgun pitched Blackwell backward. Frank saw the young cowboy who had appeared to be sleeping in the Golden Garter the night someone attempted to burn the newspaper office slip into the alley, then he turned his attention back to his fiancée.

The sheriff's orders to the men gathered in the street passed over Frank's head. Totally oblivious to the carnage around him, he murmured endearments in Amelia's ear. He stroked her hair and wept. He pleaded for her to open her eyes. But it was no use. Somewhere deep inside, he knew she was gone to some place where she could no longer hear his entreaties.

Time was swallowed up by grief, and he had no coherent sense of how long he sat in the street, cradling Amelia in his arms. Nor did he know who pried her from his arms and took her away. Someone led him, stumbling, to the Bronson home where his landlady held him and rocked him for hours as though he were one of her young sons.

At last Frank straightened, dried his eyes, and donned an armor of grim determination that carried him to the doctor's house to make funeral arrangements, then to the telegraph office to wire Amelia's mother. Long after night shrouded the town in darkness, he stood outside Amelia's office, unable to step inside. He circled the adobe building, stopping beside the watering trough where he'd watered his horse that first morning. He sat on the chipped edge, wondering how he could go on. He considered taking up Amelia's crusades, but without her, he could muster no enthusiasm for the newspaper he'd so recently wanted to make his life's work. Someone sat beside him for a time, then left without speaking. It may have been Clarence or any of the business owners he'd befriended. Sometime later, Joel Rivers found him there at dusk.

"She was a rare woman," Rivers spoke softly, paying tribute to Amelia.

"We were planning to get married."

"I thought as much." Rivers twisted his hat in his hands. After a few moments he said, "Blackwell is dead. He and one of the outlaws who rode with him are already buried up on Boothill."

"It doesn't matter. He didn't shoot Amelia."

"He was responsible for the deaths of many people."

"Tom Blackwell was a man without a heart or conscience. Still, his last action was to spare Amelia because I asked him to." Frank's voice was hollow, without emotion.

"No, his last action was to shoot at you. I figure he thought you fired that shot, when, in fact, the lead came from behind you and may have been meant for you."

"Too bad one of them's aim wasn't better. Amelia didn't deserve to die, while I . . ." his bitter words trailed off, and his gaze returned to the adobe structure where he'd experienced the greatest happiness of his adult life and had expected to begin his married life.

"She had enemies," Rivers reminded him.

"Surely no one would have shot her deliberately." His protest was feeble as he remembered the fire.

"You need to go home, get some rest. You've a difficult day ahead of you tomorrow." Rivers tried to steer him toward the Bronson house.

Frank shook off the sheriff's hand. "I have to pack up her things. I told her ma I'd send them to her. And she was working on a story. She'd want me to secure her papers."

"You can pack her clothes and personal things tomorrow, but someone already got to her papers. There's nothing left." He felt a moment's resentment that the sheriff had entered Amelia's home when Frank couldn't bring himself to even cross the threshold.

"Who did this? Who killed her and took her papers?" Anger mixed with anguish shot through him, and he demanded a name, someone on whom he could vent his anger and exact revenge.

"I don't know." Rivers shook his head.

"It wasn't Bart. I remember seeing him kneeling beside his brother."

"No, it wasn't Bart. In spite of his animosity toward her, I don't believe he would have killed her. Conrad was another matter, but he died before she did. He'll be buried tomorrow too, when the Methodist preacher gets to town." The words sent a stab of pain to Frank's heart as he remembered the plans he and Amelia had made for the preacher's arrival.

"One of the outlaws escaped, and there are rumors Kid Calloway was seen around town earlier today," Rivers went on. "Any number of people may have followed Blackwell here to get revenge and could have accidentally hit Amelia instead of the man they aimed for."

What if Joel Rivers was the man who shot Amelia, then stole papers from her house? There was something about the big man that had always bothered Frank, and several times he'd spoken words that might have been threats. *Amelia was working on something that concerned the Williams brothers and if Rivers works for them . . .* Frank's shoulders began to shake. He didn't know what to do or whom he could trust. He turned away and began to stumble up the street.

He wasn't sure how he got back to his room, but he awoke fully clothed, lying on his back on his bed. Like a man sleepwalking, he washed his face, shaved, and combed his hair before donning his black suit. He stood and knelt and went through all the proper motions as the day passed. He was vaguely aware of following Amelia's silk-lined casket to the cemetery just outside of town and of people speaking to him, touching his hand, then going on their way.

At last he was alone. He threw himself on top of the mound of raw earth, whispering endearments to his beloved and shouting curses at the villain who stole her life and his happiness. At last, exhausted, he sat beside the new grave with his head bowed.

Bart, who had lingered beside his brother's grave, joined him. They talked and cried. Bart offered him a drink from his flask to dull his pain, and Frank accepted. When the flask was empty, Bart led Frank to the back door of his saloon, which was closed in honor of Bart's brother. More drinks followed, and at length, blackness swallowed up his sorrow.

CHAPTER 8

1879

Frank awoke facedown in a patch of stinging nettle. Painfully, he pulled himself upright and looked at his hands. They were covered with welts. His face itched and burned. He lifted his hand to his aching head and discovered a lump on the back of it. His fingers came away sticky and smeared with blood. He suddenly leaned forward, violently ill.

Minutes later, he stumbled back to a path he didn't remember. He sat down beside it and placed his aching head in his hands. He needed a drink. After a few minutes, he straightened up, checked his pockets, and discovered his money was gone. It didn't take much searching to discover his horse was gone too, along with his rifle, and with them the half dozen bottles he vaguely remembered packing in his saddlebags. Not only was his Colt gone, but someone had taken his holster and belt as well. There was nothing for him to do but to walk.

He stared at the path, not knowing which way to go. He had no idea where he was or where he'd been headed, so he supposed it didn't matter which direction he chose. He trudged for what seemed hours until his feet were too sore to do more than hobble, but as he followed the winding mountain path beneath tall junipers, his mind began to clear. Being sober brought back the crushing pain of losing Amelia all over again. His life was a blur since the day he'd sat in the deep dust of Wallace Creek's Main Street and held his dead fiancée in his arms.

At the back of his mind were vague recollections of the pain-filled
days following Amelia's death. He remembered drinking with Bart at
the Golden Garter. The drinks had kept coming, and when at last he'd
started making his way to his room, he'd stumbled to the small cemetery instead. He remembered lying facedown on the fresh mound of
dirt, crying like he hadn't done since Ma and Alice died. The next
thing he recalled was the sheriff leading him to his horse, helping him
mount, and pressing a thick stack of bills into his hand—the reward
for the capture of Blackwell, Rivers had told him. He'd been just
conscious enough to figure someone wanted him to leave town. He
still had no idea whether that someone was a friend or foe.

Frank stopped by a small stream to scoop a handful of water
into his mouth, which felt like he'd been eating prickly cactus. He
went further to scrub his face and press wet leaves against the lump
at the back of his skull. For a long time, he sat by the stream and
thought about his life. Mostly he thought about Amelia and all the
dreams that had died with her. He wished he had a drink. Night
took him by surprise, and he began to get scared. He was somewhere in the mountains without a horse; he had no idea when he'd
last eaten and no clue where the next settlement might be.

Rising to his feet, he began moving down the trail. He could be
walking away from the nearest settlement for all he knew, but he
couldn't just sit down and wait for death. *I'll die here,* he thought
and examined carefully whether or not he cared.

*Without Amelia, I have nothing to live for. Still, I don't want to
die.* With a snort of contemptuous disgust, he acknowledged that
he'd become a maudlin drunk. In his eagerness to wipe out his pain,
he'd let his memories and dreams wash away. He recalled with scorn
the young fool who had dreamed of sailing to exotic ports to make
his fortune. Even if he got out of this mess, it was too late for happiness, he thought, but he could still accumulate wealth. If he could
find a way to earn enough money to buy a Sharps, he could go after
buffalo hides. He'd heard some of the buffalo hunters were making
two thousand dollars every time they went out.

He walked faster, then he recalled hearing that the great herds were
disappearing, and he slowed his pace. Amelia had said the railroads

were paying hunters to clear the beasts out of their way, and the army supported the move, since eliminating the buffalo made survival more difficult for the savages who roamed the plains. The buffalo were nearly gone. He was already too late. All right, he wouldn't hunt buffalo, but there had to be something he could do.

He could go after the man who shot Amelia. Reason told him the shooter had meant to shoot Blackwell, but he had overshot and struck Amelia instead. Joel Rivers said someone recognized Kid Calloway in the crowd that day. Somewhere in the blur of time since that tragic day, he'd heard speculation that the Kid had made a hasty shot that had gone wild. Bitterness swelled in his heart toward the man who had meant to embellish his reputation and, instead, took an innocent life.

Up ahead, a flicker of light caught Frank's attention. *Perhaps it's a homestead.* He had enough of his old survival instinct left to prompt him to approach the light with caution. He soon could tell the light wasn't a lantern set in a window, but a campfire. *This might be the same men who stole my horse and money belt.* His senses came alive and he tested each step before settling his weight. At last he peered through underbrush.

What he saw brought up his quick temper. He knew at once that he'd found the men who had robbed him. Two men had a pack open before them, pawing through it and tossing the contents about. Foodstuffs, blankets, and a leather pouch disappeared into the thieves' cache, while papers and clothing were flung toward the fire. A piece of cloth caught fire, spreading the blaze to a nearby log. A big bear of a man lay trussed next to that log. Frank didn't know how long it would take for the log to burst into flames or for the fire to spread to nearby tufts of grass, but if he didn't rescue the man, he'd soon be in worse shape than Frank.

Frank palmed his sleeve gun, thankful the thieves hadn't discovered it when they'd taken his money and left him for dead. He considered shooting them. He didn't doubt he could end one of the men's lawless careers, but the other would be on him before he could reload. As he searched for a way to capture both men, he remembered they had to have horses hidden somewhere nearby.

He began a slow circuit of the campsite, dodging behind trees and moving stealthily through thick shrubs. He knew he was getting close when he heard the restless stomp of a hoof and smelled the odor of fresh horse droppings. His movements became more careful; he didn't want to startle the horses into making any sound that might bring the thieves to investigate.

He found the horses hobbled, but not tied, a short distance away from the camp. Five saddle horses and two others, with packs on their backs, cropped grass in a small meadow. Luck was with him when he recognized one of the horses as his own. With stealthy steps, he approached the horse he'd boarded at Amelia's, the same horse that he'd gotten in trade for the one that carried him away from Harrison Duncan's ambush. For just a moment, it was like greeting an old friend, but there was no time to get sentimental. He was glad to see his rifle still rested in its scabbard. He edged closer and lifted his Winchester from its leather casing, praying the horses wouldn't give away his presence. He checked to make certain the rifle was loaded, then with it in his hand, he turned back toward the clearing.

When he reached the campsite, he could see flames dancing at one end of the log near where the man was tied. The trussed man wasn't in immediate danger from the blaze, though it wouldn't be long before the flames reached his boots. Taking a deep breath, Frank stepped into the clearing.

"Put your hands in the air!" he ordered as he stepped out of the trees. "And turn around slowly." The startled men paused, then slowly dropped whatever they were holding to raise their arms. Once the thieves had complied with the first order, he ordered them to unbuckle their gun belts and toss them into the trees. After that was done, he ordered the men to lie facedown.

He started forward to secure his prisoners when some slight motion from the man beside the log alerted him to danger. He ducked, but a rock caught his shoulder, sending his rifle flying from his grasp. He whirled about but knew he couldn't reach the rifle before his assailant was upon him. His sleeve gun dropped to his hand as he completed the turn. He fired, then dove for his rifle before either of the men he'd ordered facedown on the other side of the fire could reach it.

He grasped the stock as one of the men grabbed the barrel. His hand slid toward the trigger, and he didn't know if he squeezed it or if the man, clutching at his hand, provided the pressure that discharged the gun. With the report of the rifle ringing in his ears, he watched the other man fall backward. The slower of the two robbers raised his hands without being told.

Backing up, Frank surveyed the campsite with the barrel of his rifle slowly sweeping the clearing. One man appeared to be dead, the one he'd shot with the derringer was hunched over, holding his shoulder. Eyes watched from the ground as the bound man took his measure. Neither he nor Frank addressed the other as Frank considered the odds. He'd have to take a chance on the man.

Herding the two prisoners together where he could watch them better, he stooped to retrieve a long knife from a skillet lying beside the fire. Crouching, he sliced through the prisoner's ropes.

Rolling to his knees, then standing, the burly captive shook his hands a few times and stretched his cramped legs. He stomped his boots to free them of any stray sparks, then still without speaking, gathered up the ropes that had bound him and approached the two men cowering in front of Frank's rifle. In minutes, they were tied securely. Frank figured that resolved the question of whether or not the man was one of the thieves or another victim of the trio who had robbed him and left him to die.

Frank stared at the man lying at his feet and felt his stomach roil. If he'd had anything to eat in the past twenty-four hours, he was certain he would have lost it. The dead man looked nothing like the kid he'd shot all those years ago, but it was the boy's face he saw.

"You did fine." Frank had forgotten about the big man he'd freed. He turned to face him. He couldn't speak, but he lowered his rifle, keeping it pointed in the general direction of the bearlike man. He found he wasn't ready yet to place his full trust in the stranger. Frank watched the man who, without seeming to take his eyes off Frank either, walked toward where he'd lain helpless earlier.

The man raised a huge booted foot and began to stomp at a finger of flame that was spreading toward the depression made earlier by his body lying in the grass. When the grass fire was extinguished and the log kicked into the circle of stones that ringed the campfire, he began gathering up the scattered papers. Frank watched, but made no effort to assist him. Only when the last piece of paper was picked up did the man approach Frank again.

He stopped a few feet away, holding up the thick sheaf of papers in his hand. Waving them, he said, "You just walked into six hundred dollars. Them boys is worth two hundred dollars apiece, dead or alive."

It took a few minutes for the big man's words to make sense. The papers the man held were wanted posters, which made the mountainous man a bounty hunter.

As they made the two-and-a-half-day journey to the nearest town, Frank learned the man he'd rescued went by the name of Grif and it was a good idea to stay downwind of him. He wore a thick buffalo poncho that he said he'd acquired while hunting buffalo and living with the Indians two decades earlier. He was a rough, uneducated man, but Frank took a liking to him, and when he invited Frank to join him in his travels after collecting the reward money, Frank agreed.

Together, they rode south into Arizona, and Frank discovered that he had a knack for nosing out information concerning the men they pursued, since searching out wanted men wasn't unlike tracking the details of a newspaper story. Coupled with Grif's tracking skills and trail savvy, they made a successful team, collecting frequent bounties and seeing much of the Southwest. The pain of losing Amelia never went away, but with the passing of years, the raw edges of pain dimmed, enabling Frank to concentrate on capturing criminals. This new pursuit became an obsession, replacing whiskey as a means of distancing himself from the past and the bright hope Amelia had represented.

There was little to spend the bounties they collected on, other than food and an occasional night in real beds in some seedy hotel. As his mind cleared, Frank vowed to never allow alcohol to dim his senses again, and though he frequently sat with Grif at a saloon table, he never drank or lifted a card, and he ignored the painted women who offered an hour or two of their time in exchange for a share of the thick roll of bills he carried.

They'd been working together five years when Grif began to find his legs stiff in the mornings and his back aching when he dismounted each night. He was getting old and began dreaming of building a cabin in a mountain valley near a trout stream and only making one trip a year to some settlement for supplies. His rambling plans made Frank uneasy. He didn't want to retire to some bucolic valley, and he didn't want to keep hunting outlaws on his own, but the weight of the leather bag he now kept hidden in his saddlebag assured him of a choice in picking whatever his future might hold.

It had been a long time since Frank had thought about the future beyond capturing their next bounty, but the old man's growing infirmity and plans for retirement forced Frank to think about making plans of his own. Perhaps he'd finally travel to the exotic places he'd once dreamed of, but that old dream had lost its luster. Amelia's memory intruded to remind him of other plans he'd once made and lost, causing a familiar ache which hadn't lessened with the passage of time.

Both men began to grow fearful that the fat purses they carried might entice outlaws to pursue them instead of the other way around. At length, Frank suggested they travel to Denver or Salt Lake City to deposit their money in a bank. After some discussion, they decided on Denver.

Winter was approaching, and they discussed wintering over in the rough frontier city after depositing their money. Grif expressed some reluctance. He wasn't certain he could manage a whole winter living inside some building with too many folks around. Frank had his own reservations about wintering in the mountains. His few encounters with snow at some of the higher altitudes hadn't been pleasant.

Frank's mare was played out when they reached the city, and a friendly sheriff directed them toward a ranch three days west where a rancher was breeding and training top horseflesh. Frank figured replacing his horse could wait until spring, and he was in no hurry to say good-bye to the faithful animal anyway. He picked out a hotel where they could laze away the winter, but it soon became clear that Grif couldn't abide the noise and confusion of city life, so not long after depositing their money in a banking establishment, they purchased supplies, including heavy underwear and hats, then rode out.

A flurry of snow caught them in a high valley midway to the Colorado Star Ranch, spreading a carpet of white across the meadows and pines. It brought a peace and stillness Frank had almost forgotten existed and awoke a restless hunger for something he couldn't name. They made camp, and as they sat around a small cooking fire, Grif once more described a California valley where he'd lived with his Indian wife many years ago. Frank sensed the time was quickly approaching when Grif would head for his valley and Frank would have to come to some decisions concerning his own future. He watched the flames and thought of how his dreams had disappeared into darkness just as the smoke from the hundreds of campfires he'd watched over the years had wafted away. A hard reality intruded; he'd dreamed, but he'd done little real planning in his life other than that one brief summer when he'd planned to become Amelia's partner. Somehow, life had just happened.

When they approached the ranch, they were met by a rider who questioned them thoroughly about their business before allowing them to proceed toward the ranch house. At the ranch house, two young men met them at the door and invited them inside.

"We hadn't expected a response this quickly," one of the men began.

"The sheriff in Denver said the Star was the best place to buy a good horse," Frank remarked.

"You're here to buy a horse?" The other man sounded disappointed.

"We thought you were here about the reward," the first one said, disappointment in his voice. "Our rider said you were bounty hunters."

"That's a fact," Grif agreed. "In our line of work, we need horses we can depend on."

"We'll sell you one of the best horses in Colorado. That's no problem, but we were hoping you had plans to go after the man who shot our father."

"When did this happen?"

Frank could tell Grif was interested. Perhaps he wasn't ready to retire after all.

The brothers launched into an explanation, telling them how their father, the ranch owner, had been shot two days earlier and his horse and saddlebags, filled with the ranch's payroll, had been stolen. The rancher's sons had identified the assailant as Cole Walker, a man Frank and Grif had seen on wanted posters in several states. The bounty offered hadn't been large enough to invite their pursuit, but now the grieving brothers were upping the price on Walker's head to a thousand dollars.

The excitement of the chase filled Frank's mind. A bounty that size would buy Grif a retirement of ease and enable Frank to see the world if that's what he decided to do. He was convinced luck had brought them to the Colorado Star Ranch and would continue to shine on them. They would be days ahead of any other bounty hunters or marshals, ensuring a relatively easy capture.

The following morning, they headed north with Frank on a new mount. He hadn't haggled over a price. The mare was prime stock and the price quoted more than fair. He'd been surprised and pleased that the brothers were willing to keep the mare he'd ridden in on. They rode as far as the ranch hands had followed Walker earlier and eventually discovered the spot where the wanted man had camped to wait out the earlier brief snowfall.

"Considerate of him to leave a clear-cut trail," Grif snorted, pointing to a track near a small stream. The snow had melted as early snowfalls generally do, but the horse had left a clear impression of a horseshoe with a distinctive star centered on the top of the shoe's curve. They'd watched an old blacksmith back at the ranch remove a shoe just like it from Frank's new mount and replace it with a plain shoe. He'd explained it had been the dead rancher's

orders that when a horse no longer belonged to the ranch, the identifying shoe should be exchanged for a plain one.

They followed the distinctive print until they reached a ranch in
Idaho without catching up, though they felt certain they were
getting close. A fast moving storm dusted the ground with a thin
layer of powder just before sunset as they approached the Bar O, but
it was enough to identify the tracks leading to the ranch and assure
them they were a mere hour behind their quarry.

After scouting around the perimeter of the house, bunkhouses,
and barns, they determined that Walker was holed up on the ranch
for the night. With the large number of men in evidence around the
various outbuildings, they decided to wait until morning to
approach Walker. With luck, he'd ride out alone and be easier to
capture. Positioning themselves where they could watch the ranch,
they made a cold camp. Taking turns watching, they waited for
morning.

Just before dawn, a commotion erupted on the ranch. Men and
horses surged toward the ranch gate. Buckboards jostled for position
and men on horseback called out to each other as they took to the
road. Grif swore in colorful terms.

"What's going on?" Frank rolled from his blankets, staring in
amazement and frustration. Walker could ride right out in the
middle of that bunch, confident any tracks he left would be ground
into the mud.

"The rancher just paid off his hands, and he's sending them
home for the winter," Grif grumbled. "All Walker has to do now is
stay with the ranch hands until they start to split up and we'll lose
his trail. He must've discovered he was leaving a trail and suspected
he was being followed."

CHAPTER 9

It was well past noon when they reached a small town and decided to stop for supplies and to question some of the locals. Climbing from their horses, they fastened the reins to a rail in front of the general store, then dodged a woman carrying a wooden crate filled with groceries as they stepped inside the store. They stood for several minutes, squinting their eyes until they adjusted to the store's dim interior.

Frank watched a nervous couple pay for their purchases then head for the door. He was used to the reaction he and Grif incited from town folk. The woman glanced at Grif, then hastily averted her eyes. He suspected she would have held her nose if such an action weren't beneath her ladylike bearing. Grif headed for the counter, but a movement near the back of the store caught Frank's attention, pulling him in that direction.

"You seen any strangers 'round here lately?" he heard Grif ask the storekeeper. Frank ignored the exchange between the two. His attention focused on the man who was studying the display of canned goods a mite too closely. He was slender, dressed in heavy trousers and a cotton shirt, and appeared about average height. His boots and coat were old and worn, as was the battered felt hat that hid his eyes. Frank had seen enough cowhands and sodbusters to reckon there was nothing unusual about this one, but something about the man stirred a memory. He fit the description of Cole Walker, except he appeared to be younger than the man they sought.

"You know the man hidin' back of the canned goods?" Grif jerked a thumb toward the man Frank was observing, and Frank noticed the guilty start the man made. Frank's hand slid downward to within inches of his gun.

"Sure. That's Luke McCall. Come on over here, son, and meet these folks," the storekeeper called out. The man the storekeeper had called Luke moved toward the counter.

"Afternoon." The young man touched the brim of his hat and nodded toward Grif before addressing his words to the man behind the counter. "I don't want to rush you, but if you're ready to load my barrels of flour, I'll bring my team up. I'd like to be home before the snow sets in."

"Soon's I finish with these gentlemen." The storekeeper turned back to Grif. "Will that be all? I still have a few sweets, if you're of a mind to celebrate the season."

Frank relaxed his hand. The young farmer wasn't the man they'd been following.

"Sure, mister," Grif said. "Give me some of them hard candies. You got any chocolate creams?"

Frank shook his head. He was well aware of his partner's sweet tooth. He'd never seen a man eat as many sweets as the old buffalo hunter.

He turned his attention back to the other man standing before the storekeeper. Frank couldn't shake the feeling there was something familiar about the man waiting impatiently for his goods. He stepped closer.

"Haven't I seen you before?" he asked.

"Not likely," the storekeeper answered for the younger man. "Not unless you've been down in the Utah Territory. The McCalls settled up here the same time as me 'n Bishop Samuels." The man behind the counter went on talking, but Frank tuned him out. He knew a little bit about the Mormons in Utah Territory. If the young man was one of them, it wasn't likely he was anyone Frank had ever met. He and Grif were wasting time. There was a storm approaching and they needed to find Walker's trail before snow wiped out the tracks. He turned toward the door and Grif followed.

Icy wind stung their cheeks, so when Grif suggested they hunt up a meal and something to drink to warm their insides, Frank didn't protest. They found a cramped tavern on the edge of town and ducked their heads as they entered through the low doorway.

Minutes later Frank peered over the brim of a coffee cup at the dingy room. It wasn't much of a saloon—there were no girls, and not even a piano. It was nothing like the Golden Garter. Most of the time, he avoided thinking about Texas. Stretching his long legs toward the pot-bellied stove, he basked in the heat, relaxing for a rare moment.

"Can't figure where we lost him." Grif brought Frank back to the problem they were facing. "Tracks were clear all the way to the ferry, then that skiff of snow turned the trail into a pig wallow all the way to that big spread. I figure he rode right through the corrals, mixing with the Bar O stock, then lit out for the hills."

"He came this way, I know he did." Frank scowled at his drink. "Those tracks we cut south of town were his." Walker's ploy had worked until two miles out of town—a clear print had revealed a five-point star cut into the mud beside the road.

"Finish up your drink and let's git a move on." Grif set his whiskey glass on the table and rose to his feet. "There's a storm brewin', and if we don't cut his tracks before the snow comes, we're gonna lose him."

With a sigh, Frank gulped the contents of his cup and stood beside his partner. He didn't relish stepping outside. The temperature was dropping fast, and he hadn't slept in a bed for more than a month, but bringing in Cole Walker would set them up for a good long time.

"You expect that cowboy over at the store might be Walker?" Frank asked just loud enough for Grif to hear.

"Possible," the old man muttered, "but not likely. I never heard of Walker settlin' down, and that young man was lookin' at woman and kid fixin's. Drivin' a team too."

Shards of ice were blowing in the air when they stepped onto the boardwalk that lined both sides of the narrow street. Trailing their horses behind them, they walked the length of the short Main

Street, passing the general store and stable, paying particular attention to the horseshoe prints around the blacksmith shop. They passed a church and half a dozen homes sporting cedar wreathes on their doors before Grif suddenly knelt beside the road heading north out of town.

A broad smile spread across Frank's face as he gazed down at a clear set of tracks. Cole Walker would soon be theirs.

"Looks like he's trailin' that horse behind a wagon." Grif narrowed his eyes and glared toward the approaching storm. "The wagon will slow him down some." Without another word, both men swung into their saddles and pointed their horses north. The storm was coming on fast, and they wanted to catch up to their quarry before snow wiped out his tracks.

They weren't a half mile out of town when the sleet changed to snow. At first, the snowfall was light, and they caught glimpses of the tracks they were following. They pushed their horses as hard as they dared, knowing their mounts could travel faster than the team and wagon. As the snow became heavier, the wagon tracks filled in, leaving only a faint trail that eventually disappeared altogether.

Grif pulled his horse to a halt, and Frank reined in beside him.

"We've lost the trail," the older man shouted above the wail of the wind. "We can either continue in the direction we're headed and look for shelter, or we can try to backtrack to town."

"He can't be far ahead of us. I say let's keep going," Frank shouted back.

Grif nodded his head and set his horse in motion once more.

Between early darkness and the snow, they had to move more slowly and with greater care. The cold seeped into Frank's bones and his feet were beyond feeling. Drowsiness overcame him, placing him in danger of falling from his horse. Even so, Frank was startled when his horse stumbled and refused to take another step forward. While he struggled with the animal, Grif pulled alongside of him, placing his big mittened hand over Frank's.

"It's no use," the word's faintly reached Frank's ears. "The horses know something we don't. I'm going to check it out." Grif swung a leg over his saddle and stepped down, while keeping a tight grip on his Appaloosa's reins. After a moment's hesitation, Frank dismounted too. Snow dropped inside his boots as he attempted to walk, and pain shot through a knee as it connected with a sharp rock.

Rubbing his knee, he attempted to peer through the thick snowfall. For the short distance he could see, the snow lay in great lumps. He noticed Grif examining a lump immediately in front of him. He took his hand and brushed at the snow, exposing black rock.

"Lava flow!" Frank heard his friend shout. Moving closer together, Grif continued, "There's no telling how wide it is. We better follow along the edge until we find a cave or some place where we can shelter until the snow stops."

"What about snakes?" Frank hated snakes and had learned a long time ago to avoid places where they might be found.

"Probably hundreds of 'em hibernatin' in these rocks, but they're all sleepin' this time of year."

Frank shuddered. "I'm not sleepin' with rattlesnakes." Without further comment, he swung back into his saddle. He had no idea whether they should turn right or left, so he left the choice up to the canny old man and rode silently behind him. *If we can't tell which way to go, Walker can't either,* he reasoned, *but in this storm we could ride right past him and not know it.*

His feet were cold, and the wind seemed to whistle right through his thick, wool coat. The scarf that held his hat in place and wrapped around his face was frozen to his beard. His hands had lost all feeling, and he was beginning to worry he'd soon be unable to hang onto his horse's reins. He'd heard of men freezing to death in blizzards, and suddenly he was afraid.

Grif's voice seemed to come from a long distance away, but Frank slowly became aware his partner was pointing to a dark shape in the sea of white. Finally, he made out the word "cave." Grif's horse refused to approach the cave, but the hope of shelter revived Frank in spite of his aversion to snakes, enough to hang onto Grif's horse while Grif waded through a drift and up a sharp incline toward the black cave opening. Frank began to grow sleepy waiting for Grif to return and was startled when his partner slapped his leg and peered up at him.

"Not big enough for us and the horses. We can't risk losing the horses, so we better go on."

Frank was vaguely aware of Grif wrapping a rope around him to secure him to his saddle. His mind even recognized that Grif had attached a lead rope from Frank's horse to the Appaloosa. At some point, he was aware of his stirrups brushing through snow, and he recognized a snow-shrouded fence and knew they were following it. Then there was only endless whiteness. Eventually the cold ceased to cause him misery.

A sound penetrated the thick fog inside Frank's head, and he blinked at a light coming closer. He was no longer riding, but was on his feet with Grif propelling him toward the light.

But for his hold on Grif's buffalo robe, Frank would have collapsed. He was cold beyond feeling, and he couldn't make his eyes focus. He knew they were entering some kind of building, but it could be a house, a barn, or a line shack, and he wouldn't know or care. His only sense that seemed to be working was that of smell, and along with the air that he struggled to breathe came the scent of stew, not the sorry mess Old Grif sometimes stirred up, but stew like Ma used to make for supper. Along with the stew smell, he breathed in the sharp scent of cedar and something else he couldn't quite place. Then he remembered—popcorn!

"Come sit by the fire! You look near froze to death," a woman's voice penetrated the white fog around him. For a moment, he wondered if he had frozen to death and it was his angel ma he could hear. But no, that wasn't Ma's voice. Besides, he was pretty sure that if he were dead, he'd be feeling the opposite of all this ice and snow.

He felt hands shove him onto a chair and he heard someone— Grif, he thought—say something about the horses. Just before he passed out, pain shot through him and he realized the woman was bathing his hands and feet in what felt like scalding water. She assured him the water was cool, but to his frozen limbs, it burned like fire until he blacked out.

When he came to, he discovered that he was in a small cabin and, since he could see through a pane of glass, that snow was still falling. He could tell, too, that morning had arrived. He had no idea how long he had slept, though he vaguely remembered several attempts to awaken him.

Turning his head slightly, he discovered Grif lying on a bedroll not far away. The old bounty hunter was stretched out on his back, snoring. His stinking buffalo robe hung over a chair a short distance away, and Frank could just see a woman tending to something on a big black stove. He figured she was the woman who saved his life the night before.

He noticed she was pretty with a thick rope of yellow hair hanging over one shoulder. She was also young and slender. He wondered about her man, and if he was the one they'd been trailing.

The cabin was slowly filling with the aroma of baking biscuits, and Frank's mouth watered. It would be good to have a home-cooked meal. It had been a long time since he'd set down to a real breakfast. His mind flashed back to memories of Ma's cooking and that of Mrs. Bronson. Thoughts of eating breakfast with Amelia the mornings they delivered papers came to mind. He shut off that avenue of thought.

A sound caught his attention, and he turned to watch a little girl enter the room through a curtain that likely hid a doorway leading to the cabin's bedroom. She looked like her mother. Seeing them together brought back memories of his own ma and the little sister he had delighted in teasing. It brought back, too, the dreams he'd once had of raising a family with Amelia.

As hard as he tried to shut off the memories, watching the young man he had seen in the store enter the room carrying a baby and proceed to pass out simple Christmas gifts to his family brought a choking sensation to Frank's throat. Not for the first time, he regretted the impulse that had set him on a road far from the life he'd once known. He turned his head to shut out the sight of the little family. He didn't need the memories they incited. Marriage probably wouldn't have worked out for him anyway.

A cedar tree trimmed with odd scraps and a tin star met his eyes. With a sinking sensation, he realized it was Christmas morning. Ma had loved Christmas. She'd filled the house with the scent of fir boughs and baking. She'd also talked freely of her faith in the God the holiday represented. If that God existed, surely He'd washed His hands of Frank Haladen long before now.

Gloom filled his soul, and he wondered if Amelia would still be alive if he'd stayed out of her life. More than once, he'd suspected her death was his punishment for the innocent life he'd taken and the reason why, after six long years, he still couldn't put her memory to rest.

With a glance back toward the woman who had treated his frostbite and possibly saved his life, he hoped her husband wasn't Cole Walker, yet there was that something indefinable that continued to tell him he'd seen the man before. If he hadn't seen the man's likeness on a wanted poster, where had he seen him?

* * *

Breakfast was as delicious as the smells wafting through the room had promised. Frank didn't take part in the conversation around the table, but he derived a measure of enjoyment from watching the little girl talk and laugh with her parents and Old Grif. She was soon calling Grif "grandpa," and the old man gave every indication of enjoying the honor. The father was a little reserved and only gradually relaxed. Frank watched him lean back in his chair, his eyes narrowing to a sleepy slant.

Frank had seen that pose before—a man almost asleep, tilted back on a wooden chair with one hand hidden beneath the table, his eyes appearing closed, but in reality seeing more than most men saw with both eyes wide open. Amelia's death and the years since had driven the memory from his mind, but now he clearly recalled the youth who had trailed the man who held the outlaws' horses during the holdup in Wallace Creek. A shiver made the hairs on the back of his neck stand out. That youth was the man sitting across the table from him now. It was Kid Calloway.

Slowly his hand began to inch toward the holster resting flat against his thigh.

CHAPTER 10

"For me?" The little girl's voice reminded Frank of his surroundings. Grif was holding out one of the creams he'd purchased at the store the day before, and the child was staring at the sweet with an expression of delight on her face.

Frank relaxed his hand. He couldn't do it now. He'd have to get Grif aside, let him know McCall was really Kid Calloway and he was worth two Cole Walkers. What had been a reward of a few hundred dollars was now five thousand dollars. Harrison Duncan had raised the bounty shortly before announcing his second attempt to become governor of Texas. Frank had seen the wanted—dead or alive—poster when they first returned to Colorado a few months back and he'd read about Duncan on the back page of the *Rocky Mountain News*.

Something niggled at the back of his mind. He'd wondered when he first saw the poster why Duncan cared one way or the other about Kid Calloway. Little bits of memory seemed to be running frantically about in his mind, telling him if he would only stop to think about it, he would know why the double-dealing politician wanted the Kid dead. Frank could only think of his own reason for wanting to kill Calloway. One of the deaths attributed to Calloway's fast draw was Amelia's. He'd been seen slipping away following the shooting.

"The snow has stopped." Frank turned to face his partner, anxious to share his discovery. "We should check on the horses."

"The cattle will be needing feed. I'd best be getting it to them." Luke rose to his feet, and Frank noticed the look of concern he directed toward his wife. Frank sensed that he had a reluctance to leave his wife's side as long as he and Grif were in the house. An urge to assure the man that he and Grif didn't harm women or children caught him by surprise, and he felt depressed, knowing he could say nothing.

The older man rose to his feet too and reached for his buffalo poncho.

When the men reached the barn, Luke pitched hay onto a wagon set on runners, then left to take the feed to his cattle. Grif drifted from stall to stall until he saw the mare. Lifting a hoof, he found the star and merely grunted, as though confirming the end of their search.

"He ain't Walker," Frank said in a soft whisper.

"I know that." Grif didn't sound disappointed. "Last night whilst the woman was treatin' your frostbite, McCall told her about the mare Oscarson gave him for wages and how he plans to get a young stallion from Utah and use the pair to start a herd of fancy horses. Walker tricked us. He traded the mare for one of Oscarson's horses, but we'll catch up to him sooner or later."

"We don't need Walker." Frank paced with growing excitement in front of the mare's stall. "I remember McCall from Texas. He's worth a lot more to us than Walker." He began outlining his plan to take Luke McCall.

"Wal, I don't know." Grif scratched his beard. "We slept in his house and et his bread. It's Christmas too."

"Aren't you the one who taught me there's no place for sentiment in this business?" Frank turned to glare at his partner.

"It just don't seem right."

"You let the little girl get to you," Frank accused. "You like her calling you grandpa."

"That might be true," the old man conceded. "It's been a lot of years since a little chile spoke to me, and it's got me thinkin' 'bout things, 'specially with today bein' Christmas 'n all."

"You saying you don't want that reward money?"

"No, I'm just sayin' it ain't right. McCall and his woman have been square with us. 'Sides, I don't hold with hurtin' children." He had a faraway look in his eyes that made Frank wary.

"Look, he's getting ready to take hay to some stock out by the lava beds. We can be ready when he comes back. There'll be no chance for his woman and kids to get hurt." He let his eyes follow Luke's movements as he pitched hay onto the wagon bed.

"Oh, they'll be hurt," the old man muttered, so low Frank wasn't quite sure he heard the words.

The snow crunched loudly as Luke clucked to his team and the draft horses leaned into their harnesses. The two bounty hunters watched the wagon carrying McCall move slowly through the deep snow, the cold sending a squeaking sound into the bright, cold air.

"What if he just keeps going?" Frank asked.

"He won't," Grif said with finality. "Men like that'n always come home."

Returning to the warmth of the cabin, Frank felt a tug of conscience when Maddie McCall insisted on checking the spots of frostbite that she'd treated the night before.

Across the room, Grif knelt on the floor beside McCall's little girl, absorbed in some game the child was playing. The scents of apples and cinnamon along with some kind of fowl roasting in the oven stirred the flow of memories he'd been trying unsuccessfully to turn off all day. A melancholy sadness filled his heart, bringing a longing for home.

Feeling a tug at his leg, he looked down to see the baby use his pant leg to pull himself to a standing position. A wide, wet mouth showing two small teeth grinned up at him. Something inside him recoiled, filling him with a panicky need to free himself from the small fists clutching at his knee. He reached forward to unclasp the baby's hands, only to find one of his fingers firmly clutched by the child's small hand. He didn't know how to free himself.

The baby continued to smile his near-toothless grin. His eyes were wide and bright, and Frank found himself almost returning the smile. There was something about the smile and the light dancing in the baby's eyes that brought back a time when he'd followed Pa about, basking in his presence and striving to do everything he did.

"It's time for us to leave," he spoke abruptly to Grif. When Frank stood, the baby fell on his well-padded bottom and began to cry. His mother rushed to pick him up. While she rocked him, Frank and Grif pulled on their coats.

"Won't you stay for dinner? I have two plump hens in the oven." Frank shook his head in refusal.

As soon as the baby was asleep, Maddie hurried to the sideboard for bread, which she sliced into thick chunks while the men were still preparing for their departure. To the bread she added slabs of roasted meat, then wrapped the sandwiches in strips of cloth and placed them in a sugar sack. Two generous slices of pie joined the sandwiches before Maddie extended the bag toward Frank.

He hesitated. It didn't feel right to accept the bag when she didn't know they would be taking her husband away from her, but to refuse the offer might look suspicious. Finally he accepted the bag, tucked it beneath his coat, and reached for the door. Grif followed him out with only one last sorrowful look at the little girl, who was crying as she waved farewell.

Looking back at the woman as they exited the door, pain surfaced, unexpectedly taking his breath. *That woman could be Amelia. We could have had a son like that, and I would have built her a house behind the shop. Our children would have spent Christmas . . .* He stopped himself. Remembering the past was futile. Collecting that reward money was all that mattered now.

Neither Frank nor Grif spoke until they had their horses and the stolen mare saddled and returned to their stalls, where they would remain out of sight until needed. Frank hoped they wouldn't have to shoot Calloway. He'd rather turn him over to the sheriff in the first town they came to, collect a bank voucher, and be on their way, knowing the mare would be returned to Calloway's woman. He could see no reason to tell the sheriff the mare was stolen. He and Grif had never before captured an outlaw who left behind a family, who would suffer for the loss of their man. He was becoming maudlin. There was no reason, he reminded himself, to feel this situation was anything like the tragedy that had torn him and Amelia apart.

By silent consent, he and Grif hid in the tack room, leaving the door open a crack, to wait for Kid Calloway to return. Cold seeped into his boots, and he remembered the agonizing pain of the night before. He curled his toes several times and promised himself that when this was over, he would be on his way south, away from the snow and cold, but a picture of the young mother in the cabin stayed in his mind. He could see the little girl too, standing beside her Christmas tree, crying, and the baby holding out his chubby hands toward him, staring with those huge round eyes first in entreaty, then with a coldness more deadly than ice.

"You know what Christmas will always mean to that little girl?" Grif broke the silence.

"Yeah," Frank admitted. He almost wished he hadn't remembered Kid Calloway and the five-thousand-dollar bounty that double-dealing, would-be governor had placed on the man's head.

The jingle of harnesses sounded on the frozen air. The man they'd set out to ambush was returning. Frank tensed, one hand gripping the handle of his weapon. Calloway's speed with a six-shooter was legendary. The sooner they got this over with and collected their money, the better.

Calloway didn't release the team from the sled and bring the horses inside as they'd expected. Instead, he stepped inside the barn's dim interior without his team. He walked stiffly with his hands awkwardly extended away from his body, like a blind man feeling his way.

Calloway is snow-blind! This is going to be easy. Before he could call for Luke to surrender, Grif clapped a hand over his mouth. He jerked to free himself, and that's when he saw the man with a gun pointed at Calloway's back. Frank's grip on his own gun tightened. He turned slightly, until his own gun was pointing toward the newcomer. No claim jumper was going to steal this bounty from him and Grif!

Calloway opened the mare's box stall, then seemed to stumble, probably surprised to find the mare already saddled. The man with him stepped forward, then began to swear and wave his gun about. The intruder's anger caught Frank by surprise, then he suddenly understood. Cole Walker was attempting to steal the same horse he'd stolen once before.

"I went to a lot of trouble to get rid of that horse," Walker said. "Get another one."

"She's the only saddle horse I own." Calloway's voice was calm, though Frank knew he had to be shaking in his boots.

"Don't give me that!" There was a sneer in Walker's voice. "I ought to plug you right here. That would bring those bounty hunters who've been trailing me running. I warned you that if they interfere, expecting to collect a share of the price Old Duncan put on your hide, I'll kill them both and put a bullet through your woman's head too. She ain't worth nothin'. Her pa's dead, so he ain't lookin' for her no more. That horse will do." He pointed toward Grif's Appaloosa.

Frank felt Grif tense. The old man was touchy about that Indian pony. He'd raised it from a colt back when he was living with the Indians. Frank considered shooting Walker and taking Calloway, but Walker's next words, spoken with an unmistakable sneer, stopped him.

"It was considerate of Frank Haladen to follow you here—saves me tracking him down. It's taken far too long locating you. Duncan promised five thousand dollars to the man who silenced you for good and double money if I got Blackwell and Haladen too. I almost had all three of you back in Wallace Creek, but some two-bit sheriff got Blackwell, and that old drunk Brannigan scared Haladen into running. He had two chances at Haladen and missed both times, thanks to that stupid newspaperwoman who got in the way. Now it's my turn, and nothing's going to keep me from collecting on both you and Haladen this time."

Frank rocked back in shock. Calloway hadn't killed Amelia. Some old drunk following orders from Duncan to kill him had killed Amelia instead. Frank remembered the night that he'd walked the old drunk to his cabin and the night that flaming kerosene had been tossed through Amelia's window. Something cold tightened around his heart, bringing back the pain of his loss as clearly as though he still sat in that dusty street with his dead love in his arms.

"What makes you think Duncan will let you live after you get Haladen and me?" Calloway didn't sound scared, but his question didn't please Walker. Frank could see Calloway had managed to plant a valid concern in Walker's mind.

Frank seethed. He'd been stupid not to guess Duncan was behind his own quick exodus from Texas. The only question was whether the Wallace Creek sheriff, Joel Rivers, had been Duncan's stooge or whether the lawman had saved his life by getting him out of town. He raised his gun, sighting it toward Walker, then stifled a curse. Calloway was in his line of fire. Seeing Calloway through his gun sights brought a shocking moment of déjà vu. He'd viewed a much younger version of that face just this way once before. His hand trembled, and his mind reeled.

Feeling a slight tug on his trousers, he turned half-expecting to see round blue eyes and a near-toothless smile, but he'd only caught his pants on a nail. This time he recognized the corresponding tug at his heart. He didn't want that little boy's childhood marred as the baby's father's and his own had been by the loss of a parent. Truth was, he no longer wanted Calloway—only Walker.

Calloway moved, taking a step toward the Appaloosa's stall. He lifted the loop of wire holding the enclosure closed, then gave the gate a sudden swift shove straight toward Walker, striking him hard in the chest. Taken by surprise, Walker sprawled in the dirt, and Calloway was on top of him. Walker still clutched his gun and was attempting to raise the arm that held it.

While Frank was still shifting his own gun back and forth looking for a clear shot, Grif jumped from their hiding place into the melee. Frank hesitated a moment longer before following his partner. His high-heeled boot came down hard on the outlaw's hand, forcing him to drop his six-shooter. After that, it didn't take long for the three men to subdue the gunman. Grif's huge fist ended the fight.

Moments later, Frank looked at Walker lying unconscious at their feet, trussed like a turkey. He was aware Calloway held a gun against his pant leg, concealed by the bulky coat he wore. The gun didn't concern Frank. Somehow he knew he wasn't in any danger from the younger man.

"We'll send you your share of the reward," Frank spoke to Calloway. He made no attempt to conceal his contempt for the man lying at their feet. He caught the surprise on both Grif and Calloway's faces, but went on in an emotionless voice, "I'll be heading to Texas as soon as we drop Walker off with the closest sheriff. When I get there, I plan to have a talk with my uncle. He owns a good-sized newspaper in the town where I grew up, and he has a friend who went to work for that big Houston newspaper when I was a kid. I think they would be interested in hearing all about a certain would-be governor's past dealings. I just might manage to mention how the Calloway Kid, who survived the massacre of his family a few years back was shot and killed by some outlaw along the Arizona strip a couple of years ago."

Frank stooped. When he rose to his feet, he was carrying Walker, whom he draped none too gently over the rump of one of the saddled horses. A few twists of a rope and Walker was settled for a long, uncomfortable ride. Frank stepped into his stirrup, settled himself in the saddle, gave a curt nod toward Luke, then started toward the barn door. Grif followed.

"I don't want the reward money," Luke shouted to the departing men.

Frank turned to give him one long, appraising look, then nodded as though he understood before facing forward and riding on. Grif caught up to him a few minutes later. He was glad the old man chose to hold his tongue.

Grif nudged his horse forward to lead the way, breaking a trail through the snow. When his horse grew tired, he motioned for Frank to break trail. The animals found movement difficult, and several hours passed before they reached a windswept area Frank recognized as the trail they'd followed the previous day from the small Mormon settlement where they'd stopped the day before.

"You really heading for Texas?" It was the first time the old man had spoken since leaving the McCall homestead.

"Yeah. I've unfinished business there."

Miles passed before the old man spoke again. "You've been a good partner—the best I've ever had—and I'll miss you, but I won't try to change your mind. I understand how sometimes there's things a man has to take care of. I figure we've got enough put away in that bank in Denver to take us where we need to go and to buy that piece of land I've been thinkin' about."

"Where will you go?" Frank asked. Belatedly, his conscience reared its head to remind him that Grif was getting old and had no family. He considered asking him to accompany him to Texas, but he suspected the old man would be miserable in the more civilized parts of the state where Frank planned to go.

"Remember that little valley where we waited out the snow a few days out of Denver? I been thinkin' about filin' a claim on it. I'm gettin' too old for this, and I'm figurin' it's time to build a cabin and settle down."

They found they were in luck when they reached town. A passing marshal, headed for Eagle Rock, had waited out the storm in the small community and was just getting ready to ride out. He examined their prisoner and sent the storekeeper to fetch a woman who knew something about doctoring. She expressed doubt whether Walker would ever have full use of his gun hand again, the hand Frank had stomped on, and the marshal said it didn't matter since Walker would be spending the rest of his life in the territorial prison anyway, if he didn't hang.

The marshal gave them a voucher for the reward money that they could cash when they reached Denver, and they prepared to leave.

"You boys taking the train from Eagle Rock?" the marshal asked.

"How far does it go?" Frank asked.

"All the way to Denver." The lawman puffed out his chest. "Came in that way myself a little over a year ago."

"I'll be danged!" Grif exploded. "It's gittin so's a man can scarce wander for a week without stumblin' over them consarn railroads."

CHAPTER 11

1886

The sun was low in the sky when Frank left the hotel. He wished he'd made his decision earlier. He'd chafed at the delay since the train halted in Grayson. The conductor had made it clear that passengers heading east had little choice other than to wait until the track was repaired or travel on horseback to the next rail line. The ticket master at the depot had said it would take two weeks, maybe longer, to repair the damage spring runoff had caused, but it would take only about four days to reach the Santa Fe line on horseback if he chose to buy a horse from the local livery stable. Of course, he'd have to purchase another ticket when he reached the railhead. He'd checked into the hotel, and after two days in the dismal little town, he was tired of waiting. He went in search of the stable.

He'd sold his horse in Denver rather than worry about transporting the animal all the way to Houston, but now he wished he'd kept her. Finding the town's only livery stable, he stepped inside. The man who sauntered toward him sported a scraggly beard and a knowing grin that ruffled Frank's hackles. He almost walked out, then thought better of it. If he was going to acquire a mount, he had little choice but to deal with the man.

A quarter of an hour later, Frank rode out of the stable on a long-jawed gelding that looked like a mistake, but proved to have a comfortable gait that befitted his name, Lucky Day. He didn't have high expectations for the animal. The man he'd dickered with had been a little too anxious to sell the animal and had been willing to settle for an amount far less than the exorbitant amount he'd originally quoted. Besides, the animal didn't look like much.

Frank gave the horse his head and let him run for a few minutes. He was surprised by the big gray's speed. He responded well to each of Frank's commands, and it soon became apparent someone had invested a great deal of time into training the animal. At last, he turned back to the hotel where he gathered up his few belongings before returning to the mount that looked more like a plow horse than a saddle horse but could run like the wind.

His next stop was the general store which was preparing to close. The proprietor glanced at Lucky Day then quickly looked away before taking Frank's order. He found the requested items, but didn't encourage Frank to linger to chat. That was all right with Frank since he was also in a hurry to be on his way.

He made a neat bundle of his purchases and stowed them in a canvas bag. He had learned a great deal from Grif, including which trail provisions and supplies to pack to save space and to prevent going hungry if the journey took longer than anticipated. He fastened the bag along with a new bedroll behind the high Mexican saddle he'd purchased along with the horse.

When he finished his preparations, Frank turned his back on the town and headed south. Lucky Day was anxious to run, and Frank found it felt good to feel clean air, free of soot and ash, rush past his face. The network of railroads rapidly expanding across the country were a great convenience, but sometimes he felt a bit like Old Grif, who viewed the contraptions as a travesty against nature.

Being honest with himself, he admitted he missed the old man. They'd stayed in a hotel for a couple of months after reaching Denver, then after the snow receded enough to allow them access to the land that his former partner had acquired, he'd helped Grif build a crude cabin in a secluded valley near a picturesque mountain spring. A late blizzard had snowed them in for another month, and it had been April before Frank could continue his journey.

Flowers spread across a carpet of green and low hills rose to his right. The horse veered toward the hills to the south, and Frank let him run. As the ground grew steeper, it became rockier too, and they slowed to a walk. Trees became more numerous the higher they climbed, and Frank discovered it felt good to be back in open terrain.

Daylight was almost gone by the time Frank halted the big horse. The faint track of a wagon trail beckoned him onward toward a narrow pass between two hills that weren't quite mountains. He considered his options. It would soon be full dark, and he didn't relish picking his way through the canyon in the dark, but he hadn't traveled as much distance as he would have liked to cover before stopping. Lucky Day was surefooted, but even a good horse could stumble in the dark on an unfamiliar trail. He'd been foolhardy to begin his trek with night coming on. He decided to travel just until he found a good place to camp for the night.

Before it became completely dark, he found a spot near a trickle of water with ample grass nearby for Lucky Day. Not knowing the horse's habits, he hobbled him near the spot where he rolled out his bedroll. He'd eaten supper at the hotel before setting out, so he didn't bother with a fire. He rolled out a ground cloth to protect his bedroll from the damp ground and fell asleep to the music of the tiny stream of water splashing over rocks and the sound of Lucky Day munching on grass.

He was awakened a few hours later by the sound of horses running at breakneck speed down the canyon to the accompaniment of boisterous laughter. He was glad he was off the trail far enough not to attract the riders' attention. Chances were that the men were the kind of men better avoided.

When morning came, Frank took his time preparing breakfast. Before he sat down to eat, he gave Lucky Day a measure of the oats Frank had brought along for the big horse. His meal wasn't as good as the ones he'd enjoyed at the hotel, but he took satisfaction in the simple side pork and biscuits, washed down with coffee. When he finished, he rinsed his utensils in a small pool nearby and scrubbed them well with a handful of sand before packing them away.

The day had dawned clear and bright, and he was glad to be out in the open away from the smells and noise of the small town where

the train had halted for repairs. Lucky Day seemed to be in great
spirits and anxious to run, but Frank decided to keep him to a walk
to conserve the animal's strength for a long day of travel.

A few scraggly pines dotted the sides of the canyon, but most of
the growth appeared to be chokecherries and a variety of shrubs and
tall grasses. Shortly before noon, Lucky Day snorted and lost his
stride, alerting Frank that something was amiss. He looked around,
making certain there were no rattlers in the well-trampled, muddy
trail ahead of him. Next he checked for boulders or tree branches
overhanging the trail where a mountain cat might lie in wait.
Satisfied that the usual menaces weren't the problem, he began a
careful scan of the hills surrounding him. They were barely steep
enough to call the cut he followed a canyon. He would have considered it merely a pass between two hills had the man back at the
livery, who gave him directions, not called the place Blackdog
Canyon.

He sniffed the air and caught a faint whiff of what might be
smoke. It likely came from a campfire he decided, since there was
only a slight possibility of a brushfire with the damp ground and
new spring growth abounding everywhere. He rode on slowly,
watching for any sign of trouble. He didn't want to be caught in a
narrow canyon if a fire swept through it. He remembered the rowdy
bunch of riders that he'd heard during the night and wondered if
they'd left a fire burning.

He'd traveled a quarter of a mile before he caught sight of a wisp
of smoke in the distance. Half an hour later, he rounded a curve to
find a wagon turned on its side, its contents blackened and charred.
What hadn't burned was spilled across the muddy road and well
trampled.

"Whoa!" He pulled back on Lucky Day's reins. The animal
pranced nervously, then stood while Frank surveyed the scene.
There was no sign of the draft animals that had pulled the wagon.
He hoped that meant whoever had been traveling in the wagon had
escaped and freed the horses.

Barrels were burned down to the hoops, and the wagon box was
black with gaping holes. Wisps of smoke curled upward from its

remains, and a dozen or so arrows protruded from what remained of the boards that had formed the sides of the wagon. Charred bits of cloth lay among blackened tins and tools. Frank nudged the horse forward to slowly circle the wagon. There were few clues that might identify to whom it had belonged. He glanced over his shoulder, then stepped down from his horse to check more closely.

As he led the horse to a nearby sapling to tether him, the animal shied, and with rolling eyes resisted approaching the edge of the clearing. Frank peered toward the bushes and trees, studying them carefully. At last he spotted a patch of dull red he suspected was the hide of an animal, perhaps a draft horse or an ox.

After taking the time to tether his horse on the opposite side of the trail, Frank headed back to the spot where he'd seen the bit of hide. On the way, he noticed the metallic gleam of shell casings lying on the ground in several places. His approach sent a pair of magpies that had been pecking at spilled flour and beans fluttering to a nearby tree branch. When he broke through the already broken and twisted branches hiding the spot from the road, more birds took flight, fluttering overhead as he looked at the animal that lay there.

It didn't take long to determine that the animal was dead and that it wasn't a draft animal, but a plain old cow. A half dozen arrows protruded from its body. Frank's hair stood on end and he looked around nervously before reason overcame the hasty conclusion he'd drawn. He'd seen only signs of shod horses on the trail and around the burned-out wagon. Indians could possibly own guns, but they didn't put shoes on their horses.

Stepping away from the dead animal, he studied the ground more closely, looking for the kind of details Grif would look for when trailing an outlaw. The scattered cans and burned trunks and barrels suggested the wagon had been making a lengthy journey. An overturned lantern hinted that it may have provided the accelerant and was possibly the origin of the flames. A charred bit of lace, caught on the brake, suggested that a woman had been aboard the wagon. Numerous boot prints told the story of at least six men dismounting and walking around the burning wagon. The tracks of horses and men mingled, telling a story of chaos and confusion.

Minutes later, he found deep ruts where something heavy had been dragged across the clearing. When he reached the thick brush the ruts led to, he spotted what appeared to be smears of blood on a clump of grass and signs someone had left the scene of the burned wagon on foot.

Frank took a step toward the hint of a trail, then glanced back toward Lucky Day. Some inner prompting told him to go back for the horse before following the barely discernable trail. After a moment's hesitation, he loped back to where the animal was tied, loosed the reins, and with the big gray following as closely as a leashed dog, passed the wagon on the side away from the dead cow. Frank knew there were horses who shied away from dead carcasses, but Lucky Day seemed to have a real aversion to that dead cow. Frank reasoned that made them good partners since he wasn't too keen on running into anything dead either.

He parted the shrubs in a different place from the signs he'd noticed and planned to follow. He didn't want to turn tracks into a trail. Five years as Grif's partner had taught him caution and a bit of trail savvy.

He hadn't traveled far when he heard horses and men on the road behind him. Some feeling urged him to stay out of sight. If the bandits who had attacked the wagon were returning, he didn't want them to find him. And if the riders were a posse, he didn't want to explain a reason—he wasn't certain he understood himself—for his presence at what appeared to be a staged Indian attack.

Drawing Lucky Day deeper into the brush, he tethered the big animal to a tree, then retraced his steps to a place where he could remain concealed and still see the overturned wagon. When he reached a point where he could not only see the wagon but the road as well, he stopped to take stock. He counted seven horses and riders. They huddled together for several minutes, then two broke away to ride to the far side of the wagon where one dismounted to attach a rope to what was left of it. In minutes, the twisted metal and charred timbers disappeared into the brush beside the road it had been blocking. Several other riders dismounted and occupied themselves by kicking cans and debris into the grass that lined the track that passed as a road. Soon there was little visible evidence of the attack, and in a few weeks, when the grass grew taller, there would be none.

Whether the men were clearing the road for future travelers or removing evidence of a crime, Frank couldn't be certain, but he wasn't taking any chances. He stayed crouched a good distance from the men until they remounted and rode back toward Grayson. He stared after them until they were well out of range of any sign of movement or sound he might make. He hadn't recognized any of the men, but he hadn't been in Grayson long. He found something telling in the fact that none of the men made any attempt to locate the hapless driver of the burned wagon or the animals that had pulled it. One had pointed toward the place where the dead cow lay, but no one had checked to see whether the slight stench and cloud of birds hovering over the spot denoted the presence of a person or an animal. To Frank, that was a strong indication that the men already knew the answers that might arise in the minds of someone accidentally stumbling on the scene.

Frank studied the sky for several minutes. It was almost midday, and if he didn't want to spend another night in the canyon, he should be on his way. He had no desire to stretch this leg of his journey to five days, but something inside him wouldn't let him go. He might be merely trailing an escaped draft animal, but there was a chance he was following a wounded man. He began working his way back to Lucky Day.

The horse snorted and sidestepped nervously when Frank tried to mount him. After several misses, Frank managed to get a boot in the stirrup and swing himself up. He leaned forward, patting the horse's neck and talking in soothing tones until the horse settled down enough to be urged forward.

Lucky Day moved hesitantly, and Frank kept his senses on full alert as he watched for signs of passage through the brush and grass. Bent blades and broken twigs formed a clear trail, and when they merged with a faint path, likely formed by wild animals, the trail became easier to follow. There was something curious about the trail he followed—whoever had passed this way had walked beside the path instead of on it, even though the path had not yet deteriorated to mud or dust but was still composed of trampled grass and weeds.

Each time Lucky Day snorted or crab-stepped, Frank scanned the area for signs of a predator. The canyon was just the sort of place a mountain cat or a brown bear might search for prey. Flattened tufts of grass, an occasional drop of blood, or a muddy smear in the damp ground told him someone was ahead of him and moving away from the burned-out wagon. He wondered why a man, who was likely wounded, was moving away from the wagon road where there was at least a possibility of meeting help. It was far more likely that a wounded animal would flee toward a wilderness area, but his instincts told him he was following a person.

A wide patch of bent grass and a small pool of blood indicated that the person he trailed had stopped to rest. A glint of bright color caught his eye, and leaning closer, he picked out the shape of an arrow like those back at the attack scene. It appeared to be broken. It was also covered with brown stains. A cotton thread, caught on a thistle nearby, was enough to reinforce his conviction that he was following a man, one who had stopped, most likely to snap off a protruding arrow shaft so he could wrench the arrowhead from its lodging place without drawing either the arrowhead or the feathered shaft back through his skin. The thread was a sign the man he followed had secured a bandage around the bleeding wound.

Frank speculated concerning how serious the wound might be. The man was making no attempt to cover his trail, yet he appeared to be fleeing whatever had taken place on the road. Either he was hurt pretty badly or he was a greenhorn with no knowledge of the tactics of self-preservation.

The patches of flattened grass were coming closer together, and Frank speculated that the fleeing man was growing tired or weakening. Suddenly, Lucky Day balked with all four legs stiff, refusing to go farther.

After repeated attempts to get the horse to move on, Frank slid from the saddle in exasperation, silently berating the stable owner for selling him the overly sensitive animal. Seeing the animal's eyes rolled back, he took the reins in one hand and urged the horse to back away from whatever frightened it. Taking delicate crab steps, the horse sidled back down the trail to an aspen tree where Frank knotted the reins around a black and white tree trunk.

Before continuing the trek on foot, Frank drew his Winchester from its scabbard. He'd purchased the rifle in Denver to replace his old Browning. If Lucky Day's reaction to the dead cow he'd discovered earlier was an indication of what he'd find further up the trail, he wouldn't need the rifle, but there was no sense in trusting a hunch too far.

He soon discovered his hunch hadn't been mistaken. Near where Lucky Day had refused to continue on, Frank found where the person he'd been following had rested before crawling under a thick bush to die. Pushing back a branch covered with pale new leaves, he knelt beside the body to check for a heartbeat. There was none.

Leaning back on his heels, he studied the man, who lay straight with his arms crossed across his chest and eyes closed as though he'd known he was dying and had assumed the posture of a formally laid-out corpse in anticipation. He noted the deceased man's youth and well-worn shirt and trousers, both of which were handmade and covered in blood. A long strip of bloody fabric was tightly wound around the man's waist. Another was knotted around his thigh. Frank didn't uncover the wounds, but from the amount of blood the man appeared to have lost, he guessed the wounds were severe. He remembered the bloody arrow he'd found shortly after beginning his search.

The dead man's light-colored hair was a little long and curled against the nape of his neck. His big calloused hands showed signs of severe burns, and the soles of his worn shoes were nearly gone. Otherwise, he looked the picture of any young farmer Frank might meet anywhere in the West. There was no sign of a gun, and his pockets were empty, leaving no way of identifying the man. He wondered if someone back in Grayson might recognize him and give him a proper burial. He contemplated returning to town with the body. The delay would cost him time, but leaving the body didn't seem right.

Turning his head, Frank considered going after his horse. Lucky Day was large and could easily carry Frank and the body, but he suspected he'd have a major fight on his hands to get the body on the horse's back even if he securely wrapped it in a blanket. He'd had nightmares for years imagining the body of the young boy he'd believed he'd shot lying on that hillside. If he couldn't carry this young man back to town, he'd at least give him a proper burial.

Standing once more, he studied the thicket surrounding the place where the man had rested before crawling under the bush that hid his body from anyone who might casually pass by, but which wouldn't deter a scavenger. Frank's eyes roved around the small grassy space set in the middle of the thick bushes, noticing there were no magpies or crows waiting like specters. Something didn't feel right. He took a few steps to the spot where he assumed the dead man had rested earlier. The flattened grass covered a surprisingly wide spot, and he wondered if the dying man had thrashed about before accepting his fate. Kneeling, he touched the bent grass. It was wet, but not as tightly bunched as the grass the man had tread on in his flight up the hill. Frank found the unmistakable print of a pointed boot toe.

A chill slid down his spine. The dead man wasn't wearing boots. Frank had particularly noticed heavy shoes on the man's feet on the trail.

CHAPTER 12

Frank turned in a slow semicircle. With deliberate care, he examined each bush and tree. The warm spring sun was sending dappled shadows across the grass, teasing his senses and hinting at secrets. The dead man hadn't been alone. His partner could be anywhere, and he might assume Frank was one of the men who attacked the wagon. Frank's hand clutched his rifle tighter. He had no desire to be mistaken for one of the men who had attacked the wagon, and he had no way of knowing whether or not the surviving man was armed or if he was also wounded.

A smothered scream sent Frank scrambling for cover. From behind the nearest tree, he caught sight of a boulder a short distance away. Behind it was the most likely hiding place for the dead man's companion. He strained to hear, but the sound wasn't repeated. Once or twice, he thought he detected other sounds coming from the rock's direction, sounds which didn't seem to belong on the hillside, but he couldn't be certain.

The scream he'd heard could have come from a wild animal—an animal in pain sometimes sounded eerily human. It was also possible Frank hadn't been the only one to track the survivor of that ambushed wagon to this lonely spot, though he'd scanned his backtrail frequently and had listened for signs that someone else was moving up the hillside. The scream had stopped as though a hand had been clapped across the screamer's mouth. He needed to get closer without making himself a target.

Testing each step before placing his weight on it, Frank began a slow circuit of the rock, keeping to the thick foliage. It took more than a quarter of an hour to position himself to the side and above the boulder to where he could just glimpse the back side of it. At first he could only see a narrow strip of grass between the chunk of granite and the trees he hid behind. A slight movement brought a boot into view. By shifting his position slightly, he found the owner of the boot. He nearly dropped his rifle in shock.

A woman huddled against a tree trunk with her knees drawn up and her skirt askew. Her head was arched back, and both hands were clasped across her mouth. She was partially covered with a pitiful pile of odd, scorched rags that must have once been a patchwork quilt. Frank's heart, the one he wasn't certain he possessed anymore, constricted. The woman was in serious trouble, but she appeared to be alone.

"Ma'am," he called softly as he took a step toward her. Her head came up, and he saw her scrabbling for something that lay beside her. He ducked behind a tree. He didn't mean to be shot when he only meant to offer help.

"St-stay back." The feeble warning ended in a moan.

"Ma'am," he tried again. "I'm not going to hurt you. I found your man farther down the hill. I want to help you."

"G-Go away."

He chanced peeking around the tree and was startled to see not a gun, but a good-sized rock in her hand. If he moved toward her, she'd doubtless lob it his direction. If she did, he'd duck. His childhood playmate, Beau, had a younger sister who used to throw rocks at him and her brother, and he'd gotten quite good at dodging her missiles. A fleeting smile turned up one corner of his mouth at the memory of Betsy before his attention reverted to the problem at hand.

"I'm coming," he warned. He stepped out from behind the tree and began making his way over rocks and tree limbs downed by winter storms. When he reached the small island of grass, he was surprised by how young the woman looked. She might have been pretty, but her face was seared with the flaming red of fresh burns and etched with agony. Her hands and arms hadn't escaped the flames either. He suspected she was near out of her mind with pain.

Just as he expected, the stone hurtled toward him, narrowly missing his head. She was good, but not as expert as young Betsy had been. He continued toward her, speaking softly, as Grif had taught him was the proper way to approach a strange horse or a strange woman.

The woman threw her head back and screamed a sound of excruciating agony, making no effort to smother her cry this time. Her body arched, and a chill ran up Frank's spine. He stood as if frozen, absorbing this second shock. The woman was not only severely burned, but she was about to give birth.

His mind urged him toward her. There was no one else for miles around who could possibly help her, but what could he do? He knew nothing about babies. The only baby he recalled ever being close enough to even touch was the Calloway baby. He'd seen a few calves and a couple of colts birthed, but he couldn't see many parallels to the human baby he figured was going to arrive any minute. For the first time in many years, he wished Pa were with him to tell him what to do.

He moved closer. Compassion like he'd never known before twisted inside him, and he found himself kneeling beside the suffering young woman. He placed the Winchester on the ground and leaned toward her.

"I'm not here to hurt you. I had no part in what happened to your husband. Tell me what to do," he pleaded. "I'll do anything."

His eyes met hers and he saw the hesitation in hers. Slowly the doubt turned to acceptance, and she nodded slightly.

"He sent you. I prayed, and you came." She almost smiled, and something inside her seemed to relax for just a moment. She reached a small, burn-reddened hand toward his much larger hand and gripped it with surprising strength. A look of fearsome pain swam in her eyes, but she didn't cry out again. When the contraction ended, she once again smiled feebly. Frank's presence seemed to comfort her and renew her strength.

"I've been so afraid, but Will said I just needed faith."

"What happened?" Frank asked, trying to take in the situation.

"They attacked us just after we crossed a shallow creek. Even though Will had a bullet in his side, he whipped up the horses and made a run for it. The first curve that put us out of their sight, he insisted I get out of the wagon and hide in the trees. I jumped for the baby's sake, but I barely had time to squeeze my way into the bushes when they caught up to the wagon and began firing burning arrows into it." She sucked in her breath sharply and moaned until the contraction peaked. When the crest had passed, she continued as though there had been no interruption.

"They were shouting and swearing, saying terrible things about the Prophet and taunting Will. Then one of them hit him and he fell. At first I thought they'd killed him, then a few minutes later I saw him crawling toward the bushes where our cow had disappeared. They were so busy looting our wagon and stealing Will's horses they didn't notice at first, then one of the men took after him." She was crying now.

He placed an arm around her shoulder, awkwardly trying to comfort her.

Another contraction halted her story, then she went on, speaking rapidly as though some force compelled her to tell the story as quickly as possible. "When the man returned a few minutes later, the whole bunch took off down the road, whooping and laughing. They took our horses. I hurried to get to Will. They'd left him to bleed to death beside our cow with an arrow in his thigh. He—he was trying to stand. I wanted to dress his wounds, but he said we had to get away from there first."

"I don't understand," Frank said as he watched the woman descend into the throes of another wave of pain and felt her grip on his hand tighten. He wanted to comfort her but didn't dare touch the back of her hand with his other hand for fear he would disturb the blisters forming there and cause her further pain. When he thought the pain had ebbed, he went on.

"Why did they attack you? Was it just to steal your horses?"

His question seemed to puzzle her, but after a moment she answered in a flat voice, "Because they hate us. Because Satan has possessed their souls, leading them to hate all that is righteous and good."

"You're very religious, aren't you?" He'd never met anyone quite like this young woman. He saw her brace for another contraction. She met it silently and didn't speak at first when it concluded. He wondered if the pain were too much, forcing her to stop her explanation, but after a long moment, she continued as though compelled to make him understand.

"The Gospel matters more than anything to me and Will. Our families left Nauvoo, Illinois, after the Prophet's martyrdom and traveled to Mexico. They regretted it many times and wished they'd followed Brother Brigham. Will and I grew up and married in Mexico, but we wanted our baby to be born under the covenant. That's why we were on our way to St. George. Now Will . . ." She broke off to swipe the tattered quilt across her eyes. "Can you help us? If I can get to Utah . . ." Again she was overwhelmed by a contraction that seemed to go on a long time. It left her face covered with a fine sheen of perspiration.

Frank's confusion over her explanation was overshadowed by his concern for the woman. "You can't travel in your condition, and you should forget about continuing your journey. After the baby is born, you must return to your family. Surely they'll help you."

She muttered something, but her ramblings made little sense to Frank. After a few minutes, her speech became more clear. "Our parents are dead. They were killed in a raid by Mexican bandits ten years ago. Bishop Romney raised us, and after we got married, he moved his family to Colonia Juarez, so there is no one to return to."

"But you can't rear an infant by yourself. There must be someone who can help you."

"Once I reach Utah, the Church will help me."

"You'd trust your life and that of your child to a bunch of strangers?" His words seemed to shock her, and she was quiet for several minutes.

"Who are you?" she asked after another contraction came and went, leaving her looking even more lost and lonely.

"My name is Frank Haladen, and I'm from Willow Springs, Texas," he told her. "I've been away a long time, and I'm on my way home now." He thought it best to keep the explanation as brief and simple as possible. Knowing anything about his activities during the past twelve years wasn't likely to lend the unfortunate woman any degree of confidence in him.

"I thought . . . I've heard stories all my life about John and the three . . . " She stopped, and Frank thought the pain was commencing again. Instead, she bit her lip and glanced at him warily. After a moment, she said in a more formal voice, "I'm Elizabeth Statten. Wi-Willard and I were on our way to Utah . . ." Her voice changed to panting gasps. Her grip tightened on his hand, and this time he was certain she was experiencing another contraction.

When the pain passed, her head lolled back against the tree that supported her, and her eyes remained closed. Tears trickled down her cheeks, and he drew a square of linen from his pocket to gently pat them away. He feared salty tears would exacerbate the painful burns, though she never complained about them. Instead she seemed oblivious to the welts.

"Will. Oh, Will, I can't do this alone. You promised we would be together forever and our baby would be sealed to us. You said we only needed to get to St. George." Her voice was only a whisper.

Frank felt the change as her grip tightened once more. Her pain grew until he thought she would break, but at last it ebbed. This time, instead of sinking back to wait for the next pain, she leaned forward and spoke with fierce intensity.

"You're not who I thought you to be, but I know God sent you. It's too soon. The baby isn't due until the end of May and this is only April. I don't want him to die, and I don't believe God means for him to die. That's why He sent you. Promise me you won't let him die."

There was a glazed look in her eyes, and she appeared so near hysteria, he promised. He would have said anything to soothe and quiet her. She clenched her teeth and rode out the next pain. When it was over, she slumped lower, too tired to speak. After a few minutes, he realized she was praying.

Frank knew nothing substantial about childbirth, but the little he did know seemed to involve lying in a bed and plenty of hot water. There was nothing he could do about hauling water and heating it, but surely he could make her more comfortable. He pulled off his coat. He hadn't needed it for several hours, but there had been little opportunity to remove it. Now he offered it to Elizabeth, suggesting she lie down and use it for a pillow.

"No," she whispered. "It's better if I crouch like the Indian women do. Put it beneath my hips so that when the baby comes he won't lie on the ground."

Frank hesitated.

"Do it now," she ordered and attempted to raise herself up.

Gently, he lifted her, helping her to the position she desired. As he did so, he saw the baby's head. Elizabeth screamed, and some instinct took over inside Frank. He reached for the tiny head, turning it as he'd seen a rancher turn a calf's head to allow the mucus to drain. Elizabeth screamed once more, her body turning taut as she pushed with all her might—and the infant slid into Frank's hands. He stared at the tiny being, feeling helpless and scared. It wasn't breathing, and he'd made a promise.

"She was a mite early and delicate. Instead of slapping her bottom to get her breathing, I rubbed her good all over with a towel and breathed slow and easy into her mouth and nose, so she'd get the idea."

Whether it was a memory of his father, who was Doc to everyone in Willow Springs, describing one of the many births he'd presided over or some kind of delirious thought transfer from the young mother, Frank didn't question. He snatched up his jacket that had somehow been shoved aside and began to vigorously rub the tiny newborn.

There didn't seem to be any response to his ministrations. Despair filled his heart, and tears swam in his eyes, but he refused to give up. He rubbed the tiny chest and back as he blew puffs of air into the nose and mouth his mouth completely covered. After what seemed an eternity, he felt a movement under the hand that rubbed the small chest. It was followed by a thin wail. Laughing and crying, he gathered the infant close for a long moment. A feeling such as he'd never known before—stronger even than the intense feelings he'd had for Amelia—swamped him, yet he was filled with an awareness of the child and its mother's need for warmth and nourishment. It was up to him to provide for their needs.

Discovering he remembered more of the talk he'd heard long ago between his parents, he tied off the umbilical cord and severed it with his hunting knife, then he lost no time wrapping the baby in his coat and placing the bundle beside the young mother, who had slumped onto the tattered quilt and lay in exhausted stillness. She scarcely appeared to be alive except for her labored breathing which hadn't slowed to normal yet. He removed his shirt and did what he could to clean her up, then wrapped her in her quilt.

Kneeling beside the new mother, Frank touched Elizabeth's hair and called to her, "Elizabeth. Elizabeth, wake up. You have a fine son." She opened her eyes and stared at Frank blankly for a moment, appearing confused.

"Where is Will?" she asked. "He said I should go with him."

"Will isn't here," Frank attempted to speak consolingly. "He's gone, but you're a mother now. Your son needs you." He pushed back the folds of his coat to display the little face.

"He's beautiful," Elizabeth whispered in spite of her fatigue. "May I hold him?"

"Of course." He pulled back a corner of the quilt and placed the infant in his mother's arms. Seeing them together brought back the deep tenderness he'd felt moments ago. To ward off any possibility of letting his feelings show, he turned practical. "You need food and water, and it will soon be night. I'm going to return to my horse for some supplies. I won't be gone long."

"You'll return?" Her tired voice revealed a new fear.

"Yes, I'll be back." He checked once more to be certain Elizabeth had ample support from the tree she leaned against and the patchwork quilt was securely wrapped around her and her son before he started back down the hill.

Frank half-feared Lucky Day might have broken loose and returned to Grayson, but he was pleased to find the animal just where he'd left him. The horse nickered in welcome and Frank patted his neck affectionately, relieved the animal and all of his supplies were just where he'd left them. He regretted that the horse had been forced to wait so long, burdened with a saddle and all of his gear, but on the other hand, he was grateful for the time that would be saved by not having to saddle and stow the items again. He was anxious to return to Elizabeth and her baby.

Choosing a circuitous route rather than risking passing close beside poor Will, Frank hurried back to the small glen hidden behind a large boulder. He tethered the horse in the sapling grove, poured a small amount of water from his water bladder into a tin he'd purchased for that purpose, and placed it on the ground. While the horse drank, Frank gathered up his saddle and gear. He deposited them near Elizabeth and set about building a fire. He glanced over at her. She seemed to be sleeping. He remembered his father marveling at the strength of women in the throes of birthing their children and felt a strange pride in the strength and courage Elizabeth had shown. She'd earned the right to rest.

Night was coming on, and the temperature was beginning to drop. He shivered in his damp shirt and hurried to set a pan of water over the fire. While the water heated, he donned a clean flannel shirt, then hurried to Elizabeth's side.

"Elizabeth." He touched her shoulder and shook her gently when she didn't respond to his voice. After a few minutes, she drowsily murmured something he couldn't quite hear. The baby began to whimper, and Frank lifted him from Elizabeth's arms to carry him closer to the fire. He felt damp, so Frank delved into his meager supply of clothing to fashion a diaper from his spare pair of flannel underdrawers and used a shirt for bunting. Once the baby was warm and dry, he spread out his waterproof ground cloth near the fire and tossed one of his blankets over it. He made the baby comfortable, then gathering up a second blanket and his last clean shirt, he returned to Elizabeth.

"You need dry clothes," he told her, holding out the shirt for her to put on. She made no move to take it, so he draped it around her shaking shoulders and drew her arms, one after the other, through the sleeves. He was glad to see the shirttails reached to her knees. After fastening the shirt all the way down its length, he reached beneath it with his knife to cut away her wet and soiled skirts, which he tossed aside before wrapping her into the dry quilt and carrying her back to the makeshift bed he'd made for her near the fire. He propped her against his saddle for a pillow. She moaned, but did not awaken.

The baby was crying, making a high-pitched mewling sound like a small kitten. He was hungry, Frank figured. Elizabeth opened her eyes and made a gesture toward the baby, so Frank handed the well-wrapped bundle to her and arranged the blankets to provide support under her arm for the baby's slight weight and to ensure that in Elizabeth's weakened state she didn't drop him.

"Feed him while I fix something for you to eat," he told her. Turning his back, he set about frying bacon and mixing flapjacks. When his enamel coffeepot was hot, he walked back to a spot near where he'd tethered Lucky Day. He'd noticed a patch of peppermint growing there. He wasn't sure where the memories came from, but he did recall his mother saying tea was good for whatever ailed a woman, and she'd frequently seeped peppermint leaves in hot water, then added plenty of sugar to the brew.

Elizabeth appeared grateful for the tin cup he held to her lips a short time later. He could see she was too weak to hold the cup on her own, and he didn't want to risk spilling hot liquid on the baby, so he continued to hold it until the cup was drained. When she finished drinking, she looked around the clearing until she spotted Lucky Day.

"Coriantumr." She sounded excited and seemed about to rise, then sank back weakly. "Where's Colin? He's never far from that horse. Is Jerusha with him?"

"Who is Colin?" Frank asked.

"Why he's . . ." Her voice trailed off, and some of the wariness returned to her voice. "He lived on a nearby farm, and when two men were sent from Salt Lake last fall to check on our colony, Colin and his wife decided to travel with them on their return trip. Our village was frequently raided by outlaws, and the elders advised us to move to Salt Lake City or join the larger Colonia Juarez. The missionaries left for Salt Lake City a month ago, taking Colin and Jerusha with them."

Frank filled in the blanks himself, knowing Elizabeth had done the same. Was it possible that Lucky Day was Colin's horse? Remembering the stable owner's eagerness to sell the animal and the shopkeeper's reaction on seeing it, he felt sick. He also knew he couldn't turn to anyone in Grayson to help Elizabeth and her baby.

"I bought that horse in Grayson two days ago," he told her.

"I'm certain he's Colin's Coriantumr." Fresh tears made their way down her swollen cheeks.

"Cori—what does that mean?"

"Have you heard of the Book of Mormon?" When Frank indicated that he hadn't, Elizabeth went on. "It's a book my people consider a second witness of Jesus Christ. It's filled with stories of the people who lived in the Americas a long time ago. Coriantumr was a general over a vast army fighting a civil war. When the war ended, Coriantumr was the only one of his people left alive. Colin found his Coriantumr when he was just a colt. He was part of a wild herd that had been captured to furnish mounts for a band of Mexican fighters. They slaughtered the colts that were too young to keep up and the mares who would not leave their young. Colin found one gray colt had been only stunned and was still alive. He brought it home and made a pet of it."

Telling the story seemed to take all of her small reserve of strength, and she fell asleep again. Frank had to wake her again a short time later to place a few morsels of flapjack in her mouth and to urge her to nurse the baby. After a few bites, she fell asleep again with the baby snuggled against her side.

With both of his charges sleeping, Frank took up a task he dreaded, but knew must be done. Carrying a prospector's pickaxe he'd purchased as part of his outfit and gathering up Elizabeth's soiled quilt, he returned to the place where Will lay. Fortunately, the ground was still soft from recently melted snow, enabling Frank to dig a shallow trench. He placed Will in the quilt before moving him to his final resting place. After the grave was filled in and rocks piled on the soft soil to discourage animals from digging at it, he stood for a moment, gazing at the mound of dirt and rocks.

A man who had earned the love of a woman like Elizabeth had earned the right to have a few words spoken over his grave, Frank figured, but he wasn't a praying man. Besides, he didn't know what kind of words Mormons said over their departed loved ones. He didn't have anything against Mormons, but he'd heard rumors about their strange beliefs. Strange or not, he felt nothing but respect for Elizabeth.

Once again, distant memories of his own mother came to his rescue. Placing his hat over his heart, he prayed, *Lord, look after Willard Statten. He died a man, doing his best to look after the woman You gave him and his child about to be born. He trusted in Thee; treat him well. Amen.*

On the way back to the camp, he collected an armful of firewood. It would never do for Elizabeth and her baby to get chilled, so he'd have to risk the fire being seen from the road below. Anyway, he felt confident there was no way anyone could reach them without being heard, and he meant to keep his rifle handy through the night.

It was dark by the time he reached the camp. Nevertheless, he set about dragging several medium-sized logs from the windfall to serve as the frame for a lean-to. With the help of the pickaxe and his hunting knife, he trimmed green branches to make the shelter as tight as possible.

Before he finished, he heard the mewling cry of the infant and waited for Elizabeth to pick him up. When she didn't, he knelt beside her to give her shoulder a slight shake. He was shocked to discover that heat burned right through the heavy shirt she wore to his hand. In a gentle gesture, he moved his hand to her forehead.

Memories of the raging fever that took his mother and sister so many years ago had him reaching for his canteen and a strip of the shirt he'd torn to make diapers. Peeling back the blanket he'd used to cover Elizabeth earlier, he began bathing her face and neck, letting some of the cool water trickle down her throat, both inside and outside. After a few minutes, she opened her eyes and struggled to speak.

"Baby," she whispered.

He reached for the child whose whimpers had turned to full-scale screams. He helped her turn to her side and looked away while she settled the hungry baby. When the cries ceased, he turned back to snug the blanket around the pair.

"Too hot," Elizabeth protested.

"I know." He resumed bathing her face and neck with the cool water and urged her to swallow a small amount of it. His ministrations seemed to soothe her, so he continued the action until the baby fell asleep again. He was glad to see Elizabeth seemed more alert. She stroked her baby's head with her fingers and leaned forward a few inches to brush his brow with her lips, then settled back as though completely exhausted. She closed her eyes, and he thought she had fallen asleep, but after a few minutes she began to speak.

"Thank you," she said in a whispery voice. "You've been good to us. You're not who I first thought you might be, but you're a good man, and I know God sent you to save my baby. Please take good care of him. Will and I had so many hopes and dreams for him. When he's old enough to understand, tell him his father died to give him a chance to live. And tell him I love him."

Her words filled Frank with panic. They sounded eerily like a farewell speech. "You're going to be all right. Don't give up." Frank twisted the rag he held, letting the water drip down Elizabeth's neck before resuming gentle strokes across her temple.

"Tell him, too, the Gospel is true and he must have faith. Tell him God loves him. He loves you too, just as Will and I do." Her voice trailed off, and Frank doubled his efforts to bring down her fever. When the water from his canteen was gone, he returned to the items he'd removed from Lucky Day along with the saddle. He gathered up the water bladder and brought it into the shelter, where he resumed caring for the feverish woman.

Elizabeth stirred restlessly and called for Will. His heart ached for her as she relived a nightmare trek up the hillside, supporting her wounded husband, and Frank understood the fear that swamped them both when her water broke, signaling the imminent birth of their baby. He learned how the two of them had collapsed in the small clearing where Will had died, how she had tried repeatedly to staunch his bleeding, and how as he bled he became weaker. With his last breath before lapsing into unconsciousness, he'd urged her to pray and never lose faith.

When at last she faced the reality that he was gone, she had no means to bury him, so between contractions, she'd dragged him the few feet to the bush where she hoped his body would be concealed from the evil men who had attacked them and possibly from birds and animals as well.

Far into the night, Elizabeth's restlessness ebbed, and she grew still, but her flesh continued to burn. Frank continued his effort to bring down the fever, though his movements grew slower as fatigue caused his head to fall forward, then jerk as he tried to force himself to stay awake. The movement of the damp cloth became automatic in his hands. A sound jerked him back to awareness. The baby was awake again.

"Elizabeth," he called softly, then louder. There was no response. The baby's cries grew more insistent, but he could not rouse Elizabeth. Her breath had grown harsh and labored, and her skin continued to feel as though a fire had been kindled just beneath its surface. Even with the water he'd repeatedly trickled over and past her lips, they felt withered and scratchy. There would be no nourishment for her child. Drenching the cloth one more time in the water, he draped it over her face, then lifted the baby.

Holding him in one arm, Frank carried the baby to the spot where his barely touched supper still lay. He picked up a saddlebag and retrieved a can of milk he'd purchased for the coffee he hadn't had time to make. He'd stopped up the can after breakfast that morning with a clean handkerchief. Pulling the piece of cloth free, he looked around, unsure what the next step should be. He didn't think the little guy could drink from a cup, but he picked up his untouched tin coffee mug and poured a small amount of milk into it, then diluted it with water from the kettle he'd used to make Elizabeth's peppermint tea. Thankfully it had held its heat, situated as it was on a stone he'd placed in the fire for that purpose.

As the baby's wail rose in volume, out of desperation, Frank stuck the milk-drenched cloth in the cup, swished it around a few times, then pressed it to the baby's mouth. The tiny lips began their sucking motion, and Frank discovered if he pressed one finger, covered by the milky cloth into the baby's mouth, the hungry child could drink. Repeated dunking of the cloth gradually lowered the level of the milky mixture in the cup.

When the baby appeared satisfied or lost interest in the milk, Frank carried him back to the three-sided shelter and covered him well before returning his attention to Elizabeth. She seemed to be sleeping more peacefully. At least her breathing wasn't so harsh.

Reaching out a tentative finger, he discovered to his disappointment her fever hadn't broken. He picked up the shirt and began bathing her with the cold water again.

At times, she seemed to be talking to her dead husband as though he were right beside her. Frank found himself a little envious of the love the two had shared. He wasn't certain anyone, not even Amelia, had cared for him the way Elizabeth cared for Will.

Once he tried to talk to her, to bring her back to reality. "You haven't given your baby a name," he said. "We can't keep calling him baby." If she heard him, she made no response, and he feared her mind had gone somewhere far away and her body would soon follow.

He never gave up his efforts to bring her fever down, and toward morning, he began to fear he would soon run out of water. The stream that wound its way through the canyon was at least a half mile away, maybe farther. He couldn't leave the baby behind to go for more water and neither did he dare leave Elizabeth. Her breath became so shallow, he had to lean close to detect any sound at all. He touched her hand, seeking a sign that the fever was abating, but it was clear there was no break in the heat that consumed her.

Once more he fed the baby and carried him closer to the fire to change his makeshift diaper. It was the last one, and when daylight came, he'd have to find a way to rinse the cloths out and dry them or tear up the shirt that covered his own back.

Just as the sun sent its first rays over the top of the hill, Elizabeth opened her eyes. "Will? Oh, Will." A look of joy brought a radiance to her face. Then she was gone.

He sat beside her for a long time with her orphaned baby in his arms. At first, his mind was blank, numbed with shock and fatigue. Slowly, the fire went out and the sun warmed the small clearing that had seen both birth and death. Whether he slept or not, he didn't know, but a whimpering from the bundle in his arms told him it was time to dilute and warm another cup of milk. And the commotion coming from Lucky Day warned him that if he didn't quickly move Elizabeth to a spot beside her husband, the horse would break free and leave him stranded in the canyon with a helpless, day-old baby.

CHAPTER 13

Frank hated leaving the baby alone while he carried Elizabeth to the glen where Will was buried, so he hurried as fast as he could. He fed the baby first, tucked him in a nest formed by one of his two blankets, then moved Lucky Day to a spot farther down the hill. He buried Elizabeth in the other blanket, beside the pile of rocks that marked Will's grave, then turned away.

Methodically he dismantled the shelter and burned Elizabeth's ruined skirt, then took the time to cover the ashes of the fire with dirt and sticks. When the clearing was cleansed of any sign that anything unusual had transpired there, he picked up the still-sleeping baby and started down the hill. When he reached the new grave, he stopped beside it. He looked at the heap of rocks, then back to the face of the infant he held. Wide blue eyes stared back at him. After a moment, Frank began to speak.

"Elizabeth, I think you're close enough to hear me. I suspect your Will waited all night for you to join him, and I think you kept him waiting because it near broke your heart to leave this baby. I don't expect I'll ever take Will's place with this young one, and there's no way a man can ever take a boy's ma's place, but I give you my word, I'll do the best I can. I won't forget how important being a Mormon was to you, and when he's bigger, I'll take him to Utah and find someone who can tell him about the things Mormons consider important. You go ahead and be happy with your Will, and I'll do my best to raise this boy to be a man you'd be proud of. That's a promise . . . And Elizabeth, I don't know much about praying, but I figure you prayed enough whilst you were alive that God won't turn you away on account of me not saying the proper words . . . so . . . good-bye, Elizabeth."

By the time he reached Lucky Day, the baby was fussing again, and Frank took the time to trickle small amounts of the diluted canned milk into his mouth. He was almost out of milk and would need to reach the railhead quickly. He figured he had a day and a half ride ahead of him if he didn't stop more than was necessary to feed the baby and rest Lucky Day. Even if he rode hard, he'd run out of milk before he reached his destination. He hoped the baby would be satisfied with peach juice once the milk was gone. It was all he had.

After the baby finished drinking and drifted back to sleep, Frank secured him in a sling formed by knotting the sleeves of the shirt he'd used for swaddling for the newborn. He then unbuttoned his shirt and tucked the sleeping infant inside against his chest. He stuffed his spare socks and underwear around his small passenger in hopes they would keep him both warm and dry until they reached civilization. He buttoned his shirt back up before mounting Lucky Day.

When he reached the bottom of the hill, he passed the spot where he'd watched a group of men shove the Stattens' meager, burnt belongings into the long undergrowth beside the trail. On an impulse, he dismounted and walked toward the almost hidden pile of debris. He looked at the blackened cans and recognized a chair leg with deep char marks and a crock which might have once held milk or butter. A breeze caused a black clump lying at his feet to flutter, and he realized the lump was actually a book. He bent to retrieve it and watched as the scorched edges of pages crumbled in his fingers, while the pages themselves remained legible. Seeing the pages marked off in chapters and verses, he figured the book was a family Bible. It hadn't burned through because of its thick leather cover. He stooped to brush off as much ash as possible and was startled when indentations that were once embossed letters stamped into the leather stood out proclaiming, The Book of Mormon. He almost dropped the book back into the grass, then he gripped it tighter. Someday the book might matter to the boy—it was the only reminder of his parents Frank would be able to give him. He shook the book to clear away any lingering soot or ashes, then tucked the book in the bottom of a saddlebag.

As long as they were in the canyonlike passage between the hills, Frank was kept busy watching for signs of an ambush. He paused once, only long enough to refill his canteen and the water bladder, then pushed on. Once in the open, his thoughts turned to the future. Perhaps he'd been wrong to make the promises he had. He knew nothing about babies, and Elizabeth's child might be better off if he were raised by a woman.

That was another thing. He couldn't keep calling him "baby." Elizabeth had never said what she and Will had planned to call their son. Perhaps he ought to call him Willard after his pa, but Frank wasn't comfortable with that, though it was a perfectly fine name. Elizabeth's story about the name given her friend's horse came to mind. He figured the horse he rode was likely the same horse she had mentioned. He tried to remember what she'd called Lucky Day. It was Cor-i-ant-e-more, he thought, though that didn't sound quite right.

Feeling a stirring beneath his shirt, he patted the round lump, hoping the baby would go back to sleep and they could put more distance between them and the canyon with its threat of raiders.

"You and my horse have a lot in common," he whispered, hoping his voice might soothe the baby and let him know he wasn't alone. "You're both survivors without any family. Perhaps I ought to name you Coriantemore. I've kind of gotten used to calling my horse Lucky Day." He considered on the name for a minute, then laughed. "You're way too little to be stuck with a handle like that. How about Cory? Cory Willard Statten. Course that could get confusing. It might be best if you share my name. That way, no one will start wondering if I have a right to keep you. I'll just be letting it be known you're Cory Willard Haladen, but underneath I'll always know it's Statten, and I'll make sure you know about your ma and pa when you're old enough to understand."

The sun had set and night was coming on when Frank noticed a light in the distance. He eyed it with a certain amount of wariness, knowing it could be the campfire of the men he wished to avoid. He had every intention of reporting the attack on the Stattens when he reached the railhead, but until then, he was determined to avoid any situation which might endanger Cory. He would be hard pressed to explain his attachment to the infant; he only knew he would give his life for him, just as Cory's young parents had done.

The closer he came to the light, the more certain he became that the light came from a settler's cabin, which raised a few possibilities he couldn't ignore. Cory was awake and squirming against his chest. In moments, he would begin whimpering, and when that didn't bring relief for his hunger pains, he'd start screaming. For such a little guy, he had an admirable set of lungs. He'd stop at once and drip milk into the baby's mouth, but he'd used the last of his can of milk several hours ago.

Frank looked toward the cabin he could now see was about a half mile off the rough track he was following. If the settler was one of the farmers who were rapidly filling up the plains and foothills in this part of the country, he might own a cow. Of course the cabin might be occupied by trappers or hunters, but even they might have a few cans of milk he could purchase. There was also a chance that the raiders who attacked Cory's parents used the cabin as a place to watch for unsuspecting travelers.

After a few minutes' hesitation, Frank guided Lucky Day into a draw where he could dismount and tend to the baby. Cory blinked owlishly at him as Frank drew him from the makeshift sling. His tiny mouth puckered either in anticipation of being fed or to yell, so Frank opened a can of peaches and dipped the feeding rag into the juice. It was a messy process, but Cory seemed to like the peach juice, and Frank speared the chunks of fruit into his own mouth.

After a time, the baby appeared satisfied, and Frank prepared to tuck him back in the sling. A cool breeze rustled the long grass around them, and Frank felt a chill. His shirt was wet, and the clothing wrapped around Cory felt soggy. He was out of clothing, and he'd seen no sign of the cattails he'd heard Indian women used to absorb the wetness in their cradleboards. He'd known calves to catch a chill and die in the early spring, especially when they'd arrived earlier than expected. He would have to check out the cabin. If there was any possibility of a warm, dry place for Cory to sleep until morning, he had to do all he could to secure that place for him.

"Hello, the cabin!" he shouted once he was within hailing distance. There was a pause before a tall, thin black man stepped out on the porch. His overalls were held up by one suspender and in the crook of his arm was a shotgun. Two dark faces peered around the edge of the door and another peeked through a window.

"State your business," the man said, while not quite pointing the shotgun at Frank. Frank wondered if he should explain his dilemma or just ride away. He'd run across a few black men in his travels, but not many. Being a son of the South, it hadn't occurred to him to strike up a conversation with any of them. He'd heard about the buffalo soldiers who mostly tried to keep the Indians in check during the Civil War, and he remembered a few living on the edge of Willow Springs when he was a boy. There was a woman who came to clean Pa's house every spring and again in the fall.

Cory whimpered and moved restlessly. That made up Frank's mind. "I don't have any evil intentions toward you. I wouldn't bother you none, but I need help. My son and I are traveling alone and he's cold and wet. I was hoping I could take him inside to get him warm."

"I don't see nobody with you." The shotgun lifted a slight amount.

Frank began to sweat. "Here, under my shirt." He moved one hand slowly toward the front of his shirt. When the black man didn't voice an objection, Frank released the buttons to reach inside for Cory. As the cooler air reached the restless baby, he let out a yell. The baby's cry increased in volume as he was drawn from the sling. Cradling Cory in one arm, Frank looked back at the man holding the gun just as the door behind him was shoved completely open. It crashed against the cabin wall, revealing a large black woman wearing a gingham dress almost hidden behind an enveloping white apron.

"Careful, Purdy."

"I heared enough, Ellis. Put that gun away and git these folks inside." She charged down the porch step and straight toward Lucky Day.

"Gimme that young'n," she ordered, holding out her arms.

Frank didn't hesitate, but simply leaned forward to transfer Cory to the woman's arms. She immediately wrapped her voluminous apron around him and turned toward the cabin.

"Permission to dismount." It was almost a request, but Frank was already swinging one leg over his saddle without taking his eyes from the woman rushing Cory inside her cabin.

Ellis lowered his gun with a shake of his head. "Go on in." The invitation was more an acceptance of inevitability than cordiality, but Frank accepted.

"Eustace! Linc!" Ellis shouted, and Frank was startled by the sight of two lanky youths materializing out of the dark. "You keep an eye out. Whistle if anything appears out of the ordinary."

"Ain't nothin' sneakin' up on us, Pa," one of the adolescents swore before they faded back into the night.

Frank looked around. He wasn't sure what he had expected, but the cabin was neat and reminded him in some indefinable way of Luke Calloway's home up on the Snake River. Built of rough logs instead of planed planks, the cabin consisted of one large room with a fireplace at one end, a table with a log bench on either side of it in the center, and an iron bedstead against one wall. Three children sat on the bed, staring at him with wide eyes. A steamer trunk had been placed at the foot of the bed, and a half dozen or more three-legged stools were scattered about the room. On either side of the fireplace were wooden crates, and a large rag rug was centered in front of the flame. Purdy sat in a large wooden rocking chair with Cory on her lap. She was busy freeing him from the clothing Frank had wrapped him in, which were wet and smelly now. From her mumbled exclamations and the dark looks she cast his way, he gathered that she wasn't pleased with the care he'd given Cory.

Raising her voice, the woman said something to a girl lingering near the fireplace, holding a long spoon suspended over a black kettle. The kettle was resting on a trivet next to her. The girl set her spoon on the hob and scurried to fetch a basin of water, which she set on a stool beside the woman. She then lifted a steaming teakettle from a hook inside the fireplace and added hot water to the basin.

The girl lingered beside her mother as though waiting for further instructions while the black woman pushed up a sleeve and thrust her exposed elbow into the water. She nodded in satisfaction, and the girl returned the kettle to its hook.

Frank moved closer as Purdy placed Cory in the basin and proceeded to scrub him. Her hands were deft and the bath was completed in short order. She reached behind her, and the girl thrust a thick square of flannel into her hands, which the woman wrapped tightly around the now screaming infant. With Cory completely wrapped, the screaming stopped.

"Now, you sit down right here," she said, pointing Frank toward one of the stools, "whilst I fix that poor chile somethin' to eat."

Frank obeyed with alacrity, and once he was seated, she placed the flannel-wrapped bundle in his arms. Looking down at Cory's sweet, fresh face, Frank again felt a lump rise in his throat. He couldn't help wondering why God had chosen a man seeped in all Frank's weaknesses to take responsibility for the precious, innocent life he held in his arms.

In a moment, Purdy returned with a whiskey bottle holding a few inches of milk. The bottle had a piece of soft leather, possibly a finger cut from a pair of gloves, tied to the top that he could see would be much handier than the tortuous method he'd been using for feeding Cory. She thrust the bottle into Frank's hand. He looked at it a moment, unsure just how to go about introducing it to Cory.

"Just stick that flap on the end in his mouth, he'll do the rest."

"But . . ."

"It's goat milk. Babies take to goat milk better than cow milk, and we got us two of the pesky things," she informed him.

The hole in the end of the make-do nipple was a little bigger than needed, and Frank was kept busy for the next few minutes wiping up the trickle that persisted in running down Cory's chin, but the baby took to the feeding implement like he was starving, which he probably was.

When the bottle was drained, Frank grinned at his benefactor.

"Thanks. I was beyond knowing what to do," he said.

"You ain't done yet. Lift him so's his head rests on your shoulder and pat his back," she ordered.

Feeling awkward, Frank complied with her instructions. After a moment, a huge belch came from the baby, taking the inexperienced bachelor by surprise. The wide-eyed children perched on the bed giggled, and Frank felt he should apologize.

"Ma'am," he started.

"Land sakes," Purdy laughed. "That's what babies are supposed to do. If they don't, they git right colicky and cranky. Now supposin' you tell me how you come to be travelin' with a newborn babe. I spect he's no more'n a couple days old, and looks small at that."

"His ma gave birth to him just yesterday. She died this morning." He felt reluctant to explain further.

The woman clucked sympathetically, and Frank knew she'd assumed the baby's mother was his wife. He didn't correct her.

"How'd you come by that big hoss you rode in on?" The question came from behind him, and there was suspicion in the black man's voice. Frank had forgotten all about Ellis.

"I bought him from the stable owner in Grayson."

"Couple weeks back, a couple of them Mormon preachers came through here. They had a young man and his new wife with them and a couple of pack mules. The young man was ridin' that hoss."

Purdy took the baby from Frank's arms and placed him in the middle of the big bed while shooing her children off of it. He watched as the woman deftly folded another square of cotton and pinned it on Cory. She reached into a basket beside the bed and produced a little shirt, which she buttoned on to him. It was small but came almost to Cory's knees and was a much better fit than the flannel shirt he'd been wrapped in since his birth. When she produced a small quilt, only about a yard square, and proceeded to bundle him in it, Frank made up his mind. Black or not, these were good people, and he owed them the truth.

While watching the woman snuggle Cory close and begin a soft lullaby, he spoke to Ellis. "The Denver & Rio Grande was delayed in Grayson, and being impatient, I decided to ride to the Santa Fe railhead to continue my journey. I purchased the gray horse at the livery stable in Grayson and was told his name was Lucky Day, though I suspect it was no lucky day for the young Mormon man who set out to pass through the hills between here and Grayson a few weeks ago." He continued his story, explaining all that had happened since the start of his journey late in the afternoon two days ago.

When Frank finished his story, Ellis nodded his head and appeared pensive for a time. "We've had trouble a time or two ourselves. Had our only horse kilt by that bunch and our chickens stole. They's a bunch from over Grayson way what thinks black folks ain't got no business homesteadin' this parcel o' land, but we got the papers, all signed and proper, sayin' this land be our'n. They ain't a rail line yet connectin' further south without travelin' east first, then backtrackin', so folks headed north or south come this way right often. A few times, we let some Mormons what was passin' through sleep on the floor, and they treated us right good, but one said the storekeeper in Grayson cheated him right after he got off the train and was buyin' vittles to pack in his saddle bags. Another said he and another fella were chased for a couple of miles by white men shootin' arrows at 'em and whoopin' like Injuns."

"Sounds like the same bunch." Frank shook his head. "It doesn't make any sense why some folks are so dead set against other folks they don't even know."

Purdy insisted Frank and Cory sleep in the big bed while she joined the children in the attic bedroom and Ellis took turns with his boys watching for raiders. Exhaustion caught up to Frank, and he slept soundly, except for when Cory demanded another feeding. When morning came, he tried to pay for the canteen of goat milk and the infant feeder Purdy prepared for him, but she wouldn't hear of it. He'd noticed the family was low on supplies and dinner the night before had been nothing but watery bean soup. They'd shared what they had and likely saved Cory's life—it didn't seem right to eat their meager supplies and not repay them in some way. He was mounting Lucky Day when an idea of how to pay his debt to the family entered his mind.

"Ellis," he gripped the man's hand, "how about you let one of your boys accompany me to the railhead. I won't be needing my horse after I board the train. Your boy could bring him back here. If that Mormon comes through again, he might want him back, otherwise you'll have a horse to help with the plowing and for going to town when you need supplies. I could give you a paper saying I gave him to you, so you could prove you didn't steal him."

"Well, I don't know . . ." Ellis looked longingly at Lucky Day, and Frank could tell he really wanted the horse.

"Please, Pa," the older boy spoke up. "I'd be real careful like."

"We ain't never heerd of no trouble betwixt here and the railroad town to the south." Purdy surprised him by adding her appeal. Frank figured she was just as proud as her husband, but she had a mother's instinct when it came to her children, and she could clearly see that the horse might make a difference to their survival in the harsh land they'd chosen in which to make their home. At length, Ellis agreed to the arrangement.

Before the boy mounted behind him, Frank caught sight of Ellis giving the boy a few coins and some whispered instructions. Purdy kissed Cory and handed him up to Frank, who tucked him into the sturdy sling she had stitched from the knotted shirt. She dashed back inside the cabin and returned with a baby quilt and something wrapped in a small square of cloth which she handed to her son.

"Now, Linc," she shook a finger at the boy, "when Mr. Haladen gits on that train, you git right back here. I won't stand for no dilly-dallyin' around."

"Yes'm."

"An' you best be polite and helpful to Mr. Haladen. He gots his hands full with takin' care o' that poor motherless babe."

"Yes'm."

Frank figured it was time to leave before the poor boy got any more instructions.

* * *

Lucky Day didn't seem to be bothered by a second rider, and Linc proved to be a great help on the journey. They arrived at the railroad town after spending only two nights on the prairie. It was dusk when they first saw the cluster of lights that signified they'd reached their destination. Frank would have sought out lodging for the night, but knowing Linc wouldn't be allowed in a hotel, he chose to make camp and wait for morning.

Cory woke them just before sunup. Frank offered him the last of the goat milk, and Linc plucked up the diapers he'd spread on the grass to dry the night before and stuffed them in the cotton bag his mother had given Frank for them. The few businesses along the town's short Main Street were just opening when they rode into town.

They went to the depot first. Learning the eastbound train was due in at noon, they spent the morning making preparations for their respective journeys. Frank wired the closest marshal, giving him the facts of the attack on Elizabeth and Will without mentioning Cory. Next they visited the general store, where they found a woman behind the counter while her husband worked in the back. She proved helpful in outfitting Cory with baby gowns, thick flannel diapers, and a carrying basket lined with soft padding. She even produced a couple of nursing bottles with rubber nipples, which she claimed were the latest innovation in infant feeding devices. Most importantly, she sold him a supply of canned milk. Next came a larger valise to carry the baby's supplies and a change of clothing for Frank.

Frank watched Linc purchase a small bag of cornmeal with the coins Ellis had given him. Frank added raisins, sugar, salt, wheat flour, lard, beans, and coffee to his order, which he stuffed in his saddlebags, along with a handful of peppermint sticks. Linc's eyes grew round, but Frank insisted that the boy would need something to eat on the return trip and the rest would be a surprise for his momma. Linc held Cory while Frank took advantage of the opportunity for a trip to the barbershop for a bath and a shave.

* * *

Nearly a week aboard first the eastbound train and then one headed south had left Frank with more aggravation than the state of his suit. It seemed that every time he managed to fall asleep in the cramped car, Cory awakened him. Fortunately, the baby only awakened to be fed and have his diaper changed. He seemed to expect both items to be instantly ready the moment he opened his eyes and he seemed to like the sway of the railroad car and the clacking of the wheels. He was sleeping longer and seemed less fretful now than during the journey by horseback.

Frank took advantage of each train stop to walk about and stretch his legs. If water was available, he rinsed out the diapers. To his annoyance, several passengers objected to having the squares of cloth spread across the small stove at one end of the car to dry. He ignored their complaints and used the space anyway. A couple of middle-aged female travelers let Frank know he had no business thinking he could raise a child alone. They informed him he should find a wet nurse or a wife to take over the child's care or the child was doomed. He set his teeth to hold back a sharp reply.

He'd never given much thought to being a father, but he meant to be one to Cory. Elizabeth had trusted her child to him, and with Amelia dead, he didn't suppose he'd ever become a father the usual way. Besides, there was something about Cory. From the moment his tiny, wet body had slid into Frank's hands, he'd known he'd willingly give his life for this scrap of humanity. He spent long hours, as the wheels clacked and the other passengers snored, either holding the baby to his chest or peering into the basket watching him sleep.

The train whistle awoke him from one of the short naps his exhausted body had slumped into one afternoon, two weeks after beginning his journey. He peered through the soot-smudged window beside him. Nothing looked familiar, but as the train began to slow, he spotted a sign on the side of the depot they were approaching. It seemed to shout in tall letters "Welcome to Willow Springs." A nervous spasm caught in his stomach. He wasn't sure how welcome he'd be, but this was where he was getting off. He reached beneath his seat for his valise, securely clasped the handle of the willow basket in his other hand, and stepped into the aisle.

Five minutes later, he stood on the wooden platform, watching the train disappear around a bend, leaving a long plume of black smoke trailing behind it, the only hint that a train had passed through the sleepy little town. He looked around, trying to get his bearings. The town had changed and was considerably larger than he remembered. There hadn't been a railroad station or tracks through the town when he left it. There were new businesses, the trees seemed larger and the houses smaller, and he didn't recognize any of the children playing in the street. After a few minutes, a few landmarks appeared familiar, and he began to orient himself to the spot where he stood. To his amazement, he was standing very near the spot where he'd bid farewell to the town twelve years earlier. He turned slightly, seeing the train station where tickets were sold. It stood right where his childhood friend Beau's home had once stood.

A crushing loneliness held him immobile for several minutes. It was far worse than he'd known on that solitary ride twelve years ago when he'd left Willow Springs. Somewhere deep within him, he'd always wanted to return home someday, but now he wasn't certain the place he'd dreamed of existed anymore.

Cory made a smacking sound, bringing Frank back to the present. No matter. He had business to see to and a son to raise. He set out with purposeful strides toward a house he could barely see at the end of a tree-shaded lane that bisected Main Street.

CHAPTER 14

Frank stood outside the picket fence looking up at the white, two-story house. The tree where he'd made his escape twelve years ago still sheltered the north side of the house, and he could see a corner of the pasture where old Molly had once grazed. The yard was neat. There were even a few flowers blooming around the wide porch. His breath caught when he spotted a doll carriage beneath the oak tree. He peered closer. There was a scooter, toppled on its side beside it. A pang struck his heart. *Pa must be gone and someone else lives here now.* He almost walked away before a new possibility struck him.

He opened the gate and made his way up the path that had once been familiar. He rapped on the door and waited. After a few moments, the door swung open and he stood facing a woman, who in spite of the tired lines on her face and a small girl tugging at her spattered apron, was breathtakingly beautiful. There was something vaguely familiar about her, but he couldn't quite place what it was about her that made him think he had seen her before.

"Dan isn't here," she said. "Have you tried his office?" She brushed a lock of blonde hair that had come loose from the knot atop her head behind her ear with the back of a hand he could see was covered with some kind of flour mixture. He'd apparently interrupted her bread making.

His hunch was right. Dan had married, and his wife now reigned over the kitchen that had once been Frank's mother's. He didn't begrudge Dan any happiness, but a strange regret seized him, and he found himself at a loss for words. Finally, he managed to ask, "Doc?"

A brief smile lit the woman's face, and Frank stared like a dumb-struck adolescent as she stepped back, suggesting he enter. "Doc doesn't see patients anymore, but he's always pleased when an old friend comes to call." She gestured toward the room behind her.

Frank stepped through the door, and his eyes went immediately to a man sitting in a wheeled chair with a quilt across his lap. Pa looked old and much too thin. His shoulders were stooped, and there was a look of defeat in his slouched posture. Frank felt an unexpected ache in his heart. He took a step forward, then stopped, unsure of his welcome.

"Pa?"

Doc's head came up, and he peered at Frank as though he couldn't quite make out his features. Frank stepped closer. Something changed in his father's eyes. Shock and incredulity changed to hope and recognition. A trembling hand reached toward him.

"Frank? Has my boy come home?"

"Frank." A gasp came from behind him as the woman repeated his name.

Lowering the basket and valise to the floor, Frank closed the distance between him and his father. Guessing his father could not stand, he dropped to his knees and found surprisingly strong arms wrapped around his shoulders. He rested his cheek against Pa's and felt moisture. Whether the tears were his or his father's, he didn't know, but the lump in his throat was definitely his.

An indignant cry from the basket he'd set on the floor reminded Frank it was time to introduce Cory and see to his next feeding. He withdrew with reluctance from Pa's arms and turned to collect Cory. The woman was already bending over the basket, drawing the baby from the tangle of his quilt. She straightened with Cory cradled in her arms. The infant continued to cry and flail about with his tiny arms. She looked down at him, a considering expression on her face, then her gaze met Frank's, and there were questions in her eyes.

"He needs a dry change of clothes, and he's hungry," Frank spoke in a matter-of-fact voice as he reached for Cory, ignoring the woman's unvoiced questions and his own nervous concerns about his and Cory's welcome. She released the baby with some reluctance, then hovered near them while Frank, with practiced dispatch, changed Cory's diaper and gown. When the task was completed, he removed an infant feeder and his last can of milk from the valise. With Cory secure in the crook of one arm, he stepped into the kitchen where he combined hot water from a teakettle on the stove with an equal portion of canned milk, added the rubber nipple, then returned to a chair not far from his father's chair to begin the feeding process. Through the entire operation, he said nothing, though he was aware of the curiosity crackling around him.

He'd rehearsed a dozen speeches to explain Cory to Pa, but now that the time had come, he was filled with uncertainty. He didn't want to lie to his father, but he wasn't willing to risk any challenge to his claim to the boy either. Reason told him Cory would be accepted more readily by other children and their parents in Willow Springs if he was assumed to be Frank's natural son rather than an orphaned Mormon.

"Where's his mama?" A little girl Frank hadn't noticed before leaned over the arm of the chair to get a closer look at the baby.

"He doesn't have a mama," Frank attempted to answer her question.

The child leaned her head to one side and extended a finger to touch the bottle Cory drank from. Finally, she looked squarely at Frank and said, "Everybody gots a mama."

"Rachel!" the woman scolded.

"No, it's all right." Frank focused his eyes on Cory's small face. "His mama died."

"Did she go to sleep and you couldn't wake her up?"

"Something like that," Frank admitted.

"Sometimes I can't wake up my mama, so Willy brings me and Joe to Aunt Betsy. After awhile, Mama wakes up. Then she comes and gets us. Is Baby's mama going to come get him when she wakes up?"

"Rachel, go finish your lunch." The woman grasped the child's hand and hustled her toward the kitchen.

"It's all right. I don't mind her questions." Frank tried to ease the woman's concern, but she only seemed to straighten her back and exit the room more rapidly, leaving a few questions Frank would like answered, like why couldn't the little girl wake her mother? And who were Willy and Joe?

"Did you love her?" The question took him by surprise.

"Amelia?" How did Pa know about her? "She was everything to me," he admitted.

"Tell me about her," Pa invited in a quiet voice.

Frank had never talked about Amelia to anyone, not even Grif, but suddenly he wanted Pa to understand. "She wasn't very big, but she was the most stubborn, determined woman I ever met. She had long chestnut curls and a sprinkle of freckles on her nose and no idea how pretty she was. Amelia was good and kind and she owned a newspaper, which she ran by herself until I came along. She had a lot of enemies because of the stands she took on drinking and gambling and women getting the vote. She couldn't bear for anyone to be hurt or shunned. Still it wasn't one of her enemies that killed her, but a bullet meant for me. I've wished every day since she died that I had died instead of her." He couldn't go on, yet it was almost like a load was taken from his shoulders to share his pain with Pa. It was more than that. Keeping his grief locked inside himself had kept it fresh and burning. Sharing his memories with Pa seemed to lessen the terrible ending and brighten the good times he'd shared with Amelia.

"Don't make the mistake I did, son." Pa's voice was filled with shared pain. "Your Amelia sounds a lot like your ma. I lost you because I buried my heart in that cold grave with her. I didn't want to live without her. It took losing you too to wake me up to what I'd done. Don't let grief keep you from being the father your boy needs. Your Amelia would want you to put your son first now."

Frank was confused. Was his father talking about Amelia or Elizabeth? The realization came slowly. Pa's question had been about Cory's mother, and the answer he'd given had been about the woman he had loved. He chose not to correct the misunderstanding. He lifted Cory to his shoulder and began to pat his back the way Purdy had taught him.

"Your room is pretty much the way you left it." Pa smiled. "Betsy gives it a good scrubbing now and then, so as soon as you haul the cradle you and Alice slept in down from the attic, you should be all set. You are staying, aren't you?" There was hope and hesitation in his question.

"I'd like to—at least for a time, if that's all right with you and Dan."

"This is your home. Of course I want you to stay. Dan will be pleased to see you too. He's had some fool idea all these years that it was his fault you took off."

"It wasn't anyone's fault but my own. I was spoiling for trouble, and when the sheriff threatened to throw me in jail, I ran instead of facing the music. When I found myself in more trouble than I knew what to do with, I had too much pride to come back home, so I stayed away. I reckon I had some growing up to do before I could face you and Dan again." He looked his father in the eye, then glanced back down at Cory, who was once again asleep.

"I'm glad you're back, son. Now why don't you hand my grandson to me, and we can be getting acquainted while you fetch that cradle. If you need anything, just let Betsy know."

"Betsy?" He raised an eyebrow.

"You mean you didn't recognize her? She used to tag after you and Beau when you were boys. Seems I remember patching up a good sized gash on the top of your head one time where she got you with a rock because you and that no account brother of hers tried to leave her behind whilst you sneaked off fishing instead of doing your chores."

"She's that Betsy?" Frank glanced toward the kitchen.

"The same." Pa smiled like he was keeping a secret.

"She's Dan's wife?" He mentally kicked himself as soon as the question left his lips. He'd sworn he wouldn't find fault with Dan. It just startled him that his very upright uncle would marry a woman so much his junior. Betsy was four years younger than Frank and Dan had six years on him. That made ten years difference in their ages. He ignored the tinge of jealousy that took exception to his old playmate transferring her adulation from him to his uncle, of all people.

"No," Pa chuckled, "Dan isn't married. Betsy has never married either, though she's certainly had her share of suitors who have tried to convince her to wed. She showed up here looking for work shortly after her ma passed on and her sister wed the Steadman boy. She said she didn't want to live with Beau and his wife, and she had no place else to go. She'd heard my hip was bothering me and the colored lady who had cleaned once a week was going to California with her husband. She said she figured I could use some help keeping this big house clean and meals cooked. Dan and I talked it over and decided to give her a try. She moved into the room your mother used as a sewing room off the kitchen. That was a little more than six years ago. I believe it was the best bargain I ever made."

Pa held his arms out again. "Now let me get acquainted with my grandson while you find that cradle and do whatever settling in you need to do."

Frank hesitated only a moment before placing the sleeping baby in his father's arms. The gray head bent over Cory, and with a satisfied smile, Pa turned his full attention on the sleeping infant.

Frank turned toward the stairs. He dropped the valise inside his old room and looked around, sensing something was missing. He remembered Ma's quilt and regretted ever taking it from the room. The memory also roused the anger he'd been holding in check for a long time. It was Harrison Duncan's fault that quilt was as lost to him as Amelia and all of his once-bright dreams. Harrison Duncan was responsible for spoiling too much in too many lives. It was time he was stopped. He left the room abruptly and headed for the narrow stairway leading to the attic.

The attic was cluttered and stuffy, but it didn't take long to locate the oak cradle. He brushed a finger across the dusty headboard and remembered rocking his sister in it while Ma cooked dinner or did some household chore. He was a grown man, but he still missed his mother and the little sister he'd adored. He'd been an only child with only his Uncle Dan to play with for ten years, then his little sister had been born. Alice's arrival had filled the house with joy and laughter, dainty clothes and rebellious curls, and he'd nearly burst with pride when she took her first steps to reach him and when her first word had been his name.

Their loss was no longer the persistent ache it had been, and he could think about them now and remember how good life had been back then. He'd never given much thought to how their deaths had impacted his father's life, but now because of Amelia and Cory, he thought he had some idea. His thoughts filled him with guilt. He'd abandoned Pa when Pa had needed him the most.

"That cradle is filthy with dust. Bring it downstairs and I'll clean and polish it before you put your son in it." He turned to see Betsy standing in the doorway.

"I'm sorry, Betsy. I didn't recognize you when I first saw you."

Betsy laughed and walked toward him. "I don't think you ever really saw me—except that time I busted your head open with a rock."

"Well, you certainly got my attention that time." He chuckled and touched a spot on his head where a white scar mandated he part his hair on the other side.

"Doc sent me up here to tell you your mother's rocking chair is up here somewhere too. He said it belonged to your grandmother, and your ma had insisted on hauling it to Texas because she couldn't part with it and because it was perfect for rocking you to sleep at night. He thought you might want to use it."

"I remember she used to rock Alice in that chair." He looked around until he spotted the chair piled high with odds and ends.

"I'll move those things for you." Betsy stepped toward the chair.

Frank reached out an arm to stop her. As his hand settled on her arm, a strange awareness seemed to be reminding him this woman was no longer just Beau's little sister. "No, it's covered with dust." He withdrew his hand. "I'm already dirty, and there's no reason you should get dirt all over you as well. Go back downstairs, and I'll carry it down after I fetch the cradle."

She backed away, but she seemed hesitant to leave the attic. She continued watching him from the doorway as he moved an old pair of curtains that rested atop a box of books on the chair. He remembered Ma reading at every opportunity, not just the newspaper she edited, but she had a large collection of books she treasured. The curtains made him sneeze, and he wondered why they had been kept. If they were worth keeping, they should have been stored in one of the trunks littering the cramped space. He returned to the chair for the box, and as he set it on the floor, a thick, leatherbound volume caught his eye. It didn't seem to be covered with as much dust as the other books in the box.

He lifted the volume from the box and recognized the title at once. He turned it one way, then the other, wondering how it had gotten into his mother's box of books. He opened the cover to find its appearance quite different from the one wrapped in a square of canvas at the bottom of his valise. The text ran in a continuous flow like a volume of history or a popular novel instead of being broken into verses as the one he'd rescued for Cory did. It appeared to be both old and well used. Turning back to the front of the book, he was surprised to see his mother's name scrawled across the top of the title page.

A sound disturbed his contemplation, and he lifted his eyes to see Betsy watching him. She appeared poised to run, and for just a moment, he thought he detected a hint of fear in her eyes.

"Do you know anything about this?" he asked, holding up the book.

"I think all of the books in that box belonged to your mother." She spoke quietly and edged toward the door.

"I'm sure they did, but I wonder where she got this one."

"You might ask Dan. He cleared out the sewing room for my use. He said Doc should have turned the room into his office instead of the parlor. It hadn't been touched since—"

"I know. Pa always said a woman should have one place that was all her own, and he never entered her sewing room while she was alive unless invited. I was too absorbed with my own grief to notice he didn't go in there after Ma's death either." He suspected someone had been reading the book much more recently than his mother, but decided not to say anything until after he had a chance to talk to Dan. He returned the book to the box before picking up the cradle.

Frank barely had time to return to the attic for the chair, wash up, and change his shirt before Cory announced in no uncertain terms that he was ready for dinner. He settled in an overstuffed chair near Pa's rolling chair with the baby and was soon absorbed in Pa's recital of the important changes and issues taking place in Willow Springs and all of Texas.

He couldn't remember a time when he and Pa had ever really talked in the past. The aroma of supper preparations drifted through the air, making Frank's stomach growl and giving him a sense of peace he'd known little of for twelve years. At length, Pa's head drooped lower, and Frank saw the older man had drifted asleep.

Easing his way out of the chair, he carried Cory upstairs to his bedroom, where he settled him in the cradle. It gleamed like new, and he appreciated that Betsy had found time to polish it even while preparing dinner. Cory looked peaceful and right at home in the cradle. Frank was filled with a strong sense that it had been right to come home and claim Elizabeth's baby as his own. He dug Elizabeth's Book of Mormon out of his valise and tucked it in the bottom drawer of his bureau where it would be handy. He'd found it soothed Cory on the journey when the baby grew fussy to read aloud to him from the book.

Before leaving his room, he stood beside Cory's cradle again. Looking down at the sleeping child, he was grateful for the absence of tension with Pa and for Pa's eager acceptance of Cory. A sound reached him from downstairs and he suspected he was about to face the next big test. Dan could very well resent him for running out on him and Pa all those years ago, and he might not be eager to welcome Frank back either to his home or to the newspaper he must surely think of as his own by now. Frank had thought about the newspaper a lot ever since leaving the Snake River country. He might have a legal claim to Ma's half of the paper, but a long buried sense of fairness told him that Dan's faithfulness for so many years outweighed any legal claim Frank might have.

If Dan chose to shut him out, he'd accept that and travel to Houston, looking for a newspaper with room for another reporter. He'd been a long time coming to the realization that journal writing was what he really wanted to do with his life. He'd given up two opportunities, but he didn't intend to let anything distract him again. He hoped that he and Dan could work something out. Now that he was back home, he wanted a chance to stay and be with Pa for a time.

Leaving his bedroom, Frank left the door ajar so that if Cory awoke, he would hear him. He started down the stairs. Midway, he heard two raised voices, neither of which belonged to Dan. He paused, uncertain whether to proceed. He didn't want to cause anyone embarrassment. The voices were both female, and he was pretty certain one belonged to Betsy. He hesitated, caught between curiosity and discretion.

"It wouldn't do any good, you know that." The stranger's voice was more anguished than angry Frank decided.

"The sheriff needs to be told," Betsy's voice was adamant. "If you don't do it, I will. I should have gone to him years ago."

"You mustn't." There was panic in the other woman's voice. "You know what happened the last time you told someone."

"Yes, but what if he kills you next time."

"You know he won't do that. Anyway, it's as much my fault—"

"Don't say that. You know it's not true. If Seymour Longsworth had an ounce of honor, he would have helped you instead of making matters worse and causing you to blame yourself."

"But it is my fault. Pastor Longsworth was only trying to help when he showed me those verses in the Bible. If I submit myself in all things, God will bless me and my children. I know He will."

"Pastor Longsworth is a mealy-mouthed hypocrite," Betsy fumed. "If you'd just let Dan help you—"

"No! Surely God will strike the both of us for criticizing one of his anointed mouthpieces. I've got to be going. If dinner burns, I'll deserve his wrath."

There were rapid footsteps and the whining protests made by children. Before Frank could recover from his astonishment, he heard the kitchen door close.

There was no sign of Betsy's visitor or the little girl he'd seen earlier when he reached the first floor. He angled to catch a glimpse through the parlor window of the woman Betsy had been speaking with, but there was no one in sight. Clearly someone was in trouble, and if she was a friend of Betsy's, that somehow made it his business. He started for the kitchen, but came up short as the front door burst open. The man who stepped inside was no stranger.

CHAPTER 15

"Dan." Frank risked extending a hand. He watched the play of emotions flitting across the other man's face before recognition lit his features.

With two great bounds, Dan reached him. Ignoring his hand, he drew Frank into a rib-numbing embrace. When Dan pulled back to examine him more closely, Frank was surprised to see a sheen of moisture in his uncle's eyes. He was even more surprised by the lump in his own throat. Dan's greeting wasn't what Frank had expected. Truth to tell, he'd pictured a welcome more like that from the prodigal son's brother.

"Frank, I'd almost given up hope of ever seeing you again." Dan unabashedly wiped moisture from his eyes, and his smile appeared wide and genuine, reminding Frank of the boy he'd followed around for most of his early childhood.

"I wasn't certain you'd want me back." Frank shuffled his feet, feeling self-conscious.

"Not want you? I've never ceased missing you and imagining what it would be like to have you back home." Dan pulled a white handkerchief from his pocket and wiped at his eyes. "It was always my dream that we would work together, raise families together, and grow old together. I was too impatient, and I put too many demands on you before you were ready. I think I missed your mother so much, I tried to fill the hole she left in my life by forcing you into her place. I was wrong, and I've wanted your forgiveness since the night you left."

"I was the one in the wrong." Frank looked away and shuffled uneasily. He wasn't accustomed to admitting his errors. "I've regretted my hasty departure and hot temper almost from the beginning, but more so over the past six months."

"I never told Edmund," Dan continued, "but I hired a detective to look for you a couple of months after you disappeared. He searched for two years and never found a trace of where you'd gone. We heard rumors over the years, and each time . . . I sent someone to check, only to be disappointed. Sometimes, if the information seemed particularly valid, I went myself." His uncle clasped his arm as though afraid that he might disappear again.

"I'm here to stay, that is if . . ."

"He didn't arrive alone." He heard the whisper of sound as his father rolled his chair toward them. Dan looked at him expectantly, a smile wreathing his face, but before he could explain, his father spoke again. "My grandson is upstairs asleep."

Dan looked from one to the other, his grin growing even wider. "A son? I can't wait to meet him. How old is he and what is his name? I assume there's a Mrs. Haladen?"

"No . . ." Frank stumbled, uncertain what to say that wouldn't be an outright lie.

Betsy saved him from making an explanation. "Dinner is on the table."

"We can do our catching up while we eat." Pa urged Dan and him toward the table. Dan stepped to the back of Pa's chair, pushing it forward, then positioning it at the head of the table. The casual movement bespoke much practice in manipulating Pa's chair and left Frank with a stab of guilt. He should have seen his father's need. He should have been the one supporting and caring for Pa. He didn't even know how long his father had been confined to the chair or when he'd stopped practicing medicine.

Betsy set several steaming bowls on the table, then took the seat nearest the kitchen. Frank was pleased to see her join them at the table. Near as he could tell, Pa and Dan treated her pretty much like family, and it looked like she did a lot for them. He noticed the way Pa and Dan bowed their heads the minute Betsy joined them, like they were accustomed to saying grace. They hadn't prayed or even set down together for a meal much after Ma and Alice died.

He lifted his fork to his mouth. One thing was for sure—Betsy knew how to cook. He hadn't set himself down to a dinner like the one before him for a long time, not even at any of the fancy Denver hotels where he and Grif had stayed.

Frank's mind turned to the last two years that he'd lived in Pa's house. Pa had seen more of his patients than his family during those years. And Dan had had his hands full with the paper, trying to take over Ma's place and being awfully young to run a business by himself. Frank could see now that Pa and Dan hadn't intentionally neglected him or taken his grief lightly but had immersed themselves in work as a means of dealing with their own grief. At least they hadn't buried themselves in liquor as he had after Amelia's death.

It was strange how differently he could view Pa and Dan now. Out of grief and anger, Frank had spent most of his time with Beau back then. Thinking of his old friend, he made a mental note to ask Betsy about Beau the first chance he got. He'd like to call on Beau and perhaps resume their friendship.

He returned his attention to the conversation at the dinner table in time to hear Pa explaining that Cory was only a few weeks old and that his mother had died following childbirth. He went on to state the conclusions he'd drawn from Frank's earlier comments about Amelia and Elizabeth, whom he had assumed were one woman. He spoke of premature labor brought on by a gunshot wound and followed by a high fever. Frank caught a look of sympathy from Dan. Pa didn't give him a chance to clarify the confusion between Amelia and Elizabeth, and he was still torn between wanting to be honest with his family and his determination to keep Cody and raise him as his own son. Perhaps it was best to let the story stand, he decided.

Over roast beef and hot biscuits, Frank told of nearly being shanghaied and the drifting westward that followed. He talked about Colorado, Arizona, and the mighty rivers and mountains he'd crossed. He omitted anything to do with Harrison Duncan and the Blackwell Gang, though he did sheepishly admit to being a lackluster cowboy who turned to gambling and how his gambling career had ended after meeting Amelia. He even mentioned his friendship with the old mountain man, Grif, though he was careful not to say a word about bounty hunting.

"Did Amelia really hold a shotgun on you the first time you met her?" Betsy asked wide-eyed.

"Yes, ma'am, she did." Frank was surprised at how easily he could speak of his lost love.

"Did you believe she might shoot you?"

"I did. I learned early in life not to underestimate an armed woman." He casually brushed a hand across his head where the old scar lay and smiled when Betsy blushed.

"We'll have to compare notes, see how your experience with Amelia's newspaper compares with what we're doing here. Are you going to be here long enough to write up some of your adventures for the local folks?" Dan leaned back in his chair, watching Frank expectantly.

It was the opening Frank had been waiting for. "I'm thinking of staying if you have room for me. In my wanderings, I came across some information the people of Texas have a right to know about, a man prominent in this state's political circles. I'd like to write that story. If you decide it doesn't fit your newspaper, I'll take it to Houston and see what your friend there thinks of it."

"I'll look forward to taking a look at it. Mind telling me who the politician is you have your eye on? There are a couple of them who have aroused suspicions in me that they might not be all they claim to be. I'd like to be able to ask them a few questions and check out some of their answers." Dan leaned forward and Frank was surprised to see the same gleam in his uncle's eyes he'd seen numerous times in Amelia's when she was chasing a story. It brought a dull ache to his heart. He'd never stop missing her, but at least his encounter with Luke Calloway and adopting young Cory had restored a desire in him to move forward with his life. For the first time in many years, he had something to look forward to.

"Not yet. I meant to finish the story on the train ride here, but Cory kept me a mite busier than I expected," he finished with a wry grin that brought a chuckle from his father. In the silence that followed, a cry came from upstairs, catching Frank's ear. "And speaking of young Cory, I believe he's calling me." He started to rise.

"No, finish your dinner. I'll get him." Betsy jumped to her feet.

Frank was a bit taken aback when she rushed past him and up the stairs. For a moment, he felt uncertain as to whether or not he should follow her, but after a moment, he turned back to Dan and his father. In minutes, their conversation returned to politics. Frank knew nothing about most of the candidates mentioned but was relieved to discover that neither Dan nor Pa supported Harrison Duncan. He made a mental note to learn as much as possible concerning Duncan's opponents.

As the discussion moved closer to home, he found it interesting that old Mayor Steadman was retiring at last and that his son had plans to take his father's place.

"Didn't you say Betsy's sister married a Steadman?" Frank turned to Pa, who looked around before answering, probably checking to see if Betsy had returned and might overhear his answer.

"Yes, she married Charles Steadman. You might remember him. You're about the same age, and he and Beau got to be friends after you left. The boy isn't much of a worker, but he sure can talk. Struts around town like he's already the mayor. He and Beau had a falling out right after he married Maggie, and he doesn't allow her to see any of her family."

Frank did remember Charles. He and Beau had dismissed him as being a prissy tattletale back in Old Man Davis's school. He'd been bossy and self-righteous too, constantly getting the other boys in trouble with the headmaster, so Frank wasn't surprised that the boy he remembered had become a man who thought it his place to decide whom his wife could see. For some reason, Frank's mind flew back to the disagreement he'd heard earlier. He debated with himself on whether he should mention the incident, then decided it was Betsy's business and if she wanted anyone to know about it, she should be the one to bring it up.

"Are you going to vote for him?" he asked.

"I'm not sure." Dan pushed to his feet and walked to the sideboard. "He wouldn't be any worse as a mayor than his father, but

I'm hoping to see a stronger candidate come along." He picked up a bottle and brought it back to the table. He filled his glass, then Pa's, before reaching for Frank's.

"No, thanks." Frank waved the bottle aside. Dan looked puzzled, but returned the bottle to the sideboard. Frank turned to see an odd expression on his father's face.

"You're not a Prohibitionist, are you?" Pa lowered his voice to ask.

Frank smiled. "No, I haven't made up my mind about political parties," he answered. "I choose not to drink for personal reasons. After the escapades Beau and I got ourselves into, then the trouble I found in Galveston, I should have shied away from liquor, but I didn't. When I took up cards for a living, I learned I needed to keep my mind sharp, so I generally drank branch water. But following a severe disappointment, I resumed drinking and it nearly cost me my life. I learned then that I'm not a man who can drink in moderation. Amelia was dead set against drinking, and I suppose her views sort of rubbed off on me. The man who shot her was a pitiful drunk. I won't risk becoming like him."

"You passed through Utah a few times, didn't you?" Dan sipped slowly, watching Frank over the rim of his glass, and Frank suspected he wasn't really changing the subject. "I hear they're opposed to liquor and they let their women vote and own their own businesses."

"Grif never had any trouble finding a bottle when we went through there. As for the women, frontier women out in the territories are more independent than other women in many ways. They've had to learn to do things most women wouldn't consider doing. I only met one woman I knew for certain was a Mormon, though I saw quite a few I figured most likely were. The one woman I know was a Mormon was one of the strongest, most courageous people I've ever known, man or woman."

"You're serious? I heard they were practically slaves to their men." Pa looked as though something was troubling him, and Dan also appeared skeptical.

"Not likely," Frank laughed. "Mormon women run all kinds of businesses. Some of them even go off to college in Boston to become doctors. They run farms while their men are off preaching, and they're outspoken about their religion. Their leader, Brigham Young, says Mormon women have every bit as much business voting as their men folk. It's my opinion all women do. I'd be willing to wager the day will come when women do gain suffrage and it will be Western women who vote in national elections first."

"Was your Amelia a Mormon?" Doc asked. The question startled Frank, but he answered promptly.

"No, but I wouldn't have cared if she had been a Mormon. The only contact she ever had with Mormons was when a few came through town on their way to or from Utah. Once a bunch of cowboys gave some Mormon settlers who were just passing through a good hazing, and she got pretty upset about it."

"You know Utah's been trying to become a state, but it keeps getting held back because most folks don't figure a man ought to have more than one wife. If they ever do get to be a state, the men will have to settle for just one wife and the women won't be allowed to vote anymore. It's only in the territories folks can make up their own rules like that," Dan pointed out.

"The rest of the country needs to learn a lesson from the territories then!" Betsy said.

Frank turned to see her standing behind him, holding Cory. Her face was flushed, and she appeared upset. He wasn't surprised that the Betsy he'd known as a child had her own political views, but he was curious how much of their talk she'd heard and whether it was women voting or other Mormon practices she was defending, but he quickly dismissed his curiosity in his eagerness to show off Cory. He reached for the baby and felt the now familiar pang of joy as he settled the infant in his arms.

"Thank you, but you didn't have to . . . I mean, I don't expect you to care for my son." He wasn't sure how to express appreciation for Betsy's kindness in not only fetching Cory, but she had obviously changed him into dry clothing. Frank was accustomed to a certain dampness upon the child's waking.

"Oh! I didn't mind. He's a wonderful baby. Besides, when you start working with Dan, you can't keep him with you at the office, and I have plenty of time to watch him while you work." There was a maternal longing in her voice, which along with her obvious physical attributes, made Frank wonder why she had never married. The Betsy he remembered was strong willed, but surely that hadn't kept the local lads from appreciating her many other good qualities.

* * *

Six weeks passed before Frank closed Dan's office door one morning and laid a stack of papers before his uncle. Dan picked up the top sheet and began to read. Silently, he studied the second page, then the third, and so on until he reached the end. He still said nothing. Clasping his hands behind his neck, he rocked back in his chair and stared at the ceiling for what seemed an eternity to Frank.

"How much of this can you prove?" The question, coming suddenly into the silence, caused Frank to start. He quickly recovered and handed Dan an envelope. Dan took it, peered inside, then dumped the contents on his desk. Frank stepped back, watched for a few minutes, then excused himself, leaving Dan to wade through the stack of telegrams, letters, and affidavits from banks, land offices, and relatives of the former owners of land that was now part of the vast tracts Duncan now claimed. They verified that few of the people who supposedly sold their land to Duncan had ever been heard from again or claimed bank accounts or inheritances after selling out to Duncan. There was a badly spelled note from a bounty hunter who claimed to have captured an assassin sent by Duncan to murder two survivors of an outlaw gang who took part in the massacre of a Texas rancher and his wife, who owned the water rights to most of the water in the valley where Harrison Duncan began his empire. There was an account by one of the outlaws in Frank's handwriting, signed by an X and witnessed by Frank and a Colorado rancher, Matthew Griffin.

Frank knew his uncle would find the bottom two papers the easiest to verify. They were a bonus he'd stumbled upon. He considered them of lesser importance, but significant enough to halt Duncan's political ambition by themselves if the other papers failed to do so. First was a letter from Duncan's wife wrapped around a marriage certificate, describing the abuse she had been subjected to during their marriage, but adding that being Catholic, she had never sought a divorce and had never been served with divorce documents. The abuse wouldn't matter in a court of law since men were allowed to chastise their wives, but it did establish the fact that Duncan was married with a living wife. The second was a newspaper that had just arrived last week from Houston. Prominent on the front page was a notice of the lavish wedding of Harrison Duncan and the daughter of a well-known railroad tycoon.

Frank bent over a story he'd already proofread earlier. It didn't matter; he was too nervous to work and only wished to appear busy. He glanced toward Dan's door at frequent intervals, but it remained closed.

He'd almost changed his mind about writing the story and, even after it was written, had hesitated to give it to Dan. He was well aware that if it fell into the wrong hands, Duncan would send someone to finish the task Cole Walker had failed to accomplish. It wasn't fear for his own life that made him hesitate, but concern for Pa, Dan, Cory, and even Betsy. Duncan wouldn't hesitate to kill them if he suspected Frank had talked to them—or to punish him.

Oddly enough, it was Cory who made up his mind for him. The baby was growing fast and just last night as Frank held the boy in his arms, he'd smiled a wide toothless smile. Suddenly Frank was back in Luke Calloway's home, seeing Luke's son. If he didn't stop Duncan, he couldn't be certain either child would grow up with a father. Duncan had caused both Frank and Luke to suffer enough; Frank couldn't stand by and risk their children suffering as well. Besides he'd given his word.

"Frank?" He looked up to see Dan standing in his office doorway. With pounding heart, he moved toward him. "Sit down." Dan waved toward a chair in front of his desk. While Frank seated himself, Dan closed the door and continued to stand.

"Well?" Frank twisted in his chair to see Dan's face.

"It's too big for us."

Frank felt a stab of disappointment. "All right, I'll—"

"No, I'm not saying we shouldn't print it, but if we go for the exclusive, Duncan will silence our voice before the story can spread across the state. We'll have to take precautions."

"What do you have in mind?" Frank felt a surge of joy. Dan believed him, and he understood the risk involved.

"At first, I thought if we just omitted your byline, it would be all right. Then I realized that won't be enough, and your name should be on it. Without a byline, the story won't be taken as seriously. We'll need to find a hiding place for your documentation away from this office, and we'll need to get copies to several influential papers before our newspaper is distributed to our regular customers."

"How about setting the type, running next week's front page, then setting it aside or locking it in your safe while I take everything to your friend in Houston? He may want to write his own story instead of using mine." These were some of the points Frank had been mulling over ever since he returned to Texas. He had to find a way to stop Duncan and keep his family safe at the same time. "Can he be trusted?"

"Eric can be trusted, and he'll pull out all of the stops to have the story appear in his daily the same day as our weekly. He recently installed a new Linotype machine which can produce close to seven thousand characters per hour, which will speed things up greatly for him. We'll have to make certain copies of both papers are on the train for distribution in San Antonio and Austin before we begin deliveries to our own customers."

"I promised to send it to New York too. Mrs. Duncan wants to see it, and she wants it to run in the New York papers."

"I'll take care of that," Dan offered. "Have you considered taking the information to the Rangers?"

"Yes, I considered it, but I'm not certain I can trust them. My experience with local sheriffs hasn't given me a lot of confidence in law enforcement, and I suspect there's more than one sheriff and a few judges across Texas in Duncan's pay."

"My general impression has been that the Rangers are pretty straight. What do you say we go ahead with the story, then, once it's out, contact the Rangers?"

"Let me think about it." Frank couldn't tell Dan that a major part of his reluctance to go to the law hinged on his own fear that a close examination of the past might reveal his former connection to the Blackwell Gang. He wouldn't hang for the murder of Luke Calloway, but he might still go to prison for his part in a number of holdups and the fact that he'd done nothing to prevent the deaths of Luke's parents or the bank employees and customers who had died at the hands of the ruthless gang.

"Duncan will try to silence you as soon as the story gets out. It might be best to use a pseudonym for your byline and while you're in Houston," Dan suggested.

Frank agreed, though he wasn't certain his acceptance of the idea was based as much on protecting himself from Duncan as it was on protecting himself from the law.

"This is Monday," Dan went on making plans. "I can have the front page of Thursday's paper printed by tonight, and you can leave with the evidence on tomorrow's five o'clock train. You'll reach Houston before Eric leaves his office, giving him two days to get his story out. I'll wire him to expect you."

"Do you think Betsy will mind keeping Cory overnight?" Frank wondered aloud. "She's been more than generous to watch him days while I'm here. He still needs to be fed during the wee hours."

"She's taken to him almost like he were her own." Dan smiled. "And she's not the only one. He's given new life to your dad, and I enjoy having the little tyke around. That house has been too quiet for too long."

"I'm surprised you haven't married and filled it with your own babies. I never took you for a perennial bachelor." Frank watched for Dan's reaction to his words. A flash of pain came and went so fast in Dan's eyes, Frank wasn't certain he'd even seen it, but he couldn't help wondering if his almost-brother had also suffered a painful loss. Instead of answering, Dan returned to their earlier topic. Sensing he'd hit close to the truth, Frank felt a closer bond to his uncle.

"I suppose you've considered the possibility someone may have tipped off Duncan that you've been making inquiries about him. It might be wise to check out any strangers in town and to caution Betsy against taking Cory out before you get back."

"Yes, I thought of that, and I'll be keeping watch here and in Houston. You do the same. Do you own a gun? If I remember right, Pa only ever had that old shotgun he dragged home from the war."

"I bought a gun a few years ago." Dan opened a drawer in his desk to reveal a six-shooter. Again Frank noticed a grimness to Dan's jaw, but didn't ask questions. Dan would talk to him, he now felt certain, when Dan was ready.

"Do you know how to use that gun?" he asked.

Dan nodded, but didn't elaborate.

Frank rose to his feet. "Unless you need me here, there are a couple of merchants I'd like to talk to about ads. I promised to have lunch with Beau, and I'd like to spend some time with Cory before I leave." He'd almost reached the door when Dan's voice stopped him.

"I trust you won't be mentioning any of this to Beau."

Startled by something harsh in Dan's voice, Frank paused. "I don't intend to speak to anyone other than you and Eric. There's no reason to endanger anyone else." He puzzled over Dan's words of caution as he collected his hat and made his way out the door. Dan should have known Frank wouldn't say anything to Beau, but even if he thought Frank would confide in his old friend, that didn't account for the hardness or the note of warning he'd detected in Dan's voice. It was becoming clear to him that he wasn't the only one with secrets.

CHAPTER 16

Frank made his way to a table near a window. The Franklin Hotel hadn't existed twelve years ago. If he recalled the town of his youth correctly, a saloon had once stood on the spot the hotel now occupied. A wry smile twisted his lips as he recalled the outhouse that once stood behind the structure. Now, the Franklin was the largest hotel in Willow Springs, comfortably appointed with oak-paneled walls and rich leather upholstery. An oak staircase wound its way to two upper stories. It was the rival of anything he'd seen in Denver. Beau must be doing well or he would have surely selected a less opulent dining room for their meeting.

He'd run into Beau a number of times since returning to Willow Springs, but one or both had been in a rush each time, and this would be their first opportunity to sit down and catch up on the happenings in each other's lives since the night they'd set privies on fire and he'd run to escape the wrath of the town's most prominent men.

He'd scarcely recognized his old friend. His youthful chubbiness had turned to the portliness of middle age, though he was only a little past thirty. His hair had thinned, and where he'd once been disdainful of fancy clothes, he now attired himself in the latest fashions. Where he'd once indulged in boyish pranks, he now exuded an aura of pompous importance. He worked for the railroad, though Frank had no idea what his responsibilities entailed. Pa said he'd sold the land his mother had struggled to hang onto after her husband's death at a considerable profit.

A young woman wearing a white blouse tucked into a long, dark skirt stopped at his table to inquire if he might like a drink while he waited for his friend. After ordering a sarsaparilla and being assured it would arrive with a sliver of ice, he turned his attention once more to the window. He spotted Beau at once. On his arm was one of the most beautiful women Frank had ever seen. Her golden hair was pulled back in long curls that fell almost to her waist. A stylish bonnet sat at a rakish angle on her head, drawing attention to darkly lashed eyes, a tiny tilted nose, and a cupid's bow mouth. The windowpane made her face appear as pale as fine china. The pair stopped a short distance from the hotel entrance. Beau's back was to Frank, but his gestures indicated he was angry with the woman. To Frank's surprise, she neither showed anger in return nor seemed to exhibit any emotion at all. After a moment, she turned to make her way with graceful steps on down the walkway. She neither hurried nor dragged her steps.

"Whew! It's hot out there!" Beau slid onto the chair across from Frank minutes later. With a large handkerchief, he wiped his brow. Before Frank could respond, Beau signaled for the waitress to bring a bottle and two glasses. She glanced at Frank with a question in her eyes.

"My order stands," he told her, and she disappeared toward a long oak bar at the far end of the room.

"I thought your wife was going to join us." Frank turned his attention to Beau. He hadn't had a chance to meet Clare yet and was curious whether the woman he'd seen earlier with Beau was his old friend's wife.

"She had some excuse; I don't remember what. She's not very sociable, especially where my friends are concerned." Beau appeared distracted, but his dismissive statement whetted Frank's curiosity concerning the woman who was Beau's wife. The little he knew about her came from Pa, and though he knew that Beau and Clare's children frequently spent the day with Betsy, he hadn't yet seen their mother deliver or pick them up. In fact, he'd seen little of the youngsters themselves. They moved like shadows about the house, and he seldom saw or heard them. He had wondered what kind of woman pawned her children off on her sister-in-law with such frequency, especially when that sister-in-law was employed. He also remembered the little girl's comment about a mother she couldn't awaken and wondered if Clare had a drinking problem.

"You're looking fit," Beau turned his attention at last to Frank. "I hear you struck it rich in the California goldfields."

"Not hardly." Frank chuckled. "I tried a lot of different lines of work, but panning for gold wasn't one of them." He didn't elaborate or mention the comfortable bank account he'd accumulated bounty hunting. They drifted into a casual discussion of the West while they waited for their drinks. When they arrived, Frank sipped his slowly, savoring the cool bite of sarsaparilla against his throat. Beau downed his drink quickly and refilled his glass from the bottle the waitress had left on their table.

"Ever consider investing in the railroad?" Beau leaned back, fingering his glass. Frank was sure the posture was meant to lend an air of importance to Beau's dapper, if rotund figure, but it seemed to Frank it mostly displayed how much his friend's brightly colored vest failed to cover Beau's wide expanse of flesh.

"I purchased a few shares in the Rio & Denver Grande last winter. Took a chance on the new Pacific line working its way into the Columbia basin too," Frank admitted.

"I have connections. I could get you a job with the Union and Central Pacific."

"I don't think I'm cut out for railroad work. My heart is in news-papers . . . I think it always has been."

"I didn't think I'd see the day when Frank Haladen would settle for being Dan Ellsworth's flunky." There was a hint of a sneer in Beau's voice. "There's no money in writing little stories for him."

"When I left here, I was too immature to know what I wanted and too full of pride to listen to anyone. Dan's a good teacher, and I'm contributing some journalism experience of my own that I gained while I was away. I spent some time working on a newspaper in West Texas, and that experience is coming in handy. It served to prepare me for the journalism career for which I've found I'm suited. Mine and Dan's partnership is working out." He gave *partnership* the tiniest amount of stress.

"Would you like to order now?" The waitress returned with a notebook and pencil.

By the time they'd ordered and received their dinners, Frank noticed that Beau's bottle was almost empty and that he had only picked at his steak. Something seemed to be bothering him.

"It's good to be home," Frank confided, searching for a new topic of conversation. If Beau had problems, perhaps Frank could help out if he gave his old friend a chance to open up. "Pa and Dan, Betsy too, have made my homecoming pleasant. Of course, Cory might account for some of the attention I've been getting." He chuckled before adding, "That boy has the whole family wrapped around his finger."

"Too bad about your wife," Beau said. "Though I'm not sorry your son is keeping Betsy busy. If she'd married when she had the chance, she wouldn't be an old maid now with time to stick her nose in other people's business." He took a long swallow, and Frank eyed him with surprise. He didn't remember this negative side of Beau.

"I've found your sister both pleasant and helpful." He wasn't sure why he felt a need to defend Betsy to her brother. As boys, Beau had always been protective of his younger sisters. He was also surprised to find he resented Beau's criticism of Betsy.

"Always causin' trouble. Encourages m'wife to lay around feelin' sorry for herself. She's always cleanin' m'house and runnin' off with m'kids and findin' fault with me. She's turnin' Willy inta a blamed sissy." Beau was drunk. The alcohol was turning to self-pity. Frank had seen it happen before, turning otherwise sensible men into maudlin fools. He decided to cut the conversation short before he said more than he should.

"I need to get home." He signaled for the check, even though Beau had been the one who initiated the meeting. "I've got some packing to do and arrangements to make for Cory."

"You going somewhere?"

"I have business in Houston. I'll be leaving on tomorrow morning's five o'clock train."

"I always stay at the El Grande when I've business in Houston. I've an interest in it. If you're interested in hotels, I could help you acquire stock in some of the best hotels in the state." Beau chugged back his drink, then reached into his pocket for a notebook. He thumbed through it, losing his place several times, then starting over. At last he pointed to an address. "Good place. Tell 'em you're my friend 'n they'll take care of you."

"Thank you." Frank memorized the address quickly, then stood. After a moment, Beau indicated that Frank should go on without him. Frank hesitated only a moment before making his way to the lobby, then on to the street. He wondered where Beau's suggestions that he could assist in Frank's financial investments had come from. He didn't remember that his friend had shown any aptitude in that direction when they'd been in school.

Frank walked quickly, his mind on the unsatisfactory visit with Beau. His friend had changed a great deal—or he had. Beau had implied his marriage wasn't going well; perhaps that explained his negative attitude and his interest in financial investments. If the woman Frank had glimpsed was Clare, he suspected she spent most of Beau's paychecks on her own attire.

When Frank reached his father's house, he hurried up the steps and crossed the porch to the front door. He took the stairs two at a time to his room. Setting down the small case he used for keeping his papers intact, he looked around. Cory wasn't in his cradle, so he must be downstairs with Betsy. He took a moment to pack his valise with a change of clothes and to tuck the papers he would deliver to Dan's friend beneath them.

When he finished his packing, he hurried down the stairs, anxious to find Cory and make arrangements with Betsy for his care during the trip to Houston. Placing one hand on the top of the newel post at the bottom of the stairs, he swung around it, nearly colliding with a small figure who sat huddled behind the post.

"Look out!" He backpedaled in an attempt to avoid stepping on the child.

"I'm sorry," the boy whispered, his eyes wide with fear. "I won't do it again."

Frank grabbed the post to steady himself, and the child darted toward the kitchen, but not before Frank became aware of tears on the small, dirt-smudged face.

Standing still, Frank attempted to regain his composure. If he'd stepped or fallen on the boy, the child could have been seriously injured. His heart pounded as he considered the close call, then he wondered about the boy. What was the dirty, little urchin doing in the house, and why had he fled in terror? He'd been startled, but there had seemed to be more to his fear than their unexpected encounter. Frank estimated the child's age at about five, and though something about him appeared vaguely familiar, he felt certain he'd never seen the child before. He'd ask Betsy about him.

It was only a few steps to the kitchen. He opened the door, and all thoughts of the boy fled his mind. Betsy stood at the back door, waving to someone Frank couldn't see. Cory was snuggled in the crook of her arm, and he looked like he belonged there. The setting sun made a halo of Betsy's pale hair and painted roses in her cheeks. Her smile made him catch his breath. He'd thought of Betsy as Beau's kid sister so long, seeing her as a woman—and a beautiful woman at that—did funny things to his insides.

* * *

Frank kept his bag close to him on the trip to Houston. He took pains to watch his fellow passengers as unobtrusively as possible for any indication that he was being watched. To his relief, the trip passed in an uneventful fashion. For long stretches, he leaned back in his seat and pretended to be asleep, both to discourage conversation with his fellow passengers and to do some thinking.

Leaving Cory behind that morning had been difficult. He and the infant hadn't been apart a full day since the baby's birth. For twelve long years, he'd prided himself on his toughness and lack of sentiment, but Cory had changed that. He didn't believe he was going soft. It was more like being a father gave him an added layer of awareness. Whatever it was, he was happier now than he remembered being for a long time.

The last time he'd begun to experience hope and dared to dream, that brief bit of light had been snatched from him by a bullet. He would have gladly traded places with Amelia, but now he wanted to live, more than he'd ever wanted to live at any other time. He'd thought he wanted to live when he ran away from home and when he and Jake escaped Galveston. Running from Duncan's ambush was nothing more than an instinctive survival attempt. Without Amelia, he'd run again. Too much of his life had been given to misery and regrets, running when he should have made a stand. Now he wanted to take charge of his life. He wanted Cory to grow up in a place where men like Duncan weren't allowed to steal the lives and happiness of others. He wanted to be the kind of man who gave all the little Lukes, Lincs, and Corys a chance to grow to be men without hate and fear.

Another small boy's face flashed across his consciousness, and Frank's eyes flew open. The boy's shirt and pants had been clean and tidy, a marked contrast to his arms and face. Mulling over the brief encounter in his mind, Frank tried hard to bring the incident into better focus, as a growing suspicion took center place. At length, he became convinced the child had been covered with bruises, not smudges of dirt. Thinking that the child had somehow been injured gave rise to an uneasy sense that he should have followed through to learn who the child was and why he was in his father's house. Belatedly, he recalled his intention of asking Betsy about the boy.

He mentally squirmed in his seat, remembering that moment when he'd entered Betsy's kitchen, and all thoughts of the boy had fled from his mind. He'd expected a reduced night's sleep because of the train's early departure this morning, but his rest had suffered more from a continued repeating in his mind of that moment when he'd seen Betsy as though for the first time. He didn't want to think about Betsy that way. Amelia was the love of his life—but she'd been gone a long time. Resolutely, he turned his attention to the evidence of Harrison Duncan's crimes that he meant to show Eric, then turn over to the Rangers. Once more, he reviewed each document and conclusion he had gathered.

The miles clicked by until the conductor at last called for passengers disembarking in Houston. He straightened his jacket and reached for his hat. With the bag that held his papers clutched tightly, he made his way to the railway platform. The platform was crowded, but it didn't take him long to secure transportation to the El Grande, which fortunately was near the *Post* newspaper office.

The hotel fronted on an entire block and rose four stories high. The lobby was covered with thick carpet. Frank glanced around and grimaced. Few of the well-dressed people in the lobby wore boots, and he had the distinct impression he was outclassed. He wondered if Beau thought to somehow impress him by suggesting he stay in such a grand place. Unfortunately, he didn't have time to search for another hotel. He strode toward the desk and inquired about the reservation he'd wired in the previous afternoon. With a disdainful look, the hotel clerk turned the register toward him. Dipping the pen in the inkwell, he signed the name Floyd Wentwright and paid for two nights. The clerk then handed him a key, which he pocketed. He started toward the stairs, then changed his mind. Instead of going to his room, he crossed the lobby to the exit. He wanted this over.

It was a short hike to the newspaper office, and a young man, seated near the front of the office pointed the way to Eric's closed door. Frank knocked and was admitted at once to the assistant editor's office.

A man of about forty with sandy side-whiskers pumped his hand. "Eric Dayton," he introduced himself. "And you are Dan Ellsworth's friend?"

"Floyd Wentwright." Frank used the pseudonym he and Dan had agreed on.

"Dan said you were bringing me a story." Eric waved toward a straight-backed chair beside his desk. Frank took the chair, opened his bag, and lifted out the papers he'd brought.

"It's all here," Frank said, stacking the papers on Eric's desk.

Eric picked up the top sheet. His eyes widened. "Harrison Duncan, hmm." He appeared absorbed in Frank's notes for several minutes, then he reached for the next page. Frank settled back in his chair. A quarter of an hour later, Eric paused to look at Frank.

"There have been rumors for years about Duncan, but nothing concrete. I've tried, myself, to locate witnesses or interview someone close to him, but I've found witnesses stay lost and those who might know something will admit to nothing. If I put this together with the little I have on file and take a few weeks to check your sources, I can put together a good story by the end of the month." He grinned, suggesting he relished the assignment he'd given himself. "Tell—"

"Dan is running the story Thursday," Frank spoke bluntly. "Copies will go to all of the big Eastern papers."

"Thursday! But that doesn't give me time to—"

"Dan and I have researched every bit of the story. The telegrams and affidavits are at the bottom of that stack. You can trust Dan or lose out on one of the biggest stories of your career." He gestured toward the papers on Eric's desk. "I'll leave them with you for twenty-four hours. They better be here when I return, and if anything is leaked to Duncan, my life, Dan's, and your own won't be worth two bits. By noon Thursday, I plan to be on my way back to Willow Springs, and I intend to turn the whole lot over to the Texas Rangers on my way out of town."

Eric chuckled. "I'll take your challenge. Be here at four tomorrow."

Frank left Eric's office and made his way down the street. He was almost to the hotel when he realized he was hungry. Not wishing to eat alone in a place as fancy as the hotel dining room, he turned down a side street. Four streets over, he found a café that looked promising.

A welcoming coolness greeted him as he stepped through the opening in thick adobe walls. A glance around confirmed his expectations—the café resembled dozens of such places he'd frequented in West Texas and across the Southwest. The odors and sounds coming from the kitchen were familiar too. Somewhere in the shadows, someone strummed a Mexican guitar. He made his way to a table outside the main traffic area.

Later, with his plate wiped clean of beans and tortillas, he leaned back against a whitewashed adobe wall, feeling replete and at peace. In two days, Duncan would be exposed as a murdering scoundrel. Much of the pain and guilt Frank had suffered over the past twelve years was due to his involvement with Duncan and the Blackwells. The Blackwells were gone, but Duncan still needed to be held accountable for the lives he'd destroyed. Tom Blackwell and, Frank suspected, Luke Calloway had meant to settle the score with guns, but it was better this way. Besides, he didn't want his future to include watching over his shoulder, waiting for Duncan to send another assassin.

For Cory's sake, and to keep his promise to Luke, Frank wanted to wipe his conscience clean of his past mistakes. More than that, exposing Duncan and bringing him to justice was something Frank needed for his own satisfaction. It was necessary to free him to live again and plan for the future. Duncan wielded a great deal of power, and until he was arrested and convicted of his crimes, Frank would have to be careful, but for now, he could relax with a stomach full of good food, a warm summer night, and pleasant music playing in the background. Tipping his hat forward, almost hiding his face, his mind drifted in a somnolent fashion.

He sat up straight when Betsy's face entered his mind. She was intruding on his thoughts much too frequently. Assuring himself that she only came to mind because he had entrusted Cory to her care, he looked around the café, seeking an alternative distraction. A man at the far end of the room caught his attention. The man bore a remarkable resemblance to Joel Rivers. As he watched, the man stood, paid for his dinner, and started toward the door. There was no mistake. The man was Joel Rivers.

Frank slid lower in his seat, hiding his face beneath his hat brim. All his doubts and questions concerning the man rushed back. Rivers may have saved his life—he'd certainly ended Tom Blackwell's—but Frank had always suspected there was much more to the man than a small town sheriff.

CHAPTER 17

Frank had trouble getting to sleep that night. Whether it was the questions raised by seeing Joel Rivers or the simple fact that he missed the soft sounds Cory made in his sleep, he didn't know. It might have just been the unfamiliar bed that kept him awake.

Long into the night, he tossed and turned, remembering and berating himself for past mistakes. Toward dawn, he found himself thinking of Elizabeth and the courage with which she faced her husband's death and her son's birth. He recalled her determination to extract promises from him on behalf of her son before joining her Will. He'd seen that same courage and commitment in Luke Calloway's eyes. Something similar had burned inside Amelia, something he'd recognized in Dan and Eric. Was it possible that he recognized their commitment to a cause greater than themselves because that same light was beginning to burn within himself?

Warmth seeped into his restless body, bringing calming peace. He slept, a picture of Betsy snuggling Cory close to her while resting on the bench that sat on Pa's veranda filling his mind, and when he awoke, he could see there was no sense in ordering breakfast. Instead, he braved the hotel's dining room for a hasty lunch, followed by a solitary stroll about the rapidly expanding city.

Frank arrived at the *Houston Daily Post* promptly at four that afternoon. Eric was waiting for him. He looked exhausted, but jubilant as he ushered "Floyd" into his office and closed the door behind them.

"I'm printing five hundred extra papers," he announced, rubbing his hands together in a boyish gesture of excitement. "This will end

Harrison Duncan's campaign for the state house. He'll be run from Texas when his constituents see this story. His opponents will have a field day. I expect there will be a flurry from the other papers to add new slants and report statements by everyone close to Duncan, but we'll be way ahead. I've already got two reporters digging into his land deals and his finances. I expect to publish several follow-up stories."

Frank smiled. Dan had been right about Eric. Given the basic story, he'd run with it. It pleased him to know that Luke and dozens like him would see Duncan get what was coming to him without firing a shot.

Eric reached behind him to his desk and held up a copy of the *Post*. Bold headlines read

GUBERNATORIAL CANDIDATE COMMITS BIGAMY
Senator Harrison Duncan Under Investigation for Murder and Land Fraud

"First off the press." He handed the paper to Frank. "They'll hit the streets before the sun is up tomorrow morning." Frank glanced quickly through the story, noting Eric's style had a greater tendency to sensationalism than he'd given his own story.

"You've done well." Frank shook Eric's hand, and then Eric's expression sobered. "You're leaving town in the morning?"

"That was my plan," Frank said. "but I've learned there's a train out late tonight. I hope to be on it."

"I'll have a crate of papers on the morning train headed east and another on the first westbound to Austin." Eric grinned again, knowing his paper would cause a sensation in the capital and that would bring more subscribers. Frank was well aware his and Dan's smaller paper would also gain attention, though on a smaller scale.

"Thank you." Frank reached for Eric's hand and pumped it once more before turning toward the door. With his hand on the door-knob, he turned to look back at Eric. "You might consider hiring a guard for your press until this all shakes out."

Eric's smile turned grim, and he nodded his head in acknowledgment of the suggestion.

From the news office, Frank made his way, following Eric's instructions, to a small adobe structure in the poorer part of town. It was freshly whitewashed and on the door was a discreet sign reading, Texas Rangers. He stared at the door for several minutes. He'd been in a lot of sheriff's and marshal's offices with Grif, but this one was different. This one could determine whether the future was filled with promise or death for him. From everything he'd heard about the Rangers, they could be trusted, but if they failed to act on the information he gave them now, the odds weren't good that Frank would live long.

Evening had come, and the sun was setting when he pushed open the door and walked inside the Texas Rangers' building. He let his gaze wander over the austere room and furnishings. It wasn't much different from the offices of other lawmen, except it was cleaner than most. A door in the opposite wall suggested the building housed a holding cell or two for prisoners. A tall, thin young man, wearing a gray shirt with a star on his chest, sat at a desk. He scarcely looked old enough to shave.

"I'd like to speak to the man in charge of this office," Frank said to him.

"I'm the only one here tonight. It's my turn to tend the office." The young man didn't appear pleased with the assignment.

"You're kind of young for so much responsibility." Frank's voice betrayed his skepticism that anyone so young could be part of an organization with such a strong reputation.

"It's quiet tonight, and the others are following different assign-ments." The Ranger looked expectantly at Frank.

Frank had to make a decision. The next train would leave in a few hours, and unless he wished to wait for the Thursday morning one he was scheduled on, he needed to turn over his papers and evidence to the young lawman. Though parting with the material he'd painstakingly collected wasn't easy, some prompting told him he needed to be on that train. He held out the creased folder holding the papers Eric had returned to him.

"See that your supervisor gets this the moment he walks through the door," Frank instructed. "It's evidence involving stolen land, bigamy, and murder." He was pleased to see the Ranger handle the folder with care, locking it in the top drawer of the desk.

"I'll need your name and an address where you can be contacted." The Ranger held a pen poised over a brown notebook.

"Frank Haladen—and I'm just passing through." He felt a moment's relief when his name failed to spark any sign of recognition. Once outside the office, he found himself filled with an unexplainable urgency. Several times, he ducked into dark alleys or paused in doorways to check the street behind him to see if he were being followed. He detected nothing suspicious, but the premonition of trouble persisted.

When he reached his room, he stretched out on the bed, taking care to keep his boots off the fancy brocaded bedspread. He still had two hours before he needed to be at the train depot. For a time, he attempted to read the newspaper Eric had given him. The words danced before his eyes, and he found it impossible to concentrate. He closed his eyes, hoping for a brief rest before checking out of the hotel, but sleep didn't come. Whether it was nerves or an eagerness to get back to Willow Springs and Cory, he wasn't sure, but he felt restless and eager to be on his way.

Giving up any pretense of resting, he rose to his feet. There was plenty of time before he needed to be at the depot, still he gathered his few belongings and placed them in his bag, folded the newspaper and stuffed it in his jacket pocket, then snuffed out the flame in the bedside lantern that had been provided for his convenience. When he was ready, he opened the door leading to the hall. Again, he felt a strong premonition that danger lurked nearby.

He hesitated a moment before turning away from the main staircase. It took only a moment to find a back stairway, presumably meant for the use of hotel staff. Treading as softly as his boots allowed, he made his way down the stairs to a large kitchen, teeming with cooks and waiters scurrying about their business. He watched for a moment, then strolled casually to a door, hoping his sense of direction hadn't become muddled and he'd find himself in a pantry.

Stepping through the door, he breathed a sigh of relief, discovering he was where he hoped to be, in a narrow alley lined with trash barrels. He started toward the street, but hearing the clatter of horses' hooves entering the far end of the alley, he ducked behind one of the barrels. From there, he watched a trio of horses pick their way toward him, though none of the riders seemed aware of his presence. All three dismounted and hurried through the door he'd exited moments earlier.

He had a hunch that they were looking for him, but he wasn't sure why he was so certain he was the object of the riders' backdoor entry into the hotel. The only people who had seen the newspaper story so far were Eric's employees. There was a possibility that one of them might have let something slip, then there was the Ranger. He was sure he hadn't been followed from the Rangers' station and he was registered at the hotel under a different name. The three men who had rushed into the hotel certainly didn't have the appearance of lawmen, so he doubted they were Rangers. Anyway, he doubted that no matter how good the Rangers were, they weren't good enough to have traced him so quickly. That left Duncan's hired thugs. He also considered the possibility that he might be suffering from a case of paranoia.

Leaving his hiding place, he hurried to the end of the alley. From there, he caught a glimpse of a small cluster of men watching the front of the hotel. Staying in the shadows, he moved down the street a block before crossing. Before hurrying away, he had a good view of the section of the hotel where his room had been located. A light shone from the window, and shadows could be seen behind the curtain. He didn't know whether to be glad or sorry he couldn't attribute his uneasiness to paranoia. He began walking with brisk steps toward the depot.

His boots weren't made for hiking, but he made good time. When the station came into view, he approached it with care. Standing in the shadows, he surveyed it for several minutes, then circled it to observe the squat structure and wooden platform from every angle. Once he was certain no one was waiting for him, he entered the building and crossed to the ticket counter. It took only a moment to trade his return ticket for a seat on the train leaving that night. He took a few minutes more to arrange for the telegrapher to wire Dan, letting him know their plan had succeeded and he would be on the earlier train.

He joined the few waiting passengers on benches near a large window where he could keep watch on the door. Nothing appeared amiss, and the train was due to arrive shortly. Though the wait seemed longer, it was only a few minutes before the long drawn out whistle of the approaching train sounded.

Hearing the whistle and feeling the boards beneath them tremble was the signal for the passengers to leave the station and move to the platform. They moved quickly, suggesting most were familiar with the train's schedule and knew it would pause but a few minutes to take on water and pick up the mail pouch. Frank glanced about as he followed the others out of the station and onto the platform. He saw nothing unusual.

The train slowed, and cars began flashing by. As soon as the great wheels ground to a halt with a flash of sparks and the hiss of released steam, the porter lowered the steps. One lone passenger disembarked, and there was a flurry of movement as the half dozen waiting passengers hurried to board the eastbound train.

Frank passed a number of seats filled with sleeping passengers continuing east. At last he spotted an empty pair of seats. Sitting on one and stretching his legs across the other, he prepared to follow the sleeping passengers' example. As he settled himself, he felt the train begin to move. While lifting his hat to lower it across his face, he glanced out the window.

A man was running toward the train, which was already moving. For just a moment Frank's eyes met Joel Rivers's and he knew recognition was mutual. The train picked up momentum, leaving the platform and the running man behind.

* * *

Frank turned one way, then another, unable to find a comfortable position. Each time the train slowed, he braced himself and peered out into the darkness. He couldn't get Joel Rivers's face out of his mind. There didn't seem to be any logical reason for the man to be following him—unless he was somehow connected to Harrison Duncan. What were the chances of seeing the man twice in little more than twenty-four hours if he wasn't following him?

Before Amelia's death, she'd been researching a story about the railroad line that was rumored to be buying up a right-of-way near Wallace Creek. She had found something disturbing in the discovery that all of the land the railroad planned to purchase belonged to the Williams brothers, and the holdings were all recent acquisitions. She'd mentioned her suspicion once that Bart and Conrad Williams were only fronting for someone else. She had never named the man, but now he wondered if that man was Duncan. It was the sort of thing he would do, and his recent marriage to the daughter of a railroad baron suggested he had more than a passing acquaintance with railroads. It made sense too, that Duncan might have an agent in Wallace Creek to keep an eye on the local pair. Joel Rivers could have been that agent. He was a crack shot, and he was the man who shot Tom Blackwell. He could be planning to finish the job Cole Walker had failed to complete.

The train made frequent stops and starts to pick up or set down passengers and freight. Between the questions running through Frank's mind and the jerking motions of the train, he finally gave up on sleep. The sun was up and the air was beginning to lose its morning coolness when the train slowed, then gradually halted at the small depot in Willow Springs.

Before making his way to the exit, he visually searched the train platform and the area surrounding for as far as he could see around the train station. He didn't see Dan, but he didn't see anything threatening either. An old man was seated near the station door, a wooden figure and his pocket knife in his hands, and beside the steps the porter was letting down, an elderly woman gripped a small boy's hand in one of hers and a carpetbag in the other.

He caught a movement farther down the platform. A man was stepping away from the train. He recognized him at once as Dan and felt some of the tension melt away. Dan's action was the assurance he needed that the story about Duncan had been printed and Dan had hand-delivered the newspapers, destined for eastern cities, to the mail car. He watched as Dan hurried toward the path that led from the train station to the town's business center. He wondered for a moment why his uncle didn't wait on the platform for him, then he realized that Dan wasn't just rushing away. He was hurrying toward someone.

Raising his eyes, Frank was surprised to see a woman standing in the shade of a large tree in a backyard just beyond the station. He couldn't resist the smile that his lips formed. Perhaps Dan wasn't the confirmed bachelor he'd thought him to be. Trying to get a better look at the woman, he wondered if she might be someone he knew. His eyes widened when he recognized her as the woman he'd seen with Beau the afternoon before Frank departed for Houston.

All appeared quiet, so Frank gathered up his small bag and hurried toward the exit. From the top step, he again glanced around. He caught a glimpse of the woman's skirt as she stepped behind the tree she'd waited under. She wasn't alone now. Dan stood beside her, and they seemed to be arguing. Curious, he decided to move closer and find out what he could about the situation.

"Sir, the train is ready to leave." He became aware he was still standing on the step, and the porter was urging him to move on so that he could tuck the portable step back inside the car. Frank leaped to the ground, just as a loud whistle sounded and the train began to tremble.

When he looked up again, searching for Dan, he saw his uncle still stood beneath the tree's wide branches. Dan make a gesture as though reaching for the woman's hands, then, changing his mind, let his hands drop to his sides. Intrigued, Frank walked toward them. They were so wrapped up in their own exchange, they didn't notice his approach.

He couldn't see the woman's face, but the anguish on Dan's was apparent. "You must go. It's too dangerous for both of you here. You know I'll give you the money for tickets and to get settled." They hadn't noticed Frank's approach. Something about Dan's fervor made Frank uneasy.

He halted, suddenly wary of intruding on a private conversation. He didn't hear the woman's response, but Dan raised his voice to a hoarse whisper, tinged with bitterness. "I won't follow you, and I'm not asking you to break your vows. I just don't want to have to write your obituary."

Frank stopped. He was taking a step back when a bullet whizzed past him to slam into the tree beside Dan and the woman. Throwing himself to the ground, Frank looked around for his assailant. Pandemonium had erupted. Dogs were barking, and people were running for cover. He thought he recognized Beau disappearing behind the far side of the train station. Taking a chance, he scooted toward a privy that was set off a few feet from the path he lay on. It was half-concealed by shrubs. Expecting to feel a bullet in his back, he darted behind the structure, drawing his gun as he ran. From this new position, he had a good view of the station platform, station, a long stretch of track, and the closest street. A westbound train was approaching, but he didn't see any sign of a gunman.

Businessmen and customers along the street peered from windows toward the railroad platform. A few hardy souls, guns in hand, fanned out and appeared to be looking for the person who had fired the shot. Frank glanced toward the tree where he'd last seen Dan. He could see him crouching behind the tree with a revolver in his hand, but there was no sign of the woman.

CHAPTER 18

After a short time and no further shots, the town seemed to settle down. Someone managed to calm the dogs, and Frank made his way toward Dan. He avoided the path by cutting straight across the open space between his hiding spot and the tree where Dan had taken shelter.

"Did you see who fired that shot?" he asked as he joined Dan beneath the tree.

"No," Dan's response was abrupt. His eyes didn't meet Frank's and it became clear he was watching something or someone behind Frank.

Turning casually and letting his derringer slide into his hand again, Frank could see nothing that might alarm Dan. Most of the locals were returning to their businesses. Their guns, except for a few shotguns, were out of sight, and the general attitude suggested that whatever the danger had been, it was over now. Two portly gentlemen were walking toward the place where he stood and would soon pass right by them. He'd seen the first man around a few times. He was the stationmaster. The other man was Beau.

"Good morning," he greeted Beau. Beau inclined his head slightly and went on his way without acknowledging Dan. There was definitely bad blood between the two. He watched Beau and his friend continue toward Main Street, then turned back to Dan.

"What's between you and Beau?" he asked.

"Nothing."

"Don't give me that. I'd have to be blind to not see the antagonism between the two of you." Frank stood his ground.

"I'd rather not discuss it." Dan changed the subject, "Everything went smoothly with the paper this morning. The boys should be finishing up deliveries about now, and I sent copies to every big Eastern paper I could think of, along with a couple copies for our congressman and senator in Washington. I even managed to get the first couple of copies off the press on the early train this morning to Austin."

"Eric did the same." Frank grinned wolfishly, then sobered. "There may be repercussions. I'd like to go to the house for a change of clothes, see Cory, then meet you in your office to discuss in detail all that's happened. You might want to see Eric's paper too."

* * *

Frank was whistling when he raced up the steps to the veranda that covered the front of the house. Pa was asleep in a large chair that Dan had placed on the porch for his comfort, the wheeled chair parked close beside it. Deciding against awakening his father, he pulled open the front door and stepped inside the house.

Singing came from the kitchen, and Frank turned in that direction. He set down his bag and eased the kitchen door open. He smiled to see Betsy with flour to her elbows, rolling out piecrust. On a thick quilt placed on the floor nearby, Cory waved his arms and smiled with contentment.

"Hello," Frank said, keeping his voice low to avoid startling either of them.

"Oh!" Betsy looked up. With one hand, she brushed a lock of hair behind her ear, leaving a streak of flour across her cheek. "I didn't expect you until this afternoon. I was planning pie for dinner." She smiled and seemed just a bit flustered.

"Don't let me stop you." He laughed before stooping to pick up Cory. He snuggled the baby close and whispered loving nonsense in his ear. It felt good to feel the small body tucked against his chest again. "Was he good?" He looked toward Betsy.

"Of course, he was good." Betsy laughed now. "Cory's the best baby in the world."

"You don't think he's a little small, do you?" Frank had never stopped worrying over whether or not Cory got enough to eat. He had no idea how much of the canned milk the baby should drink or when he'd be able to handle other food. His father had assured him that his son was healthy, but it seemed to him that a woman would know more about babies than a man, even if that man was a doctor.

"Goodness, no. Both Willy and Joe were smaller than Cory is now when they were three months old, especially Willy."

"Willy and Joe?"

"You haven't met Beau and Clare's children?" Betsy turned back to her piecrust, dumping a circle of dough into a tin plate a bit too vigorously. It seemed to Frank that her fingers trembled the slightest bit as they moved around the tin, pinching the edges of the dough into a pattern. She seemed to regret mentioning her brother's little boys. He couldn't remember even hearing their names before, though he was aware that they frequently spent the day with Betsy.

"No, I haven't had the opportunity of meeting Beau's wife or children, except for the little girl who was here the day I arrived. He's a busy man, and his wife doesn't seem to be anxious to make my acquaintance." If he didn't know Betsy was too much a lady to make such an indelicate sound, he'd swear she snorted.

"Beau has changed." Betsy kept her eyes on the fluted piecrust she was trimming. "He isn't the friend you remember."

"We haven't spent much time together since I returned, but I know he isn't happy and that he works long hours to support a wife who doesn't appreciate him and who won't exert herself to look after her children properly."

"You know nothing!" Betsy's voice was sharp. She raised her head, and he could see he'd touched a sore point.

"Then tell me about them. You seem to care for her children more than she does."

"That's not true. Clare loves her children more than anything."

"I'm aware they're frequently here," Frank went on, hoping he could make Betsy see that though her intentions were good, the children really needed their mother's attention. "They move like shadows around this house, and if I try to speak to them, they flee to you in the kitchen. Beau told me their mother neglects them and you spoil them. It's not good for the children to be so coddled by you, though I'm sure you have the best of intentions. They need their mother, but as long as you're willing to assume Clare's responsibilities, she'll continue to be more concerned about fashionable hats and gowns and never learn to be a good wife and mother."

"Don't criticize Clare! She does the best she can." Betsy looked as if she might throw her pie at him.

"Whoa! You might hit Cory." He tried to keep a teasing note in his voice. He didn't want to upset Betsy, and he certainly didn't want to fight with her, but for some reason, it was important to him that Clare not take advantage of Betsy's kind nature.

"I'm sorry." Betsy looked stricken. "I'm tired, but that's no excuse.

"Did Cory keep you up last night?" He jostled his son in a careful rocking motion. The baby's eyes were almost closed. She wasn't acting like the efficient, calm woman he'd become accustomed to meeting in his father's house.

"No, Cory didn't keep me awake. Willy didn't feel well . . ."

"Did he stay the night?" Before she could answer, he remembered the boy he'd almost stepped on before leaving for Houston. "Is he the child who was here before I left? The one with bruises on his face?"

Betsy nodded her head slowly and looked away. She seemed reluctant to discuss Willy, but Frank persisted.

"Why did his mother bring him here? Pa doesn't see patients any more, and after an accident that left bruises like that, he should have been home where his parents could look after him and comfort him. Beau must have been beside himself worrying, with the child here instead of in his own bed."

"Beau doesn't worry about Willy; he hates him." Betsy slammed the pie plate back on the table and whirled about. She dashed out the back door, letting it slam shut behind her. Frank stared after her in shock, then took a step toward the door.

"Give her a few minutes before you go after her." Frank was caught up by his father's voice. He turned to see Pa had gotten himself back in his chair and had wheeled to the doorway that separated the parlor from the kitchen. There was an expression of great sorrow on his face.

"Pa, what's going on? Betsy—"

"I heard most of what the two of you had to say. Betsy is reluctant to talk about Beau. He's her brother, and it fills her with shame to speak of him. For a long time, she hoped that by helping Clare and the children herself, no one would need to know."

"Know what? Why should Betsy be ashamed of her brother? I had dinner with Beau two days ago. I got the impression he's disappointed in his marriage and that Betsy's interference is part of the reason the marriage isn't going well."

"Sit down." Pa gestured toward a straight-backed kitchen chair and Frank sat. "I've ignored what was right before my eyes much too long. I thought it was none of my business, but I'm an old man now, and I've come to the conclusion that suffering is my business."

"Pa, you always made suffering your business. I doubt there's a person in this town whose suffering hasn't been eased by you."

"I devoted my life to fixing physical complaints, but there's another kind of suffering and I've never been good at easing that kind of pain. I didn't want to see how much your ma hurt because I wouldn't allow her to join the Mormons like she wanted."

"Ma wanted . . ."

Pa went on, ignoring Frank's startled exclamation, "I dismissed your sorrow after her death because you were just a boy, and I figured you'd outgrow missing your ma, and I pretended not to see how Dan was hurting, seeing his sweetheart married to another man. I told myself there are a lot of men who knock their wives around and there's no law against it, 'less he kills her, so I should mind my own business. But when Betsy brought Willy to me a few days ago, something changed. I'm through keeping quiet about Beau and about a lot of other things. Some folks are plain mean and selfish. Now give me that baby and you get out there and listen to Betsy. Keep your mouth shut and just listen."

Frank stared at his father. The words seemed to bounce back and forth inside his head. *Ma had wanted to be a Mormon? Dan was in love with a woman who chose someone else? And Beau beat his wife?* It was too much to absorb. Wordlessly, he shifted Cory to Pa's arms, then turned toward the door through which Betsy had run from the house.

Shading his eyes with his hand, he searched for her. She wasn't anywhere in sight. He crossed to the stable and glanced briefly inside. Seeing nothing but Pa's seldom-used buggy and gear for two horses, he turned his attention to the pasture. There was no sign of Betsy.

Spying a narrow band of fruit trees on the far side of the pasture, he recalled lugging water from the creek to water those trees when they were mere sticks poking up from the ground. Now they were tall and broad, covered with peaches ripening on their boughs. A picture of Betsy sitting high in a walnut tree that grew behind the Widow Mason's house a long time ago came to mind. She'd climbed there to escape her brother's teasing and to be alone to read the book Old Man Davis had loaned her. He had a hunch that the peach orchard had replaced the walnut tree as her refuge.

When he reached the trees, he found Betsy sitting on a hummock of grass with her arms wrapped around her skirt, holding it tight against her drawn-up knees. He knew she was aware of his presence, though she didn't look up. Sitting down a short distance from her, he watched her. After a few moments, he pulled a long blade of orchard grass from the clump nearest him and stuck it in his mouth.

"Pa said I was wrong about the things I said. He said, too, that I should listen to you." That didn't sound quite right. He tried again. "Betsy, we've known each other a long time and I trust you to be honest with me. You were always truthful, even when you said I deserved being hit in the head with the rocks you threw at me. I was an arrogant beast who teased you and encouraged your brother to run off with me to play, when he should have been helping you and your mother."

A brief smile turned up one corner of her mouth, then her face resumed its solemn look.

"Please, will you tell me what happened to my old friend?"

Betsy was quiet so long, Frank began to doubt she would tell him anything, but at last she mumbled a few words. She kept her head down, and her fingers were busy twisting a long flower stem which was completely devoid of petals or leaves. Her words sounded something like, "He didn't really change; he was always selfish and mean."

"Beau?" The single word expressed Frank's shock. It was enough to ignite Betsy's temper.

"Beau was big enough to get a job and help with our family's support before you ran away. He seldom went to school anyway, as you may recall. Ma took in sewing to feed us. She became ill a few months after you left. She couldn't work, and I was too young to find steady employment, so she decided to sell the few acres Papa left her, but Beau got upset and convinced her she shouldn't. He said Papa promised him that land and she had no business selling it. She agreed not to sell it because she thought the land was important to Beau and there was possibly one other way to get the money she needed. Her hope was that the contents of Papa's cellar would bring a good price, enough anyway to tide us over until Beau graduated and found a job. That plan didn't materialize either. She discovered Beau had already helped himself to every bottle. The cellar was empty."

"I didn't know . . ." Guilt consumed Frank as he remembered the many times he'd drunk from those bottles. She shook her head, and he realized Betsy was already aware he had helped Beau empty some of those bottles.

"I'm not certain when it started, but Beau has a serious drinking problem. He's well on his way to becoming the laughing stock of the town, the town drunk." She lifted her head and looked at Frank for the first time, pride and defiance in her eyes.

"I knew he drank, but I didn't know his drinking had become a problem or that it was taking food out of the mouths of you and little Maggie." He couldn't help remembering the lunch he'd shared with Beau a few days earlier and the annoyance he'd felt at his friend's inebriated state. Why hadn't he been disturbed by that side of Beau all those years ago?

"Even though we were living on the town's charity and the little bit I made cleaning other people's houses, he couldn't let Mother sell that land because he'd already sold it. As soon as Beau turned eighteen, he was legally the head of our family and the property passed from Mother's control to his, so he sold it to buy liquor."

Frank recoiled with shock. He would never have believed his old friend guilty of such perfidy, but as he'd said before, Betsy never lied. Without conscious intention, he picked up one of her work-roughened hands. She didn't withdraw it, but went on with her recital.

"After Mother died, Beau sold our house and the twenty acres around it to the railroad without making any kind of arrangements for a place for Maggie and me to live. With nowhere else to go, Maggie married Charles, and I came here to Doc."

She took a deep breath while Frank squirmed guiltily, thinking of his own drinking problem before he realized where the liquor was taking him. If what Betsy said was true, and he didn't doubt her, then Beau was no better than the old man who had shot Amelia. His heart broke to think of the two little girls he'd once thought of as almost sisters suffering and fending for themselves.

"When Beau drinks, he's mean," Betsy continued, and there was bitterness in her voice. "You used to tease Maggie and me, but you were never mean to us. Beau has always been mean."

Beau's callous disregard for the old schoolteacher, trapped in his outhouse by a fire he and Beau had set came back to haunt Frank. Slowly he became aware that Betsy was still talking.

"Maggie's husband won't let Beau near her. He doesn't hit me anymore either because Dan threatened to shoot him if he ever sees me with another black eye. There's nothing Dan can do about Clare. She's Beau's wife and the law is on her husband's side."

Frank went still. Several incidents were beginning to paint an ugly picture in his mind. There was only one more question he wanted answered by Betsy, then he would seek out Dan.

"The little boy? I think you called him Willy. Did Beau do that to him?"

Betsy burst into tears. "Beau has always been cruel to Willy. He doesn't believe Willy is his son." She gulped a couple of times, then plowed on. "I told Beau that if he just can't stand the sight of the child, I would take him, but he refuses to give him to me. But this time, he almost killed him. Clare tried to protect Willy, but Beau broke her arm, and she passed out. I think he might have murdered them both if I hadn't arrived when I did."

Frank bowed his head as nausea threatened to overwhelm him. He could hear Betsy crying and reached out to place an arm around her shaking shoulders. Suddenly, she was in his arms. They clung tightly to each other, sharing their grief.

"Something has to be done," Frank fumed. "I'll not stand by and see a woman and child tortured, perhaps murdered."

Betsy straightened, pushing her hair back with one hand. "I've tried to persuade Clare to take the children and disappear. I've saved a little, enough to get her to a safe place. She had money when she arrived here, an inheritance from her parents, but Beau gained control of it as soon as they married, and there's nothing left of it. She could go west, or she could go to Philadelphia where she was raised, but he's convinced her she can never get away, that wherever she runs, he'll find her and drag her back. She believes that if she even attempts to leave, he'll kill Willy."

Frank stood and offered a hand to Betsy. "I don't believe there's nothing that can be done. I'll think of something, I promise." Betsy took his hand and rose to stand beside him. He found himself mesmerized as they stood facing each other. An emotion beyond their shared grief touched a place deep within him. Though her eyes were swollen and her cheeks damp, she was beautiful, and something urged him to close the small distance between them. He bent his head.

A glint of sunlight on metal beyond the trees caught Frank's attention. "Down!" He pushed Betsy to the ground and rolled with her to a depression in the ground where the grass grew deep. A bullet struck the ground where they'd stood. Several more shots followed in rapid succession, the lead digging deep into the peach trees around them. Sheltering Betsy the best he could, he drew his own gun. He held his fire, not wanting to give away their position. Besides, the derringer was ineffectual unless fired at close range.

Shots erupted from behind them, startling Frank into fearing they were surrounded by enemies. It took a moment for him to realize the new shooter wasn't shooting at them, but at their attacker. The first gun turned silent, but Frank stayed put and kept Betsy from showing herself. After a few minutes, he shifted to see who their rescuer had been. He was greeted by the sound of footsteps hurrying away.

"I think we're safe now." He stood and, after a moment, helped Betsy to her feet. She looked around, but didn't release his hand.

At length, she asked in a tremulous voice, "Do you think Beau . . ."

"No." He was almost running by this time, dragging her with him. "There's someone far more dangerous than Beau who wants me dead."

CHAPTER 19

Concern for Cory and Pa lent speed to Frank's steps as he rushed back to the house. He burst through the back door, still clutching Betsy's hand. She was gasping for breath but made no attempt to free herself from his hold as he tore across the kitchen and charged into the parlor. There he found Pa in his chair, still cradling Cory in his arms. Frank stopped and Betsy pulled her hand free.

Pa looked up, a question in his eyes. Seeing their disheveled appearance, he looked disapprovingly at his son. The sound of their running feet or their gasping breathing woke the baby as well, and he began to cry. Both Betsy and Frank rushed toward him. Frank reached the infant first, swooping him up in his arms.

"There, there," he murmured, patting Cory's small back.

"He's probably hungry again," Betsy said. "I'll prepare his bottle." She hurried from the room.

"Wet too," Frank grimaced and started toward the stairs. When he returned, both he and Cory were attired in fresh clothes, and Betsy sat at Pa's feet, a warm bottle of milk in her hands. Frank reached for it and settled in an easy chair to feed the baby. By now, feeding Cory was a familiar task, one he enjoyed and one he'd missed during his brief stay in Houston.

While the baby ate, Betsy told Pa someone had shot at them. She described the incident in detail.

"I read about that Duncan fellow in the paper this morning," Pa said when she finished. "Do you think he found you this quickly?" he addressed the question to Frank.

"I haven't had a chance to read the paper yet." Betsy turned to Frank too. He sensed hurt that he hadn't mentioned anything of the story to her. He remedied that by launching into a synopsis of the account given in the newspaper. He didn't want to alarm her, but he felt it best she know enough to be careful and to protect Cory and herself if anyone should come to the house looking for him. After a brief sketch of the details concerning Harrison Duncan, he warned that the man might send someone to Willow Springs to take revenge against Frank for spoiling his ambition to become governor.

"I've read about Senator Duncan before," Betsy said. "He's opposed to women voting or owning property. Didn't he recently marry a railroad heiress?"

"Yes, but he already has a wife in New York. She is a wealthy woman and the reason he is opposed to women owning property. New York has a law allowing married women to own and control their own inheritances, including property."

"Sounds like a good law to me," Betsy said, and Frank remembered that she got nothing from the sale of her father's land or her childhood home.

When Cory finished his milk, Frank lifted him to his shoulder to firmly pat his back. He caught an indulgent smile on Betsy's face and didn't mind. It was all right for family to know how he felt about his son and even be a little amused by his obvious pleasure in caring for the boy. Someday he would try to explain to Betsy what the boy meant to him and how the baby had ended twelve harsh years of drifting without purpose.

When he was sure the baby was asleep, he carried him upstairs and placed him in his cradle. He left his door propped open, so the baby would be heard when he awakened, then hurried downstairs. Under his jacket, he carried a Colt. The smaller derringer, he held out to Betsy.

"Do you know how to shoot?" he asked. When she nodded her head, he demonstrated how to operate the small gun. "I have to get back to the newspaper office now, but I'll be able to concentrate better knowing you have a chance of protecting yourself. Put the derringer in your apron pocket," he told her. "You probably won't need it, but just in case."

"I'm not helpless you know," Pa's voice interrupted them. "Betsy, you keep the back door locked, and I'll keep an eye on the front." He lifted the quilt off his legs and Frank saw a large, wide bore revolver nestled in his lap. "I heard the gunfire," he explained.

"Good. I'm glad you're prepared to keep Betsy and Cory safe," he said, acknowledging his father's weapon. "I have to go. Dan might be in danger. Anyway, he'll be wondering what has happened to me, so I best be on my way. I'll stop by the sheriff's office and let him know what happened here, then I'll be back as quickly as I can." Frank stepped to the door. He took the precaution of peeking through the curtain before opening it.

* * *

"I don't know who shot at us or who shot back at him," Frank finished, filling Dan in on the events since they had parted that morning.

"No one seems to know who fired that shot near the rail station this morning either," Dan said.

"But you think it was Beau Mason and he was aiming at you, not me," Frank spoke with the bluntness he'd learned from Grif.

Dan looked uncomfortable, but he didn't deny Frank's guess.

"I want to hear your side of it." Frank looked squarely at Dan. "Pa told me there was a woman you cared about, but she married another man. Am I wrong to guess that woman was Beau's wife, Clare? And is that the reason for the animosity between you and Beau?"

"There's more to it than that."

"Betsy told me about his drinking and that he's mean when he drinks."

"Which is all of the time," Dan snorted in contempt.

"She told me he hits Clare and he beat up his kid too. She even told me Beau blacked her eye a few times until you put a stop to it."

"But I can't stop his attacks on Clare." There was anguish in Dan's voice.

"She's the woman you were talking to this morning, isn't she?" Frank lowered his voice. "No matter what your feelings are for her, you need to stay away from her. If Beau is as violent as Betsy claims, seeing you two together will precipitate greater violence, and she'll be the one to suffer."

Dan pushed his chair back and rose to his feet to pace back and forth across the small office. "I've stayed away from her as long as I can. I saw Willy, and I learned from Betsy that Clare's arm is broken. Beau has forbidden her to see a doctor to have it set. Betsy told Edmund, and he gave her supplies and instructions for wrapping it, but it needs to be set by a doctor, and I don't want it to happen again. I can't bear for her to go on suffering like this. When I saw her this morning, I broke my own rule by approaching her and offering her money to take her children and leave him, but she won't go."

"Perhaps she loves him or she thinks her children need their pa even if he isn't a good one." Frank couldn't help sympathizing with Dan who was clearly suffering.

"She doesn't love him. She never has." There was venom in Dan's words.

"Then why did she marry him? From what I learned of her, she had money when she arrived in town and didn't need a man to support her. Or was it because of Willy?"

Dan's face grew red, and he looked like he might punch Frank. "That's the story Beau has let out, that I left Clare with child and he married her out of compassion for her predicament. That's a lie. We were very much in love, but we never went beyond the bounds of propriety. We were engaged to be married, still she encouraged me to go west to search for you when we got word your horse had been confiscated by a sheriff because her current owner failed to pay a debt he owed. I returned as soon as it became evident the man knew nothing of you, but I was too late."

"Sorry. I was with a man who did his horse trading in the dark. I didn't even know about the trade until I went to saddle up the next morning and discovered a new mount where I'd left my old mare the night before."

Dan clasped his hands together, his elbows resting on the desk as he leaned forward to make his point. "Clare was the new schoolteacher. She lived alone in the little house reserved for schoolteachers, the one where your old schoolmaster used to live. When I returned a scant six months later, Clare and Beau were already wed, and she was well into her confinement. She wouldn't speak to me, and it wasn't until Beau's sister Maggie showed up at the house one day to beg your pa to help Clare, who had gone into labor early, that I learned what had happened. It seems Maggie's husband and Beau were friends, and young Steadman knew about Beau breaking into the schoolteacher's house and forcing himself on her two days after I left. He then convinced her she was damaged goods and I would no longer want her when I returned. He threatened to go to the school board with a tale about her loose morals if she didn't agree to marry him. When she learned she was with child, she gave in. Maggie said Clare was covered with fresh bruises when they stood before the preacher and that right after the wedding, Beau took over the inheritance Clare's parents had left her. He insists she wear the latest fashions and he struts around town, boasting about taking the most beautiful and fashionable woman in town away from me."

Frank felt sick.

"Do you want to hear the rest of it?" Dan's voice turned harsh. "Willy arrived early, before Clare and Beau had been married the requisite length of time. He was small, sickly, and looked nothing like Beau. That's when the rumor began that he's my child. Beau ignored Willy's obvious immaturity and concluded Clare had tricked him. He accused her of trying to pass off my child as his. He physically attacked Maggie and Betsy for going to Ed for help, though Clare and Willy both would likely have died without a doctor's help. When Betsy confronted him, he said Willy should have died and struck her. Maggie came to Betsy's aid, and he hit her too. That's when Steadman ordered Maggie not to see Beau, Clare, or Betsy again. He was protecting Maggie, but he was also protecting his political future from being tainted by the scandal."

"Dan, I'm sorry."

"You'd better get back to the house," Dan changed the subject. "Whoever shot at you earlier might return and be more than Betsy and Pa can hold off."

"I promised them I'd stop by the sheriff's office." Frank rose to his feet, but before he reached the front door, a boy burst through it.

"Telegrams!" he shouted, waving a handful of yellow slips of paper. Frank noted the boy's announcement was plural.

Dan took the papers and began reading. He grinned and passed the first one to Frank. Together they pored over the telegrams, which were mostly congratulatory and came from editors in other cities and a few politicians.

"Uh oh," Dan pointed to one of the telegrams which was different from the others. "Eric sent a warning that Duncan has disappeared. He's not at his ranch or the office he uses in Austin when congress is in session. His new wife is packing up to return to Daddy. Do you think he might be coming after you?"

"I don't know. He mostly uses underlings to do his dirty work now, but he was personally involved in the attack on the Blackwell Gang. He can shoot and doesn't hesitate to kill." Frank felt uneasy. Pa was an old man, unable to walk on his own, and Cory was a helpless baby. Betsy was all that stood between them and trouble. "I'd better be on my way." He thrust the telegrams he held at Dan and hurried out the door.

He moved with rapid steps down the boardwalk that fronted the Main Street businesses, keeping watch for anyone who looked out of place. Several times, he searched the roofs ahead of him. The sheriff's office was between the newspaper office and Pa's house, and though he was reluctant to take the time to stop and report the shooting, Frank stepped over the threshold. Two men were in deep discussion on the far side of the room.

"Sheriff?" He wanted to get this over quickly and be on his way. Both men turned, and Frank stumbled back a step. The man wearing a sheriff's star on his shirt was a total stranger, but the one in the gray shirt of a Texas Ranger was Joel Rivers.

The slight flex of Frank's shoulder was automatic. When the derringer didn't drop into his hand, he remembered that he'd left it with Betsy. He'd be a fool to reach for the larger pistol beneath his coat. He leaned his head to one side and waited.

"Frank Haladen. We meet again." He couldn't read Rivers's eyes to know whether the man was glad to see him or preparing to shoot him. Rivers had always been an enigma to him.

"Rivers," he acknowledged the other man.

"We just missed each other last night." Rivers sounded amiable, as though they were old friends. "I reached town a short time ago and was asking the sheriff here for directions to your home. He said he hadn't met you, but he understood you were the old doctor's son and that I could probably find you down the street at the news office."

"I'm headed home." Frank kept an eye on Rivers, watching for his reaction. "But I thought it best to stop in here to report a shooting to the sheriff."

"Was someone killed?" the sheriff asked.

"No, but someone took a couple of shots at Betsy Mason and me a short time ago down in Pa's orchard."

"That was you?" Rivers cut in. "Just after my train got in, I set out on a short walk to stretch my legs and get a feel for your town. I saw what I took for a courting couple in a grove of trees. I was about to step away, leaving them some privacy, when I heard a gunshot. I was on a slight elevation and could see a fellow drawing another bead on the pair. I fired a few warning shots, assuming the fellow was a jealous husband or an estranged lover, to keep him from becoming a murderer."

Frank didn't know whether he believed Rivers or not. "Did you get a good look at the person who shot at us?"

"No, but I've a pretty good idea who he is now that I know you were his target. I just can't figure out how he got here before I did."

"And why are you here?"

"It's a long story. Perhaps I could tell you while I walk with you for a bit." Rivers reached for a felt hat that rested on the sheriff's desk.

Frank made no objection. He was anxious to discover what Rivers wanted with him, but he was even more anxious to satisfy himself that his family was safe.

Once the sheriff's door closed, Rivers didn't need any coaxing to begin his story. "To begin with, I suspect your shooter is Cole Walker, and he followed you here on the same train from Houston that brought you."

"Walker? That can't be. I teamed up with an old bounty hunter after I left Wallace Creek. He and I captured Walker and collected a reward on him at Eagle Rock up in the Idaho Territory." Frank shook his head. "The marshal there said he would personally take Walker back to Colorado to face murder charges."

"He did, but a new deputy in Denver got careless, and Walker escaped. The Texas Rangers got word to watch for him. He was spotted leaving Senator Duncan's office in Austin two weeks ago, then there were several sightings in Houston. I had business at the El Grande hotel last night and saw him leave there in a hurry with two other men. I followed him to the train depot but was too late to catch him before he boarded the train. He swung aboard a cargo car just before the train picked up speed."

Frank thought about Rivers's story and wondered how much of it was true. It would explain the shot right after he arrived, and Walker could have followed him to Pa's house and waited for a second chance at him.

"How did you find me? I didn't leave an address with the Ranger I talked to in Houston."

"I traced you back to this town a long time ago. Figuring you were headed home was just a lucky guess."

Frank's uneasiness grew. He'd been right to suspect Rivers knew more than he let on. But how did Walker learn he was in Houston? Still unsure if Rivers could be trusted, he asked, "Why did you get me out of Wallace Creek? I didn't care whether I lived or died back then."

Rivers shook his head. "When I learned it was just a run of bad luck that put you in Wallace Creek and your feelings for Amelia Carlisle were genuine, I did a little snooping and learned Bart Williams couldn't take the chance you might sober up and continue Miss Carlisle's investigation into his and Conrad's acquisition of land along the proposed rail route. When Tom Blackwell addressed you by name, pieces of a puzzle clicked into place for Bart. You were the other outlaw who escaped Harrison Duncan's massacre of the Blackwell Gang. Bart couldn't afford to have Duncan discover the man he was searching for had been right under Bart's nose for months. Neither could he risk your discovery that Duncan was the financier and a major beneficiary of the little project that promised to make him a wealthy man. With Conrad dead, Bart stood to gain a fortune if you didn't spoil it for him. I followed him that night and discovered the trap he'd set for you."

"Why didn't you just arrest me, or is that what you have planned for me now?" Frank's tone was belligerent, and he didn't care. He'd spent twelve years expecting his past to catch up to him. He only regretted that it was happening just when he was finally getting his life together and was looking forward to a future with Cory and working with Dan. He wanted to take care of Pa and enjoy the closeness with his father that they had denied themselves for too long. He thought of Betsy and wondered if she might have become part of his future too.

"You were a kid when you got involved with the Blackwells, and I figured you'd suffered enough. Besides, arresting you would have tipped my hand." Rivers ignored his tone.

"Then why are you here?"

"Last night, when I returned to the Ranger's office, I discovered you'd been there and you'd left enough evidence to fill in all of the holes in an investigation I've been pursuing for fifteen years. I mean to see Duncan hang."

"Fifteen?"

There was something dark in the Ranger's chuckle, and Frank stopped to look at him. Rivers stopped too and faced him. "Did you think you and Luke Calloway were the only ones who hated Harrison Duncan enough to want vengeance? He destroyed my sister. She was just sixteen when she met him and thought him romantic and dashing. They married, then when she denied him access to her share of our father's fortune and he learned she had a legal right in New York to control her own income, he attempted to kill her in order to inherit it. She survived, but has spent the past fifteen years in a quiet room, doing little more than staring at the wall."

"But I wrote to her, and she sent me a wire."

"Mother handles all of her correspondence. She sent me a wire informing me of the inquiry from Floyd Wentwright and the town from where it came. When I saw you last night, I wondered if you might be Floyd Wentwright. When I saw the *Post* this morning, I knew that I was on the right track and that you were in danger. I caught the next train."

CHAPTER 20

"Dan received a telegram saying Duncan has disappeared." Frank paused in front of his father's house, noting idly that it needed painting. There was no sign of Betsy or Pa, but the enticing aroma of peach pie floated on a late afternoon breeze. He remembered Betsy shaping pie shells in the kitchen before she ran to the orchard. He thought of the way Betsy felt in his arms as he'd rolled with her to safety earlier that day and the way the taste of flour and sugar had lingered on his lips as he'd walked with her back to the house.

"I, too, received word from headquarters in Austin that Duncan is nowhere to be found. I'll be watching for him, but I think Walker is the greater threat to you now," Rivers speculated. "Go eat your supper. I expect your girl is waiting for you." He turned about.

Frank watched him walk away, his words lingering in Frank's mind. *Your girl.* Was Betsy his girl? Suddenly he wanted her to be.

The ordinariness of that evening was almost unbearably sweet. Pa congratulated him and Dan on their scoop. The dinner Betsy set before them was perfect, right down to the peach pie topped with sweetened dollops of cream. Cory smiled and blew bubbles from the crook of Frank's arm. He found himself watching Betsy, and each time their eyes met, she blushed and a tiny smile lifted the corners of her mouth. It was good to be home.

After dinner, Pa played with Cory and insisted on giving him his bottle while Frank helped Betsy with the dishes. Dan said he'd take first watch over their press as they had discussed doing until Duncan was caught and took his leave.

"You don't have to dry dishes," Betsy protested when Frank picked up a dishtowel.

"Sure I do." He picked up two plates, dried a top and bottom, then shuffled the plates to dry the other top and bottom surfaces.

Betsy laughed. "You do that like someone who has had practice drying dishes. I thought you were a gambler."

"My ma taught me well."

When they finished, Frank stepped into the parlor to find Cory sleeping soundly. He looked down at the baby and felt the now familiar tug at his heart. He would never forget Elizabeth Statten's courage, and he would always regret that he couldn't save her, but he would never stop thanking God that he had been there to save Cory. He was grateful too that Elizabeth had trusted him to raise her son. He thought of the promise he'd made to her and the strange discovery that his own mother had wished to be a Mormon. Once Duncan was safely behind bars, he'd find out more about the religion that was important to these two strong women he admired—and he'd keep his promise to acquaint Cory with its teachings. He'd start by bringing his mother's Book of Mormon down from the attic. Her book would probably be easier to read than the burnt and brittle one from which he read a little to Cory each day. Cory wouldn't understand it for some time, but Frank was determined it would become familiar to both of them.

"I'll take him up to bed," he said to his father as he lifted the sleeping child. "You look tired. An early night might do you good as well."

"You're right. I feel more tired than usual, but before I go, I want to say something I should have said a long time ago. I love you. I always have, even when I was caught up in my own grief. I'm glad you came back, and I'm grateful for that precious boy of yours. Be a better father than I was." He gave the wheels on his chair a push, sending him rolling toward his bedroom. Frank caught up to him, halting the chair.

"I'm glad I came back too. I think I always knew that you loved me, and when I was left alone with Cory, all I could think was that I needed to take him home." He leaned forward and gently brushed his lips against the old man's brow.

* * *

Frank had a hard time getting to sleep. He was tired from the trip and the events of the day, but sleep wouldn't come. There was a mugginess in the air, and his mind returned over and over to Dan's dilemma as his body turned over repeatedly seeking a comfortable position. He thought losing Amelia the way he had was actually less painful than Dan's experience. He couldn't imagine living in the same town as the woman he loved, knowing she was married to someone else who was beating her and being unable to help her.

He shifted, hoping for a cool breeze through the open window. Thoughts of Duncan and Cole Walker played on his mind. There were warrants out for both of them. He didn't care about a reward, but he wished Old Grif were nearby to help him track them down.

At length, he drifted to sleep, only to be awakened a short time later by Cory. Stumbling out of bed, he made his way to the cradle. It took but a moment to discover the baby needed changing. A full moon shone through his bedroom window, making changing the infant's nightgown and diaper possible without lighting the lantern. His bedding was wet too. Fortunately, Betsy had left a stack of clean linens handy.

Cory continued to whimper and make smacking sounds, suggesting he was hungry. After pulling on his pants, Frank nestled the baby in the crook of his arm and made his way down the stairs to the kitchen. He was pulling a can of milk from the cupboard when he heard a sound behind him. A glance over his shoulder told him that he had awakened Betsy.

"Let me do that." She reached for the can and efficiently mixed the milk with warm water from the teakettle, which sat at the back of the stove. When the bottle was ready, she offered to feed Cory so that Frank could return to his bed.

"It's too hot to sleep. I think I'll take him out on the porch to feed him."

"Do you mind if I join you?" she asked, hesitation in her voice.

"I'd enjoy your company." He led the way to the wide bench that had graced the porch as long as he could remember. He sat down and indicated that Betsy should sit beside him. They sat side-by-side for a long time without speaking, listening to Cory's hungry gulps and to bullfrogs croaking in the distance. A train whistle broke the silence, then faded away, leaving stillness in its wake. Cory finished his milk but didn't drift back to sleep. Though no longer whimpering, he kicked his small legs and waved his arms, a sure sign he had no wish to be returned to his bed. Frank rocked him gently, hoping he would tire soon.

"Dan told me about Clare and him." Frank kept his voice low.

"She knows she made a mistake agreeing to marry Beau, but since she's his wife, she tries to make the best of it. She attends church faithfully, so when I couldn't reason with Beau or convince her to leave him, I talked to Reverend Longsworth. The old hypocrite told her all her misery was her own fault for enticing a man who wasn't yet her husband and praised Beau for his charity in marrying her. He said she's to blame for her marriage being bad and warned her she'd go to hell if she broke her marriage vows. Then he went right to Beau and told him his wife was complaining about him"

"I don't suppose that helped the situation any."

"No, it didn't. It was the reason Willy came so early. I've been afraid to do any more than try to reason with her since." Betsy sighed. "She won't listen to me, and Beau's violence is escalating. I'm afraid for her."

"It's tearing Dan apart."

"It's why he works late most nights."

Frank felt a stir of uneasiness and wondered if he should check on his uncle. Cory sighed softly—he was almost asleep. Frank would check on Dan after he returned Cory to his cradle.

They sat companionably for several minutes, then Frank asked, "You knew the Book of Mormon we found in the attic belonged to my mother. How did you know?"

"Her name is inside the book, and she wrote her testimony of why she believed it to be true on the flyleaf." Betsy paused, then continued in a soft earnest voice, "You might as well know I've read it—many times. I find comfort in it, and I've come to believe it is true. I've heard the Latter-day Saints send missionaries to many places to tell the people about their beliefs. I've hoped for a long time that one day they would come here."

"I promised Cory's mother I would teach him about Mormon beliefs and someday take him to Utah for some kind of ceremony that would unite them for eternity."

"Are you going to do it?"

"I gave my word."

Betsy was quiet for a long time, and Frank became aware that both she and Cory had fallen asleep. Her head tilted toward his shoulder. He lifted his arm, circled her shoulders, and brought her head to rest against his chest. He had a feeling she belonged there. He thought about that for a long time.

His head was beginning to nod when an explosion several blocks away sent flames shooting into the sky and jerked him fully awake. Betsy pulled herself upright, and Frank stood to get a better view. With Betsy beside him, he hurried down the front steps, intent on discovering the source of the explosion. The flames seemed to be rising from the center of town.

"It might be the news office. I better check on Dan. Here take . . ."

A second explosion erupted behind them, throwing them to the ground. Frank barely maintained the presence of mind to avoid landing on Cory. Debris rained on top of them, and Frank used his body to shelter Cory from it.

"Betsy!" he called her name.

"I'm all right. Cory?"

"He's safe." Frank struggled to his knees and turned to look back. What was left of his home was in flames. Burning debris lit up the old oak tree like a giant, misplaced Christmas tree.

"Pa!" Thick smoke rolled toward them. He reached for Betsy, helping her to her feet and thrust Cory, who was now screaming, toward her.

"Go to the sheriff's office. You'll both be safe there," he shouted.

"Doc," he heard her cry as he raced toward the back of the house. Neighbors were pouring out of nearby houses, but he ignored them as he ran.

The back of the house was gone; the kitchen, Betsy's room, and Pa's had disappeared. Nothing but smoke and unidentifiable lumps and shards remained. He could see through the remnants of the house's frame to the staircase. Flames shot up it. Pieces of the ceiling dropped into the flames, and what was left of the roof sagged ominously.

"Pa! Pa!" he screamed, running toward the spot where Pa's bedroom had been. Someone grabbed him from behind, and he fought to free himself.

"He's gone. There's nothing you can do." Joel Rivers refused to let go of him. Slowly, reality set in and his shoulders shook with great, gasping sobs. Pa was gone, and he had wasted so many years not really knowing him.

"Come back to the sheriff's office. We need to talk," Rivers coaxed, leading him toward the road. He remembered he'd sent Betsy with Cory there, and suddenly he couldn't walk fast enough. Dazed, he passed his neighbors who had formed a bucket brigade. *They needn't bother. Pa is dead, Cory's cradle is gone, even Ma's book is nothing but cinders. There's nothing left to save.*

With shoulders hunched, he stumbled into the sheriff's office. Cory's cries and the gentle sounds Betsy made as she tried to shush him reached out to him. He rushed across the room and fell at Betsy's feet, burying his head in her lap. He felt her hand smooth his hair. A lump lodged in his throat, making speech impossible.

"I'm sorry," she whispered. "Doc was a good man. He always treated me more like a daughter than a servant. He loved you more than you ever knew, and you made him happy just by coming home."

"I thought I'd lost everything. Then I thought of how easily I could have lost you and Cory tonight. I don't know what kind of lucky chance made us decide to go outside . . ."

Betsy placed a finger on his lips. "I don't believe it was luck or chance. I think a Higher Power saved us for a reason only He knows."

"Frank, are you all right? Betsy? The baby?" Dan burst into the room. His hair was disheveled, and his face and ragged clothing were covered with soot. Frank rose to his feet and went to meet him.

"We're fine, but Pa—"

Dan cut off his words with a massive embrace.

"I know about Doc. I was on my way home when someone set off a charge of dynamite at the back of the newspaper office. I ran back, hoping to save something. Fortunately, only the storeroom burned. We lost our paper supply, but the press appears to be undamaged. I keep a couple of barrels of water near the paper, and I was able to tip them onto the flames. Then I heard a larger explosion. By the time I reached the house, you had gone. Someone said you were here and Doc was dead. No one seemed to know anything about Betsy and Cory." He walked over to Betsy to give her a brief hug. Frank took Cory and placed an arm around Betsy.

"I'll make this brief," Rivers spoke over the other conversations in the room. "The sheriff will find a place for everyone to sleep. He's learned someone stole a case of dynamite from the railroad's supply shed at Three Mile last evening. Whoever it was didn't break in. He had a key to the shed. The engineer on the train that went through here at five reported he saw the door hanging open, so I rode up there with the stationmaster to check. I could see where a heavy box had been dragged into the bushes. There were two clear sets of boot tracks. We found the box, but it was empty."

"Do you think it was Walker and Duncan?" Frank asked.

"Walker, but not Duncan. There's been a Ranger watching for Duncan on every train headed this way since yesterday's paper came out. Wherever he is, he didn't come this direction," Rivers assured them. "I'll be checking for tracks behind the Haladen house as soon as the sun comes up."

"I'll go with you." One thing Frank had learned as a bounty hunter was how to track a suspect.

"Betsy!" A high-pitched squeal preceded a whirl of color catapulting across the room. Betsy took a step toward the woman, and the two embraced in a flurry of questions and answers accompanied by a surplus of tears. Finally, Betsy stepped back. She looked up at Frank.

"Do you remember my little sister, Maggie?"

"Indeed I do." He took Maggie's hand. Maggie smiled brightly at him before turning back to Betsy.

"Come, Betsy. You must come home with me. We have plenty of room."

"But Charles . . ."

"Oh, pooh! Charles is learning he can't always get his own way. Besides, he was angry with Beau, not you."

"I can't leave little Cory. Frank can't take him with him when he goes with Mr. Rivers to search for the men who blew up his house. And I'll need to go shopping for a new bottle and more milk."

"Bring him with you," Maggie suggested. "And don't worry about a thing. Your shopping can wait until you're rested. I'll take care of this little guy." She scooped Cory from Frank's arms, winked at Frank, and started for the door. Frank had a pretty good idea how Maggie meant to take care of Cory. If he hadn't heard the mayor-to-be's pretty wife had a four-month-old son, Betsy's vivid red cheeks would have been hint enough.

"Go ahead, Betsy," he told her. "You'll rest better at your sister's house than you would at the boarding house. I'll be by as soon as I know anything."

Once the door closed behind the sisters, Rivers cleared his throat. "I didn't want to say anything in front of his sisters, but there's a good chance Beau Mason unlocked the shed where the explosives were stored. He has one of only two keys."

Dan looked stunned. "As much as I would like to hang Doc's murder on that weasel, it couldn't have been Beau. I saw him board the five o'clock for Houston last night. He was running, barely made it, but he did leave on that train."

"He still could have unlocked the shed but had no part in setting those charges," Rivers mused. "There were indications two men dragged that box from the shed to where we found it."

"I think I'll wander over to the telegraph office and see if I can learn anything. I might even stop by and question Mason's wife," Rivers said. "She might know where he was yesterday afternoon and what was behind his hasty trip."

"You won't find Mrs. Mason at her house," Dan said to the lawman, then faced Frank. "He hurt Willy again, made his nose bleed and bruised a couple of ribs. Clare came to me last evening at the office after Beau left. She said she'd changed her mind about accepting my help. She feared her husband would kill the boy the next time he flew into a rage. She wanted to leave before he returned. I put her and her children on the midnight train, headed east."

CHAPTER 21

It was just beginning to become light when Frank and Rivers made their way to the stable behind the burned-out ruin of the Haladen house. The sheriff had decided not to accompany them, figuring he needed to stay in town to watch for further trouble, but he'd loaned Frank a hat and gun. The area immediately around the house was severely trampled and lent no clues, but an empty kerosene can was discovered next to Pa's buggy. The kerosene was likely used to set the fire, which then served as detonator for the dynamite.

Frank looked back at the ruins, wondering if Pa's body would be found. Dan had promised to lead a search for whatever remains had survived as soon as the rubble cooled sufficiently. Frank turned with lingering regret back to the search for the man responsible for Pa's death. But for Cory's fussing, he, Betsy, and the baby would likely have perished in the fire as well.

In the orchard, they found a single set of prints made by Mexican-style boots and a tree where scuffed and worn bark indicated a tether had been tied. Around the tree were hoof prints, and the grass had been cropped, indicating a horse had waited there. Beyond the orchard, they met a farmer searching for a missing horse. He led them to a copse of trees where a horse with a broken leg lay. They could only presume the animal had stepped in a badger hole in the dark. There was a strong probability that Walker had transferred his gear to one of the farmer's horses and left his own suffering animal behind.

The discovery seemed to confirm Rivers's theory that two men were responsible for obtaining the dynamite, but one, Cole Walker, had acted alone in its use. Rivers ended the animal's misery, and the two men returned to the orchard for Pa and Dan's horses. As he'd done once before, Frank gathered supplies from Pa's cellar. Once they were mounted, Frank and Rivers headed in the direction the dead horse had likely been traveling. They figured Walker was planning to lose any pursuers in the thick hills and trees to the north.

Before noon, Frank spotted tracks that seemed to confirm their suspicions. Walker, if it was Walker, was pushing his horse hard but making little attempt to conceal his trail. He was either confident he wasn't being followed, or he was confident he could shake anyone trailing him once he reached the brush- and tree-covered hills.

By early afternoon, they were deep in the hill country. Trailing their quarry through the thick vegetation reminded Frank of the mountain passes and forests of the West with their ample supply of hiding places and opportunities for ambush.

Water was plentiful, and they stopped with increasing frequency beside springs and streams. Occasionally, they found indications that the man they followed had paused to refresh himself or allow his horse a few sips of water.

Frank knew his tracking skills were better than most, but no great amount of skill was required to follow Walker. The horse he'd stolen was a heavy-footed plow horse that frequently gave its rider a hard time and interfered with Walker's ability to conceal his passage through the forest. Warm droppings beside the trail at last told Frank that they were closing in on their quarry. He grew hopeful they would capture Walker and be on their way back before darkness obscured the trail.

Trees blocked the sun, bringing early dusk, when they came upon a narrow draw. Frank pulled Pa's horse to a halt and looked around. Something didn't feel right.

"He can't be far ahead," Rivers whispered. "Let's keep going."

"The signs are too obvious," Frank whispered back. "He's discovered we're following and is planning a trap."

"You're sure?"

"Sure enough." He dismounted. "Let's walk a bit." He broke trail, following the pine-covered rim of the narrow gorge instead of following Walker into it. They tramped for more than a mile, and darkness had fallen before Frank spotted the flicker of a small flame below and some distance ahead of where they stood. He pointed, and Rivers nodded his head. In silent agreement, they led their horses away from the gorge. Leaving them tied to a couple of saplings in a small clearing back from the rim, he and Rivers began working their way closer to the edge of the narrow canyon for a better view.

From directly above, they could see the fire was small and tucked beneath a rocky overhang where it wouldn't have been seen until they were right on it had they followed Walker into the narrow cut. Frank could barely make out the shape of a coffeepot resting in the coals of the fire. An oblong, blanket-wrapped shape lay a short distance away from the fire, propped against a saddle. The silhouette of a horse could be seen at the edge of the trees, and a deceptive calm lay over the almost hidden camp.

The camp was a decoy. He knew it. There was no question that Rivers knew it too. If they rushed the camp, they'd feel bullets in their backs. A familiar shiver snaked its way down Frank's spine. He'd felt it before, just when he and Grif had begun to move in on one of the outlaws they'd pursued. Walker was close, waiting in ambush; he was watching the camp from someplace nearby, just as they were. He might abandon his gear, but he wouldn't abandon his horse. He was waiting for them to attack the camp, then he would have the drop on them.

Rivers signed for Frank to remain behind, covering his back, while he moved closer to the camp. He intended to draw Walker out. Instead of watching Rivers move silently from one vantage point to the next, Frank scanned every rock and tree along the steep bank for any movement or flash of moonlight on metal. He studied every shadow. Peripherally, he was aware of Rivers's progress down the embankment, but his attention focused on who else might be watching the Ranger's movements. The closer the other man came to the dummy camp, the tighter Frank's nerves grew.

Rivers was almost to the camp and nothing. Every instinct told him he wasn't wrong about the camp being a setup. Walker was too canny to build a fire or to camp in a low spot when he was on the run. The camp couldn't be real, but why hadn't the man they pursued shown himself? Walker was no greenhorn; he wouldn't set up a false camp, then head out on foot. No way would he leave his horse behind—unless . . .

Frank jumped to his feet. He ran, leaping over logs, crashing through brush. He prayed he wasn't too late.

The restless shuffle of hooves and a nervous whinny told him he wasn't wrong. Walker wouldn't leave his horse behind unless he knew where to find another one, a much better one that came with a saddle and gear to replace what he was leaving behind. He was stealing Pa and Dan's horses.

Frank crashed through the brush and lunged for the man who already had one foot in the stirrup of Dan's horse. He hit hard, and the two men tumbled to the ground. A fist crashed into Frank's temple. Frank followed with an uppercut to Walker's jaw. They rolled nearer the horses, exchanging blows, and the panicked animals thrashed about, kicking indiscriminately. Frank felt a glancing blow from a shod hoof graze his shoulder. Walker rose to his knees, then lurched backward, assisted by a blow from Pa's mare. Frank caught him with both arms, which he closed around the other man's chest, pinning the outlaw's arms against his sides. Walker jerked and kicked, trying to free himself, but Frank held on while attempting to roll clear of the horses.

Walker managed to get his six-shooter clear of its holster, and Frank felt a pang of regret for the chivalrous gesture that had deprived him of his sleeve gun. Tightening his hold on Walker, he attempted to immobilize him, but felt the cold metal slide against his stomach. If Walker got his finger on the trigger and was able to direct the weapon, he would kill Frank. Frank couldn't release his hold to knock the gun away or draw his own.

Desperation gave him little time to think of a plan. Drawing back his head, he crashed it hard into Walker's face. Feeling the crunch of splintering bones and the splatter of blood, he hoped they were Walker's. He heard a gunshot, but it sounded far away, and he was falling, though he was already on the ground. Maybe he was in the sky. He could see strange lights, not really stars, circling closer. Then the darkness was complete.

He awoke with a hangover worse than any he'd ever suffered after a night of drinking with Jake or anyone else. He put his hand to his head and discovered liquor wasn't to blame for his headache. He had a lump on his forehead the size of an egg, and he hurt all over. He hadn't felt this badly since he'd been left for dead by thieves on a Colorado mountain trail after Amelia's death.

"You've rejoined the living, I see." He heard Joel Rivers's voice, but he couldn't quite focus on the man's face. He remembered Cole Walker and the fight. He attempted to sit up. The movement was too abrupt, and he nearly lost consciousness again.

"Walker?" he managed to mumble.

"He'll live. He's got a busted nose, a couple missing teeth, and a bullet . . . uh . . . where riding back to town on that plow horse will be none too comfortable."

The ride back to town wasn't a pleasure for Frank either. Between double vision and not being able to tell up from sideways, he barely managed to hang onto his horse. The sun was up before they reached Willow Springs, and its heat and brilliance intensified the pain in his head. When they reached the sheriff's office, Rivers helped Walker and Frank to bunks in separate cells, then he collapsed in the sheriff's chair with an order for someone to call a doctor.

Frank lay on the jailhouse bunk and closed his eyes. He was too tired to appreciate the irony of an old fear come true. Rivers had put him in jail; the only difference was that there was no lock on his cell door.

The next time he opened his eyes, he noticed that the bars on his cell ran up and down and there was only one pretty woman kneeling beside him.

"Frank. Wake up, Frank." Betsy stroked his face. "There isn't much time. Please wake up."

"I'm awake," he mumbled, "or this is the first decent dream I've had in ages." He couldn't get his fill of looking at Betsy.

"Cory? Where's Cory," he asked.

"He's fine. He's with Maggie. Frank, I brought you a change of clothes. Your pa's body was found, and Reverend Longsworth insists on holding a service and giving him a decent burial in just an hour. I wanted to wait, but in this heat . . ."

"I understand." Frank swung his feet to the floor and pulled himself upright, wincing at the stab of pain in his head brought on by the movement. After a moment, the pain subsided, and Betsy helped him get his boots off. She then returned to the front office while he dressed.

It seemed the whole town showed up at the church to bid Doc good-bye. The church was filled to capacity, but Dan had saved a place for them beside him on the front row. Frank's own thoughts and silent tribute to his father blocked out most of the sermon, but he took comfort in the music. When the service ended, he and Dan, with Betsy between them, followed the casket to the cemetery.

Again, his own thoughts filled his mind as the pine box was lowered into the ground. He thought of two graves on a distant hillside and of Elizabeth's firm belief that she and Willard would be together again. He found it comforting to think of his parents together again.

* * *

Frank missed Cory; he missed Betsy too. He wanted to be with them instead of spending his evenings alone. After the second night spent at the boarding house, Frank showed up at the sheriff's office to see if there was word of Duncan. He was surprised to find Joel Rivers still there.

"Glad you stopped in." Rivers seemed to be in a particularly expansive mood. The town's new young doctor must have given his approval for the Ranger to transport Walker to Austin. "I was about to go looking for you. This came this morning." He handed a telegram to Frank.

Duncan body found stop Pushed from train stop Suspect shot by railroad detective stop Unidentified shooter's body lost in lake stop Proceed to Austin with prisoner stop

It was over. He felt an urge to cheer, but it was surely unseemly to be pleased over any man's demise. "What do you suppose happened?" he turned to Rivers.

"It's just speculation on my part, but I think that when Duncan's new father-in-law learned his precious daughter wasn't legally married and Duncan's house of cards was about to fall, he made a few discreet arrangements. Beau Mason worked for the railroad, and we learned he received two wires only a few hours before he boarded that westbound train, the same one Duncan sneaked aboard in Austin. Mason may have been ordered or bribed to get the dynamite for Walker, or Walker may have forced him at gunpoint. I don't know, but if I were a betting man, I'd place my money on Mason's body being the body in the lake."

"You don't think he killed Duncan, do you?" The Beau Frank remembered would never have found the courage to attempt shoving a man as big as Duncan from a train car platform.

"He may have," Rivers conceded. "But I suspect he was merely a convenient patsy, a man who was no longer useful to the railroad."

"Are you going to stay in Texas now Duncan is gone?" Frank asked.

"For a time at least. I came here filled with hate and itching to put a bullet in Duncan, but I learned there are a lot of men like Duncan, and I can do more to stop them by wearing a badge than by assassinating just one such man. I may visit my mother and sister for a time, but I'll be back. I'm a Texan now."

Frank started for the door, but stopped before he reached the door. "How did you know I rode with Blackwell?"

"I was there. I joined up just after Duncan hired the outlaws to eliminate the Calloways, so Duncan never knew I was with the gang. What happened at that ranch made me sick, and I was planning to sneak away. Not even for a chance to shoot Duncan, could I stay with men who were that depraved. Then Duncan rode into camp. Fortunately, I'd gone off by myself to sit by the spring and think. I was afraid he might recognize me, so I crept down to the river to hide out in the willows. I saw you and Tom leave. The next morning, I lashed a couple of logs together and floated downstream.

I followed Duncan's movements for a few years until I discovered he was buying up land and reselling it to the railroad. He'd just bought a couple of large parcels near Wallace Creek when I learned the town was in need of a sheriff. I shaved my beard, cut my hair, and visited an acquaintance in the governor's office."

* * *

When Frank left the sheriff's office, he made his way to the burned-out shell of his boyhood home. He stood there a long time, remembering and making peace with the past. A breeze lifted bits of soot and fluttered the pages of a charred book resting in the ashes. He stooped to pick it up, not at all surprised to find himself holding the same charred book he'd held once before. It was blackened more, and some of the pages were missing, but it was Elizabeth's Book of Mormon that he'd left wrapped in heavy canvas when he placed it in his bureau drawer. He dusted it off a bit. He had a feeling that it was important to Elizabeth that Cory have the book.

Looking at it gave him the final push he needed to move forward with plans that had been stewing in his mind for some time. He turned toward the Steadman house, walking briskly now. He found Betsy hanging clothes on a line behind the house while Cory slept in a basket atop a pile of clean linens. He approached her.

"Sit with me a moment." He pulled her down beside him on the dry grass beside the sleeping baby. She didn't protest but seemed pleased to see him. He told her about Duncan and Rivers's theory concerning Beau's continued absence. She didn't cry, but appeared sad, remembering the brother of her childhood. Her memories weren't all bad, Frank knew.

"Betsy," he reached for her work-worn hands and held them between his calloused palms. "I want to go back out West. It's a land better suited for me than this place, and there's space there for new memories to be made. This has always been your home, but I'm thinking there's little to hold you here now. I'd like you to go with me. I can't imagine beginning a new life without you. Will you marry me?"

She didn't immediately answer, and Frank wondered if he'd misread her regard for him. Finally she said, "I've loved you since we were children. I prayed every day you were away that God would keep you safe and bring you back."

"I can't say that I've loved you so long, but through all the time I was away, I never forgot you. I'm not even sure I can say when my regard for you turned to love. I can only say I love you now, and if a dying woman I respected a great deal was right in her faith, I'll love you forever."

Pulling her closer so that she sat between his legs with her head resting against his chest, he said, "I need to tell you about that lady. Her name was Elizabeth Statten, and I haven't been honest with you about Cory. I never meant to lie to Pa or to you." He started slowly, thankful she couldn't see his face as he told her about Amelia and about Elizabeth. When he finished, he added, "I loved Amelia, but it was the selfish love of a boy who hadn't quite become a man yet. In time it may have ripened into a mature love, but we weren't given time. She'll always hold a special place in my heart, but I'll never know if I could feel for her what I feel for you. You bring peace to my soul, and I love you with a love beyond all else. With you I am complete."

She turned slowly, meeting his eyes. The light he saw there was all the answer he needed. She smiled, and he bent his head to brush his lips against hers. Her hand caught the back of his neck, holding him to her. When he at last lifted his head, he released a wild whoop of joy.

Cory, startled awake, began to cry. Frank lifted him into his arms, snuggling and soothing him until his cries stopped, then he placed his lips against the baby's ear and whispered, loudly enough for Betsy to hear, "We're a couple of lucky guys, little cowboy. Betsy just promised to be my wife and your ma. Ain't she the best?"

* * *

Bidding Dan farewell brought a lump to Frank's throat. They stood on the wooden platform waiting for trains that would carry them in opposite directions. Frank had signed over his share in Pa's property and the printing press to Dan. Dan was heading north with the press to join Clare in Philadelphia. He had yet to tell her about Beau. He said he would leave it to Clare to consult an attorney concerning whether to file for divorce or wait for Beau to be declared dead. Whatever her decision, he meant to stay near her and look after her and her children. In time, if she agreed, they too would go west to look for a town in need of a newspaper.

Betsy had walked off a little way with Cory, and now the two men watched her return.

"She's a good woman," Dan said. He'd stood beside Frank a few hours earlier as Frank and Betsy became man and wife. "Life hasn't always treated her well. Many times when I became discouraged thinking Clare and I would never have our chance to be together, I thought of marrying her myself. Something always stopped my asking. I think it was knowing she deserved to be loved more than I could love her."

"I plan to love her forever," Frank said. "I made some promises I intend to keep." He knew Dan thought he was referring to his marriage vows. Only he knew that the promises he meant to keep went beyond those made in the village church. He meant to find out if Elizabeth was right about forever.

ABOUT THE AUTHOR

Jennie Hansen graduated from Ricks College in Idaho, then Westminster College in Utah. She has been a newspaper reporter, editor, and librarian. In addition to writing novels, she reviews LDS fiction in a monthly column for *Meridian* magazine.

She was born in Idaho Falls, Idaho, and has lived in Idaho, Montana, and Utah. She has received numerous writing awards from the Utah and National Federation of Press Women and was the 1997 third-place winner of the URWA Heart of the West Writers Contest.

Her church service has included teaching in all auxiliaries and serving in stake and ward auxiliary presidencies. She has also served as a den mother, stake public affairs coordinator, ward chorister, education counselor in the Relief Society, and teacher improvement coordinator.

Jennie has also been active in community affairs. She served a term on the Kearns Town Council, two terms on the Salt Palace Advisory Board, and was a delegate to the White House Conference on Libraries and Information Services.

Jennie and her husband, Boyd, live in Salt Lake County. Their five children are all married and have so far provided them with ten grandchildren.